Bird

of

Paradise

G.J. Paterson

Bird

of

Paradise

G.J. Paterson

Ex Caliban Publishing
Los Angeles, CA 91040

Cover Design & Interior Images
Typeset & Layout

Jo-Ann Byers Mierzwicki

www.*Ex Caliban*.com
an imprint of
Pendraig Publishing
Los Angeles, CA 91040
www. *Pendraig Publishing*.com
Printed in the United States of America

ISBN: 978-1-936922-64-2

To:

HBT3 and TM,

who always understood the importance of
"the embrace of love and resistance."

And to:

Patricia, always.

Acknowledgements

*T*he line *"the embrace of love and resistance"* is from Walt Whitman's astounding poem, *"I Sing the Body Electric."* To me it expresses that love is love and that it should always resist the crushing blows society can bring to bear against it.

There are so many people that have helped me over the years that I literally cannot list them all. There were a lot of people in England, from Terri Becket to Frieda Harris, who opened their homes to me and my bicycle while I was gathering information. And there were friends in the States who helped me with the first shaping and reshaping of the book, including Marian Kelly and Melanie Rawn.

Then there are the *"beta-readers,"* including but not limited to: Bobby Beeman, Jon Ciesla, Kip Coddington, Content Love Knowles, Melanie Rowlett, Rita Tilson-Vasak, Judy Weidner and the rest who poked and prodded me toward a much, much better manuscript. There are also people whose support never flagged like: Tori Bradley,

Neil McKenzie, Donna Siebert, Patsy Sutton, Terri Wilson and Mike Herrara. In that number I include my sister, Nora Sekine. And my wonderful Dad, Arliss Moses, who I miss very much.

I must also mention Paul Allen, Spencer Brown, Patrick French, Lucas Green, Kirk Holt, Toby Jenkins, Mary Jones, Dennis R. Neill, Denise Polonchek, Stewart Wallace and so many, many more at the Dennis R. Neill Equality Center whose tireless work the parity of LGBT people in Oklahoma and the whole country is inspirational. I want to thank the members of the Rainbow Writers Group at the Center, especially the core members of the group, Scott Goodpaster, Travis Hall, and Roger Morris. And I also want to thank my Tuesday morning S.A.G.E. (Support and Advocacy for Gay Elders) friends: David, Eduardo, Gordon, Guthrie, Jerry, John, Kim, Marlena, Ray, Sol, and Stanley, among others.,

Additionally, I want to thank Johnny Womack for being such an enthusiastic supporter and for suggesting I contact my wonderful and amazingly patient publisher, Peter Paddon at Pendraig Publishing. I also want to mention Angela James and her excellent course, *Before You Hit Send*, which every aspiring author should take. Then there is my friend and mentor Josh Lanyon, along with the incredibly multi-talented Rodney Orpheus, whose help and support is without measure.

I'd also like to thank Patricia's brothers and sisters, especially Heather and Walter Pearson. Not to mention, Leslie and all the *"Utah Patersons,"* who have all helped us so much during our seemingly interminable starving artist phase.

But most of all I want to thank my partner of 33 years and spouse of 5 years, Patricia, who has always believed in me and in this book.

Whatever mistakes are in this book are my fault and not theirs. They have, one and all, been so supportive and helpful that no author could ask for better research assistants and certainly not for better friends.

"*It never was about the musician or the instrument — it was about the laser notes in a hall of mirrors, the music itself. It was going to change the world for the better and it has. Maybe not as fast or as much as we wanted, but it has and it still will. Whether your name is Mozart, or Django Reinhardt, or Robert Johnson, or Jimi Hendrix, or whoever is next; who you are doesn't matter so long as you can open that conduit and let the music come through. It is the burning edge, whatever it sounds like and whoever is playing it. It is the noisy, messy, silly, invincible voice of life that comes through the LP on the turn-table, the transistor radio, or the Bose in your new Lexus that makes you want to get up out of whatever you are stuck in and dance. It is Dionysus and the Maenads all over again. No one can control it and I pity whoever tries. I am old now and only a house cat sunning herself in the window — but I was a tigress once, and I remember. I still remember.*"

- G. J. Paterson,
Tulsa, OK, 2013

WEDNESDAY, DECEMBER 20, 1978

One 1

"So, what'd you think of that last lot?" Derek Quinn asked as he shut the heavy front door.

Allyn Sterling brushed past him without pausing. Only the slight unsteadiness in his gait betrayed the amount of alcohol he had drunk in the course of the evening. He went through the foyer and crossed the huge, dark den to the fireplace.

"Derek, old son," he said as he bent to retrieve a poker and stir the embers, "by the time you'd dragged me all over southern California and we got round to that last dive I couldn't see the stage, leave off hear the band."

Quinn sauntered into the room and tossed his coat onto one of the overstuffed leather chairs. He watched as Allyn added a log to the fire. "You weren't as far gone as that."

"Yes I was. So were you. That's why I drove us home."

"I knew there must have been a reason."

"I drive better than you, pissed or not," Allyn said. "Benedict Canyon Road is no place for an amateur like you to drive drunk after two in the morning."

"Probably, but I wonder why the forces of order have threatened to lift your license so many times."

"Bollocks." He pushed the hood of his cloak back from his head and stretched out his hands to the fire. The glow played on his face and glimmered in his red-gold hair. "All right, then. The singer was okay, the guitarist fair, the bass player should do less coke, and the drummer couldn't keep time if it meant his life."

"Few American drummers can," Quinn said. He watched Allyn closely. *You'll talk yourself into touring again at this rate.*

If Allyn was aware of the scrutiny he didn't show it. He unfastened the clasp at his throat and let the dark blue cloak slip to the floor behind him. Underneath, he wore bell-bottom jeans and a bronze satin poet shirt. His unconfined hair cascaded in curling waves past his shoulders.

He crossed the den to the corner by the sliding glass doors. For a few moments he knelt in the darkness, then laughed as the strings of lights came on, revealing a blue spruce tree sagging a bit under the burden of so many hand blown ornaments. An antique angel dressed in satin and lace adorned the treetop. Allyn restacked the packages he had moved and stood up, dusting his hands together to dislodge the silver glitter that stuck to his fingers. "How do you suppose they came to be off?"

"Shouldn't be left on if no one's about."

"Yeah? Well, frankly, Scrooge, I haven't a clue why you're dragging me to all these places to listen to bands. We haven't used a warm-up band any time these past few years." Allyn bent to retrieve the cloak, frowning as some of the glitter clung to the fabric.

"Never, really. Unless you count the early days, traveling with those Dick Clark things in the sixties."

"Forgetting your own history? *We* never did that. That was you and White Mare. We played a bit with other bands in — oh, I don't know — nineteen seventy or that, like." There was glitter in the blond curls now.

"Road show stuff, still." Quinn shrugged. "I don't much like it myself but, I dunno, lots of fellows are doing it. Times change. It is nineteen seventy-eight after all."

"You needn't remind me." Allyn flung the cloak over a chair and examined it more closely.

"And anyway, I've been meaning to discuss that with you."

Allyn turned to look at him. "Yeah, I suppose you have. Can it wait until I've had a look in at Carys?"

Derek smiled at the thought of the child sleeping down the hall and accepted his victory with grace. He moved to the well-stocked wet bar. "Would you care for something?"

"Whiskey, please." Allyn said as he crossed the den and disappeared into the hall that led to the bedrooms.

Quinn busied himself with bottles and glasses, humming softly and considering his next move. The ice bucket was full, but the tongs were missing.

"*Quinn*!" Allyn's distant voice was ragged with alarm.

"Allyn?" There was no response. He strode down the hall to the only open door. Light streamed out. He stopped in the doorway and looked inside. Allyn stood in the middle of the room with a paper in his hand. "What is it?"

"She's gone!" Allyn shoved the paper at Quinn. "Someone's taken her."

He took the paper gingerly, trying to hold it only at the edges. His hands had grown cold and shaky. He took a deep breath to steady himself and looked at what was written there.

The typed message was simple:

> *DO NOT CALL THE POLICE.*
> *WE WILL CONTACT YOU.*

Bird of Paradise
G.J. Paterson

He looked around the room. The bed was rumpled, the pale blue lace spread thrown back and the ivory sheets disarrayed. It had been slept in, at least for a while. A stuffed lion with a ragged mane and only one button eye sat squarely in the center of the mattress. The sheer lace curtains on the window moved in the breeze. The cool draft blew past him. The air smelled of wet earth and rain.

Quinn tipped his head back, looking up at the ceiling for a moment. A shiver ran through him. His veins whispered of certain hunger to come. *No*, he told his aching body, *there is no time for that now.*

"Where was the note?"

"Under Muffin's paws."

Quinn turned and put the note carefully back under the stuffed lion's paws. "Don't touch anything else."

"What?"

"There might be fingerprints."

"I've got to go look for her."

"And where will you look, I wonder." Quinn shook his head. "Let's go back to the den and figure this out."

"How the bloody hell can you be so fucking cold!" Allyn shouted, his voice ringing in the small room.

"Someone has to be," Quinn said grimly. He raised his hands in appeasement as Allyn's fists clenched. "Not, now. Fighting me won't help us. We have to think what to do."

"Do? We can't do anything, that's what the note says!" Allyn's voice had gone low, never a good sign.

"We have to call Miltie at the very least."

"It says not to call anyone."

"Put down your sword, old son. It says not to call the police. There's nothing in it about calling our manager."

"What if Miltie's in on it?"

"Miltie?" Quinn scoffed. He turned and headed back to the den, knowing Allyn would follow. "I trust him with my life. With all our lives, if it comes to it. He'd never dream of doing something like this."

Bird of Paradise
G.J. Paterson

In the den, Quinn picked up the whiskey bottle then sat it back down. They had to be clear-headed for this. He looked at Allyn, thinking of Carys and noticing how the firelight tangled in her father's hair. *I have no idea how I can think of that when she is in trouble.* He shook his head. "We're going to call Miltie," he explained. "Then we're going to have a chat with Noel."

"How can he help?" Allyn's anger had a new target. "He's no use as a fucking bodyguard!"

"It's his day off. I don't know if he's even here. Miltie will know what to do. I think we'll need the police, myself."

Allyn began to pace before the fire. Quinn watched him for a few moments. "Stay put. I've got something to do."

He walked down the hall to his room, fumbled with the switch and flooded the space with light. The only order in the room was the row of four guitars — two acoustic and two electric — standing before a battered old Fender amp. The light gleamed on the engraved silver pickguards of the Strats.

In the bathroom, Quinn picked up a small polished rosewood box from the top of the white porcelain tank, took out two glassine envelopes and dumped their contents into the bowl. He watched the two powders, one white and one ivory, swirl and mingle. He tore the envelopes into tiny pieces and tossed them in as well. He set the box back in its place and flushed the toilet. Watching to make sure everything went down, he realized he was licking his fingers. The bitter, medicinal taste made him grimace, but there wasn't enough to give him any kind of buzz.

He washed his hands and walked out of the bathroom, to find Carys' nanny, Lydia Calhoun, standing in the doorway. Her gray hair was in disarray. She held her rose-colored robe closed with one hand. Her face was pale.

"What's wrong, Mr. Quinn?" Her voice was querulous.

"Someone's taken Carys."

"Oh, no!" Lydia gasped and sat down as though her legs were cut from under her, slumping against the wall.

"Allyn!" he called. "Come help. Nanny's fainted."

Allyn ran into the hall. He knelt by the woman, chaffing her wrists. She stirred and after a few moments sat up. Allyn helped her get to her feet.

"There now, old girl," Quinn said as bracingly as he could. "It's all going to come right. You'll see."

Allyn put his hand on Quinn's arm.

"You do believe that?" Fierce blue eyes met his own.

"We'll find her, old son," he said. "We'll find her."

Two

2

"*Where the bloody hell were you when she needed you?*" a man's voice roared.

Paul Taglia stopped in mid-stride as he entered the den.

A quick glance around the spacious area took in several civilians and three patrol officers. Everyone seemed frozen by the shout.

The speaker stood by the fireplace, arms crossed. He was a tall man with dark blue eyes and a mane of wildly curling blond hair. Standing beside him, a slender man with long dark hair put a hand on his arm. Light but effective, the restraint stopped the impending attack.

"Well, Moody?" The blond man's gaze was locked on a big man across the room. "Where were you?"

"Me?" Moody bellowed at the challenge. "I was on my day off! Where were you? Out drinking and drugging with your 'mate'?"

"You fucking, maggot-brained idiot!" The blond man shook free and started for Moody.

Taglia stepped in to catch Moody's arm before the blond man reached him. He signaled an officer. "Put this guy by himself in the parlor. Make sure nobody leaves until we get this sorted out." The patrolman took charge of Moody and hustled him toward the foyer.

"Glad you finally made it, Sergeant," said a familiar voice behind him.

Taglia turned to find himself face-to-face with his partner, Jeff Kincaid. The man's pale blond hair didn't quite hide the few strands of gray that were beginning to show. His clear, light blue eyes had intimidated more than one criminal during their five years as partners.

"Sergeant? Is it Formal Day and I missed the memo?" Taglia asked. He knew they were a study in opposites: Kincaid always dressed in business casual, while Taglia dressed for the street. Kincaid's hair was short and neatly trimmed. His own brown hair was collar length and shaggier. But they made a good team. They had been friends too, but Taglia wasn't sure about that now. "So, *Lieutenant*, have you been here long enough to bring me up to speed?"

Kincaid pulled out his notebook and began to read. "Patrol was dispatched at four-eighteen this morning. Report of a missing child, white female, aged eight, four foot one and slim. Her name is Carys Althea Sterling. Father is Allyn Sterling, the blond guy with the hair. He's twenty-eight."

"*Allyn Sterling* is her father?" Taglia shifted to look back at the man by the fireplace. He felt a lurching moment of unreality. He had never thought he would be in the same room with this man. "Jesus! You're right. That is Allyn Sterling."

"You know this guy?"

"Well, no. Not personally. He's the singer from Leviathon. I've been a fan for years." Taglia couldn't keep the admiration out of his voice. "That makes the other guy Derek Quinn, the guitarist."

"Right," Kincaid continued. "Derek Edward Quinn, thirty-one. Both of them have British passports and their visas are up to date.

Quinn was dressed in a gray silk shirt with a narrow black tie and faded jeans. He had dark eyes, dark just past shoulder-length hair and was junkie thin. Taglia frowned for a moment. *Funny — on the street I would bust you for breathing. It'd stick, too. Something you were doing would be bound to be illegal somewhere.*

Kincaid said, "The other people here are the girl's nanny, and the band's manager. You've already met the body-guard. Patrol has started collecting statements, but I saved Quinn and Sterling for us. Let's talk to Sterling first."

Sterling sat down in a chair. Quinn leaned against the mantel, one boot heel resting on the edge of the hearth. The pair watched them approach.

"I'm Lieutenant Kincaid, and this is my partner, Sergeant Taglia. We're from Missing Persons. I know this is hard for you, but we need to ask you some questions."

Sterling nodded. "Yeah. Anything to get Carys back."

"Okay. So tell us what happened this evening."

"Derek and I went out drinking at various clubs, listening to bands." Allyn looked up at the two detectives. "We got back about three. I went to check on Carys, but she wasn't in her room. I found the note on her bed."

"What time did you leave to go to the club?"

"Around nine, I think."

"And you got in at three, but you didn't call us until after four. Why?"

"It was my idea." Quinn's dark gaze was steady. "The note said not to involve the police, so we weren't sure what to do. I called Miltie — Milton Ables, our manager. Once he got here, he insisted we call you."

"Do you have any idea who might have taken your daughter, Mr. Sterling?"

"No. Most people don't know about Carys. I try to be private about my family. The only people I talk to about her are either the band or other friends."

"Would Carys have left with anyone?" Kincaid asked.

"No. She's a smart girl, and she knows better," Allyn said. "Besides, how would anyone get in here to take her, anyway? We have a security system and a live-in bodyguard — for all the good he did. They must have known the code for the system somehow."

"Can you get me a list of everyone who had access to the security codes for the house?"

"Yeah. Anything you need."

"Where's your bodyguard?"

"He's the big guy in the front room," Taglia said. "Uniforms are talking to him."

Kincaid nodded. "Okay. What's his name?"

"Noel Moody," Allyn replied.

"Is there a Mrs. Sterling?"

"Yeah, but Demetra and I've been separated for two years. She's a model and is usually out on photo-shoots. Doesn't give her much time to be a mum. The last we heard, she's in Majorca."

"What about child custody issues?"

Quinn smiled as if at some private joke. Taglia studied him. He was handsome under the air of dissipation. His smile made him seem younger. Taglia wondered what the smile was about.

Sterling shook his head. "Like I said, Demetra's not big on being a mum. Carys visits her, but she stays with me most of the year. Demetra has her for a few weeks each summer and an occasional holiday."

"So you don't think your wife might have taken her?" Kincaid asked.

"It'd stun me. Her main interest is in my money."

"Any chance she'd kidnap Carys to get more of your money?"

There was a flash of temper in Sterling's eyes. "Forget Demetra! She didn't take Carys. What else do you want to know?"

"What do you think happened?"

"What do *I* think? Isn't that what you are supposed to do? I think someone wants money from me." Allyn's eyes narrowed.

"I agree." Quinn said.

Kincaid glanced around the room, gestured with one hand. "Do you own this place?"

"No. We have it on hire. My home is in Wales. I wish now we'd never left."

"Who else was in the house during the time Carys was taken?"

"Just Lydia Calhoun, Carys's nanny. Lydia's the nice old gal over on the couch. And Noel Moody, of course."

Kincaid turned his gaze to Quinn. "What about drugs?"

If Quinn was startled it didn't show. "There are none in the house for anyone to try to steal." Allyn, Taglia noticed, turned his face away from the detectives as Quinn spoke.

"I'm sure that's true enough." Taglia understood the bitter irony in his partner's voice. Any drugs in the house would have been dumped before the first cop arrived on the scene. "Is there any chance Carys's kidnapping could be drug-related? Maybe someone you've dealt with?"

"No," Quinn said. "Carys's abduction has nothing to do with drugs."

Taglia saw that the man's pupils were pin-pricks. *And what kind of drugs are you using, Derek? I was right about you being up to something illegal.*

"No dealers?" Kincaid persisted. "No one who might *think* you have drugs in the house?"

"Absolutely not."

Kincaid turned his attention back to Allyn. "Is anything missing — other than Carys? Any valuables?"

"Nothing I've noticed. But then, I didn't look."

"What about jealousy? Anyone jealous of you and your success?"

"How the hell should I know who's jealous of me? It's not like any of my 'success' has come easy. Shit! I've worked hard for what I've got. Now the one person who matters more than anything else is stolen." Allyn's voice broke.

"We're doing everything possible to get her back," Kincaid said.

Allyn nodded then stood. "Give me a couple of minutes, please?"

"Sure. We'll go on when you're ready." He watched as Allyn walked toward the hallway leading to the bedrooms, and then turned to Quinn. "I gather you've known Mr. Sterling a long time, Mr. Quinn?"

"Please, just call me Quinn. 'Mister' reminds me of my father. And yeah, I've known Allyn ten years next month. We met at a club where he was performing with a band. The next day I asked him to join Leviathon. You've heard of us?"

"I haven't spent the last ten years in Tibet. You're all English, I guess.

"Don't let Allyn hear you call him English. He's Welsh, and Gil's a Scot," Quinn said with a laugh. "It's rather like calling someone from Georgia a Yankee. Touchy bastards. But yes, we are a British band. There're four of us. Allyn sings lead. I play guitar. Gilbert McConathy is our bass player, and Avery Potts is our drummer. Milton Ables is our manager. He's the older gent over there sitting with Lydia on the couch. He was at the hotel when we called. He hasn't told the others about Carys yet. That's the only reason the whole band isn't here."

"What hotel are you staying at?"

"I'm not at the hotel. I have a room here. The other blokes are staying at a hotel in Bel Air – I don't remember the name. Miltie can tell you, though."

Kincaid frowned. "Why aren't you staying at the hotel with the others?"

Quinn shrugged. "There's a small studio here in the house, and it was easier for me to be here while Allyn and I were working on some songs together. After that, I just... stayed."

Kincaid shook his head then took a moment to review his notes. "So what brings all of you to Los Angeles?" he asked at last.

"Carys has always wanted to see Disneyland, so he arranged to bring her over this past August. I arrived in October."

"It's December." Kincaid glanced at the decorated tree in the corner. "Almost Christmas."

"True. Which is where I come in. Allyn and I are the immovable object and the irresistible force on a number of subjects, and one of them is touring. We haven't toured or released a new album since seventy-six.

"The problem is, every time Allyn comes off the road, he swears he'll never go out again. The only way to get him moving is with music. That's why I turned up on his doorstep with a bundle of new songs back in early October. Before he knew it, I'd called in the rest of our lot, and we were all here and in a studio downtown."

"You're recording a new album?" Taglia tried to suppress the interest in his voice.

"Just done. We wrapped it up this week past."

"But you're still here," Kincaid said. "Why?"

Quinn shrugged. "Allyn decided to stay through the holidays. I'd always planned to be home, but I've no family so here's as good as anywhere for Christmas. Some of the others'll be going home in the next few days, though. I think Gil already has his plane tickets."

"What's the possibility this is a publicity stunt?" Kincaid asked.

"None at all. Miltie's a good man, and the idea would never occur to him. Besides, none of us would stand for it."

"I wasn't thinking of Miltie. I was thinking of Allyn."

"She's *his* daughter." He stared at Kincaid as if that explained everything.

"What about you?" Taglia found himself asking.

"I beg your pardon?" Quinn stared at him. "That's contemptible."

"Maybe," Taglia said, knowing that he had the man's full attention. "And maybe not. I saw the look on your face when Allyn was talking about Demetra."

Quinn said. "It has nothing to do with Carys. She thinks of me as her uncle. I'd never do anything to put her in jeopardy."

Kincaid cleared his throat and considered his notes for a moment. "If it's not just about the money, do you have any idea who would do this? You've known Allyn ten years. Do you know if he has any enemies?"

"Everybody loves Allyn. He's had rows with a handful of people, but Allyn's not the enemy-making sort. No one we know would do something like this. It seems to me most likely money is the answer." Quinn crushed his cigarette out in a nearby ashtray. "Tell me, are you arresting Moody?"

"Why? Do you think we should?" Kincaid's voice was casual, but his expression sharpened. "Do you think he knows something about Carys's disappearance?"

"I don't know. I don't think so. I do think he's negligent, and I don't want him here in the morning. If you aren't going to arrest him, I'm going to see that Miltie gives him the push tonight."

"We don't have any reasons to arrest anyone yet," Kincaid said. "If you do let him go, make sure he knows to stay in town."

Allyn walked back into the room. His eyes were reddened and bloodshot as he crossed to where they stood. Taglia noted that he and Jeff were about the same height, something over six feet. His clothing was rumpled and he needed a shave.

"He's right, you know. Moody is right. I failed her." Allyn cleared his throat. Quinn reached for his shoulder, but the singer jerked away. "No, Derek. I should've been here with her, not out at some fucking club with you."

He turned his eyes to the detectives. "Please," he whispered. "My little girl. Will you get her back?"

Kincaid said, "We're doing our best, Mr. Sterling. Our very best. I promise you."

Taglia smiled and caught his partner's eye. *Do you know how much I admire your compassion for strangers in trouble, Jeff?* Kincaid returned the look, a brief flicker of unity. Then Kincaid sobered, eyes going frosty, and he turned away.

Taglia suppressed a sigh. *But where is your compassion when the trouble is ours?*

Three   3

Taglia glanced up from his manual typewriter as Kincaid walked into the Missing Persons squad room, followed by Captain Raul Ortiz.

"...I've already taken care of ordering a phone trap and trace, plus a tape recorder," Kincaid was saying. "Paul and I are going to get some clothes in case we have to stay there overnight, then we'll be heading back to Sterling's place to set up a command post. I've left a couple of uniforms there until we arrive, just in case."

"Sounds good, Lieutenant. Have we got all your paperwork?"

Kincaid glanced at Taglia, who nodded, pulled the paper from the typewriter and handed over his report. "Just finished."

Ortiz scanned the paperwork in silence then passed it on to Kincaid. "There's some politics with this kidnapping you need to know about. The Chief is very concerned that this case be handled quickly and quietly."

"We always do," Taglia said.

"I know, but this case is big. Apparently England considers Leviathon to be a top export. The amount of money these men pay in taxes to the British government would stagger a mule. If anything goes wrong here, this won't just be a field day for the local press, it could have international repercussions."

"We'll handle it like always, Captain," Kincaid said. "If there's any way to get Carys Sterling back, we'll do it."

"One more thing," Ortiz added. "We're keeping this case quiet. Nothing goes out over the air. We don't know if the kidnapper has a police scanner, but the media does. We're assuming none of our frequencies are safe, and all communications about this case from now on are by phone lines only."

"You've got it, Captain," Kincaid replied. "Is there anything else?"

"Nope. I'll be here when you need me. Good luck."

They walked out into the thin wintry sunshine, side-by-side and silent. Taglia felt the silence as a weight on his shoulders. *Shit. We've hardly spoken since Sunday morning, and now we get thrown together on a high-pressure case for God-knows-how-long.*

In the employee parking lot, Kincaid paused by his car, a copper-colored Honda Prelude. He fiddled with his car keys, gazing off into the distance.

"Hey," Taglia began, "do you want to go somewhere and talk? I mean, you know... about Saturday?"

Kincaid glanced at him at him then turned away. "It must've been a helluva party. I don't remember much after Vincent proposed his toast."

Okay. Is this how we're going to play it?

Kincaid changed the subject. "Must be hard to grow up surrounded by people like that."

"What kind of people are you talking about?"

"Well, for example, Carys is a pretty name, but it's very unusual. Weird, in fact. I bet kids in school give her hell about it. I wonder if Sterling even thought about that when he named her?" Kincaid shook his head. "At least it's better than some of the other weird names we hear out here. Zowie Bowie. Moon Unit Zappa and her brother Dweezle. Imagine growing up named Zowie Bowie. It's enough to give a kid a complex."

"Everybody out here has complexes anyway. Besides, how do you know what David Bowie named his kid?"

"I read it in *People*."

"You've never read *People* in your life!"

"Standing in line at the supermarket. What do you think about the case?"

"I don't know yet. No snap judgments, right? It's amazing, though, meeting those guys and everything. Allyn Sterling is my favorite singer, and Derek Quinn — he's got to be the best guitarist in the world."

"What's he got Segovia hasn't got?"

"About a zillion dollars."

"Doesn't means he's better, Paul."

"Have you ever heard him play?"

"Of course. I even know 'Bird of Paradise' is one of their songs, but it's too damn noisy for me."

"Oh, yeah. I tried to get you to go with me to Leviathon's concert last time they were in town, but you wouldn't. I wonder what the new album will be like? Anyway, I think they're terrific. My mom got me their first album back in sixty-nine, and I haven't missed one since. I've seen them every time they've been in town, except for the first because I was in 'Nam. Their light shows are always incredible."

"I didn't realize you were such a fan," Kincaid commented.

Taglia tilted his head. "I am a fan. Always have been."

"It's not art, Paul."

"Why not? You listen to that Gypsy guitarist and all his old jazz stuff," Taglia rebutted. "Is that art?"

"Django Reinhardt. Of course his music is art."

"Rock and roll is too, the way Leviathon, and Led Zeppelin, and The Who, and the Stones, and all those guys play it. I mean it's all about the blues and stuff. I think you don't believe it's art because you don't know anything about it. You haven't learned to appreciate it — like you keep telling me about Italian opera."

"C'mon, you can't mention Alice Cooper and Toscanini in the same breath." Kincaid shook his head. "We'd better go. Besides, we'll know more about Leviathon later today. More than I ever wanted to know anyway."

Taglia looked at him, swallowing hard against a lump in his throat. "You know we have to talk about what happened Saturday night."

Kincaid frowned. "We got drunk. I got drunk. You got drunk. That pretty much sums it up."

"No it doesn't." Taglia said, but he found himself talking to Kincaid's back as his partner got in his car and shut the door.

Oak Pass Drive wound its way to a wealthy residential neighborhood up in the hills. Although paved, it was an older road, rough and discouraging to those who might go exploring. A tall hedge masked the house they were seeking from the road. Taglia eased his black and gold Trans Am through the gate in the hedge.

Fifty feet beyond the gate, the driveway took a sharp curve and expanded into a wide parking area. There were a couple of unmarked cars drawn up in front of the carport, blocking in a forest green Jaguar XJS and something low-slung and probably fast, shrouded by a canvas cover displaying the Lotus mark.

Kincaid gathered up his notepad, got out of the car as soon as it stopped rolling, and looked around.

The large wood-and-stucco ranch-style house was painted brown with a cool sage green trim. Lawn and gardens, faded now in winter, swept in all directions.

A patrolman let Kincaid and Taglia in. They found Quinn in the spacious den. "Good morning, Inspectors," he said.

"Morning," Kincaid replied. "Is Mr. Sterling up?"

"He's an early riser. He's in the back garden. There's a Japanese pond he likes to sit by." He glanced toward Lydia Calhoun as she emerged from the kitchen, heading toward the bedroom hallway. "Lydia, will you show Lieutenant Kincaid to the pond?"

"Of course," she said.

Kincaid followed the woman as she opened the sliding glass door and stepped out onto a broad patio under an overcast sky.

"This way," she said. They walked away from the sheltering corner of the house, and she shivered as the cold wind slipped over them. Kincaid took off his jacket and draped it over her shoulders. She smiled her thanks. After a moment she said, "I can't manage to think clearly this morning, somehow. I'm that worried about Carys, and Mr. Sterling is taking it hard."

Kincaid glanced down at her as they walked along the brick-lined path. "Ma'am, do you have any ideas who might have done this?"

"No idea at all, I'm afraid. I wish I did."

"There's no one, anywhere, who might want to get to Allyn for any reason?"

Lydia was silent for a moment then said, "It's not my place to tell you this, but if there were anyone who wanted to hurt him it would be Demetra."

"Would she do this?"

"I don't know. I can tell you she's a cold woman with quite a temper. Very different from Mr. Sterling."

"What about fans?"

"Fans? What do you mean?"

"I don't know. You tell me. Fan mail? Weird mail? Hate mail? Who writes to them?"

She stopped walking. He pulled up short rather than run into her. "All of them get mail, but most of it comes to Mr. Quinn and Mr.

Sterling. Mr. Sterling gets hundreds of letters. It depends on whether or not he's done an interview or gotten a write-up in some magazine. Also whether they've put out an album or are on tour. Most of the letters are nice, of course. We do see the odd bit of ugliness from time to time. John Birch-types, religious zealots —" she sniffed, "— and a few others."

"What kind of others?"

"There aren't many. Kate — Mr. Ables' secretary — keeps a file at the office in London. When I started seeing disturbing letters arrive here, I asked her what to do about them. She told me to file them and deliver them to her when we return home. Over the years she's received a number of letters from such people. I had no idea."

"I'd have thought no one knew the address," Kincaid said.

"This address isn't published, but these things do get around after a bit. Some mail comes to us directly, and some is forwarded from the record company. Mr. Sterling's gotten over a hundred letters since we arrived. We'll take the good ones back to London where the office can send a photo to the writers. Only ten or so have been bothersome. I don't read them, you know. Just the first bits, and if they're at all worrisome, I put them in the file."

"Ten." Kincaid frowned. "All from the same person?"

"Oh, heavens, no! Most of them never write more than once or twice. There've been a few exceptions. I've filed about half a dozen from what appears to be the same man. I can tell it's the same person because he calls Mr. Sterling 'Peacock.' The letters came here. We haven't had one from him in a week or two. It's been a relief. His were nasty."

"Hate mail?"

"No, not hate, although he doesn't like Mr. Quinn above half. No, it's more... umm... I think the unfortunate man has some serious problems." She clasped her arms across her chest. "It got so I could tell from the envelope if a letter was from him, even though he never put a return address."

"What does Mr. Sterling think?"

She looked away. "He's never seen them. We want to keep him from worrying, Inspector. You must see Mr. Sterling is sensitive. We felt it better he didn't know he received this kind of mail. It would distress him."

"'We?'"

"Mr. Quinn, Mr. Ables and Kate. I had to agree."

"I'm sure you do a good job, ma'am. We'll need to see those letters of yours. Could you arrange it for me?"

"Certainly." She looked relieved. "I'm leaving with Mr. Ables, but I'll get them for you before I go."

The path led them through a gap in a low hedge, dipping down into a hollow to reveal an intricate Japanese garden hidden from the house. A large fishpond lay in the center of the hollow, surrounded by graceful trees. On the far side stood a stone lantern framed by two bronze cranes. Beyond the pond a wrought iron fence hugged the yard as the canyon wall fell away, revealing a spectacular view of sky and the valley far below.

Allyn sat on the grassy bank beside the pond, a dark blue cloak wrapped around his shoulders, its hood covering the back of his head. A few feet away a patrol officer kept watch.

The singer was feeding breadcrumbs to the big, brightly colored koi swimming up to take the food from his fingers. The water swirled and churned around them as they poked their heads out of the water, jostling each other in their eagerness. Their big open mouths sucked the food down. The sun came out from behind a cloud, and light blazed in his tangled hair and gleamed on the silver jewelry on his wrists and hands.

"Hullo, Lydia. Lieutenant Kincaid." Allyn tossed the remaining bits of bread into the water and stood, shaking out his cloak. "Have you heard anything?"

"No, but we're working on it. We have an entire squad of detectives on the case. We need to discuss plans."

"Doesn't seem there is much to discuss." The singer gazed across the pond at the bronze cranes. Kincaid noted he had taken the time to shave. "It's all quite simple to me. Find Carys. Find her. That's all there is to it."

"Sorry, but there's more," Kincaid said.

"I suppose I should feel comforted." The singer strode away toward the house, his cloak billowing behind him.

"Please try to allow for his worry," Lydia said as she and Kincaid followed in Allyn's wake. "He loves his daughter dearly. If someone had wanted to do something horrible to him, they couldn't have chosen better."

"What about Quinn? Would somebody do this to get at him? He and Mr. Sterling must be pretty close if he's staying here. Some people you can't get at except through their friends."

She stared at him. "I don't think so, but if it were, it wouldn't be much help. His list is endless."

"Is it?"

"Oh, Lord, everyone's been after Mr. Quinn at one time or another. Why, even our Harry."

"What do you mean?"

"Harry Stuart. He works for the band. He's been with us forever. Derek had an affair with his fiancée. Unfortunately, the girl was running in company much too fast for her. Mr. Quinn wasn't at fault, though Harry has always thought so."

"What wasn't his fault?

"She died, Inspector. In Mr. Quinn's hotel suite after a recording session in Paris years ago. She got into some tainted drugs. Those were the days when Mr. Quinn... I mean he used to do...."

"What kind of drugs?"

"Heroin, I'm afraid. Megan died of it."

"Stuart forgave him?"

"Mr. Quinn was ill for days," Lydia said. "The doctors said the adulterant was strychnine. We were afraid we would lose him."

"When did this happen?"

"Oh, nearly four years ago, I believe."

They had reached the patio. The clouds were closing in again overhead, and the freshening breeze smelled of rain. "And this guy still works for you?"

"Why, yes. Of course."

Kincaid stared at her. "After his girlfriend died?" He shook his head in disbelief. "Why?"

"Loyalty, Inspector," Lydia said with her hand on the door. She didn't meet his gaze. "It's very important to Mr. Quinn."

Four 4

Quinn watched Allyn open the sliding glass door and come into the house. The tension in the man's shoulders and the fatigue lining his face tugged at him. Allyn unclasped his cape and draped it over the back of a chair. His movement spoke of grief and exhaustion. *This is killing you. Does no one else see it?*

The singer's blue jeans had been washed often enough to lose their bright indigo and mold themselves to his thighs as if made for him. Embroidered sunflowers ran in a bright, intricate chain around the neck and wrists of his linen peasant shirt. Quinn guessed it was a gift from a fan. Besides silver bracelets and rings, Allyn wore a heavy silver buckle set with turquoise and coral on a tooled and painted belt. The colors were long since faded, but the theme of mountains seen from a distance through trees with golden leaves could still be made out. From his left earlobe hung a tiny silver feather.

Quinn sighed. *I wish you could take comfort from me. At least you still wear the buckle.*

The dark-haired cop's voice intruded. "We're agreed then," Taglia said to Ables. "All non-essential persons will return to the hotel." As he spoke, the sliding door opened again and Lydia entered, followed by the blond detective.

"*We* haven't agreed to anything," Allyn said. "But it would be nice not to be alone in this."

"The police know best how to handle these things, Allyn," Ables said.

"Gentlemen," Taglia soothed, "no one is suggesting Mr. Sterling be left alone. Lieutenant Kincaid and I will be here around-the-clock until this is resolved."

Quinn pulled his cigarettes out of his shirt pocket and studied the pack. He cleared his throat. Everyone in the room turned to stare at him.

"It's rare," Quinn said in a low voice, as though he were only thinking aloud. "Rare to find Allyn and I in agreement over anything first time through, but for once I find I must concur. Someone from the band should stay."

"Who then?" Ables asked. "I could go get Gillie if you'd like."

Quinn smiled. "I shall be the one who stays."

"Uh, Derek," Ables said. "Don't you think it might be better if one of us..."

"No." Quinn held Allyn's gaze. "I don't."

"Now look," Kincaid cut in, "the security problems involved –"

"– are no greater for two than for one."

"We can probably manage," Taglia agreed.

"What do you think?" Ables appealed directly to Allyn.

Allyn tipped his head to one side quizzically and spoke to Quinn as though there were no one else in the room. "Still out to protect your investments?"

"If you like," Quinn replied.

The singer turned away. "Stay then."

"How far should we go?" Ables asked. "The hotel we're in isn't far, but we could move if necessary."

"Your hotel will be fine, I'm sure," Kincaid replied. "We'll assign some officers to be on site in case of any trouble. Our concern is this might be more than a simple kidnapping. We're concerned about the safety of all the members of Leviathon. I don't recommend any of you go anywhere by yourselves until this is over. We're going to place this house in lockdown. No one will be allowed to leave or enter without police clearance, once you and your party are gone. And by the way..." he turned his attention to Sterling. "Carys' room is considered a crime scene. You'll have access to anywhere in the house but her room."

Ables turned to gaze at Quinn. The guitarist lit a cigarette and hoped his face showed neither surprise nor dismay.

"Are you sure you want to go through with this?" Ables asked quietly. "Gil or I would be more than willing to stay, you know."

"I have said I will stay."

"It's bound to be a bit awkward."

"So is fucking but that's never stopped me." Quinn exhaled a cloud of smoke. Ables shrugged and fell silent. At length Quinn sighed, relenting. "There now, Miltie, old lad," he said. "I have my reasons."

"I hope you know what you're doing," Ables grumbled.

"So do we all, ducks," Quinn said soberly. "So do we all." He got up and strolled toward the bedrooms.

Allyn rapped at the door.

"Come in," Derek said, voice muffled from inside the room. Allyn opened the door and paused, watching with interest from the doorway as the guitarist put a cigarette to his lips and fumbled in his pocket for his lighter. It took both hands to keep the flame steady enough to light the tip. "Well," he snapped. "What is it then?"

Allyn raised his eyebrows. "Nothing much. Save that you've got one lit already."

Derek looked down at the ashtray on the table beside him. "So I do," he muttered.

Allyn closed the door. He waited until Derek had carefully rubbed out the new cigarette and replaced it in his pack before saying, "Are you running short?"

Derek squinted at him. "Does it show as bad as that?"

"I've known you these ten years." Allyn shrugged. "I know what to look for. I daresay no one else would notice. Except for the police, and hopefully they won't."

"So much for that," Derek said. He sat down on the bed and stared up at Allyn. "I'm not short, chum. I'm flat out, except for one small bump in the nightstand."

"Lord!" Allyn was shocked. "You understand I'm grateful with you staying and all, but this presents a problem."

"Dead right there, more's the pity." Derek laughed a little. Only the tremor in his hands betrayed his anxiety as he poured himself a stiff shot of whiskey from the bottle on the table.

"Drink up. That'll help."

"Yes," Derek agreed, drinking off about half the glass, "and in three days I should be about right. But I'd be no good to you completely pissed, which is the only tolerable way through it. Would you care for some of this?"

"Yes, please." Allyn held out his hand. Derek filled up the shot glass again and handed it to Allyn, reserving the bottle for himself. "Not to mention that I'm not entirely certain if we have enough alcohol on hand."

"We've broached our last case of this lot," the dark haired man agreed. "I think the cognac and the champagne are holding out well enough."

"You're useless on champagne," Allyn pointed out as he sipped his whiskey.

"I don't like to admit it, but you're perfectly right there. At this rate I'm going to be driving the porcelain bus far enough without the bubbly. Never could see how you can knock it back like you do."

"French blood."

"You don't have any French blood!" Derek protested.

"Don't know that. I'm a bastard, you know. Father could have been anyone. Might have been French."

"You are not a bastard!"

"You call me one often enough." Allyn laughed ruefully and downed the last of his drink. "Besides, this hair didn't come from a bottle. No one else in the family has it."

"Throwback to your Saxon ancestors," Derek said. "Besides, I've seen pictures of your mum."

"My mum was a lovely dark haired little lady."

"So she was. More's the mystery. Here's to her."

Derek refilled Allyn's glass and they drank the toast. "And here's to your father," he added, lifting the bottle, "whoever he was."

"This is good, you know. But I can't get it out of my head that a gram of prevention would beat a gallon of cure all hollow. You've well and truly put your foot in it this time." Sterling frowned. "I dunno what to do."

"Me neither," Quinn shrugged. "I'm sorry for it for your sake, though."

"There must be a way," Allyn said a bit grimly. "I can't worry about two things at once like this. And frankly, old son, you aren't the more important of the two."

"I am well aware of that. And as it should be." Derek took a deep drag on his cigarette.

"Oh, now here's a thought." Allyn sank down to sit on the bed beside him. "What if we have someone bring it round?"

"How do you figure? The cops will never let us have someone else back up here."

"Not for you, perhaps." Allyn ran both hands through his hair and laughed. "Not for you."

Five 5

aglia stood in the carport, watching Ables and Lydia get into the limousine. When the hedges finally cut the cars off from his view, he turned and went back into the house, careful to lock the door.

He wandered back into the den. No one was around. He figured Kincaid had gone to unpack. The musicians were probably off talking somewhere. He didn't mind. Having a few minutes to himself was nice.

He glanced around the luxurious den. It was decorated with lots of leather furniture, expensive silk drapes and a plush carpet. The Christmas tree and the piano gave the place a personal touch, but the abstract art on the walls could have come from any bank building, bland and unremarkable.

Taglia took a seat in the conversation pit and opened a large picture album on the coffee table. The first few pages were all old black-and-white snapshots. Fascinated, Taglia examined them in detail. Allyn was much younger in them, perhaps in his teens, on stage with a band. *I don't know those other guys. Must be before he joined Leviathon.*

The younger version of Allyn Sterling's mass of hair was, if anything, a trifle longer in the pictures, and he hadn't yet grown into his lanky frame. He leaned on the shoulder of the guitarist beside him, much as he leaned on Quinn's shoulder from time to time in Leviathon's concerts. The strikingly handsome guitar player had a lean face and long, straight fair hair.

Taglia examined the photos more closely. In one of the early shots he noticed Allyn wore a peace button on his unbuttoned shirt. Taglia sighed as a distant ache of alienation whispered through him. He had missed the Summer of Love. He had spent 1969 in a banana jungle running from enemy fire, or pursuing those fleeing from him, and doing his best to ignore the turmoil he carried inside.

Several pages had color shots of Quinn and Allyn together. The backgrounds might have been travel posters from all over the world. Balinese temples, the Taj Mahal, a market place in what might have been Morocco, Himalayan villages, the Sphinx, a Turkish mosque — all were backdrops for the now-famous musicians, doing all the usual tourist things. There were pictures of them sitting on camels in front of a pyramid and shots of them feeding the pigeons in St. Mark's Square.

Taglia flipped through the last two pages of the travel pictures. He guessed this sequence had been taken in the Rocky Mountains. In them, Quinn wore jeans and long-sleeved shirts, hiking boots, and a wide-brimmed hat. Allyn wore nothing but cut-offs and hiking boots, with a pack slung over his shoulders.

The series ended, replaced with shots of Allyn with a beautiful dark-haired woman. With her ivory skin, high cheekbones and wide green eyes, her face might have come to life out of ancient bronze.

There followed a seemingly endless number of photographs of a little blonde girl growing up in an old stone-and-timber house on a hillside. There were pictures of her with a lamb and a kitten, several with a rabbit and some with a tiny black and white pup. The prints ended with a shot of her standing next to the carport of the house here on Oak Pass.

"Hullo."

Taglia glanced up as Allyn walked into the room. "Hi. I hope you don't mind me looking at this."

"No. It's all right. It's there to look at. That's why we take the bleeding things to begin with, innit?" The singer smiled. "Where's your partner?"

"Around somewhere. I think in his room. Did you need him for something, Mr. Sterling?"

The singer smiled. "Please, call me Allyn."

"I can get him if you want, Allyn." The name was clumsy on his tongue. He'd never dreamed he'd be on a first-name basis with his favorite rock star. He put the open photo album aside and started to rise.

"Not necessary." Allyn perched on the coffee table, knee to knee with Taglia. "I'm sure you can help."

"Me?"

"Yes." Allyn leaned forward, his lips curved in a slight smile which somehow managed to shiver its way through Taglia to the base of his spine. "The truth is a bit of a problem has come up."

"What is it?" It was difficult to get the words out. Taglia took a deep breath meant to settle his nerves. Instead it filled his lungs with the warm spicy aroma of the man's presence.

"Derek was just speaking with Harry over the phone." Allyn tugged his fingers through his hair and toyed with one lock, pulling it forward across his shoulder and wrapping it around his fingers. "He's one of our people. Been with us for eons. Guess you could call him our head roadie. He's down at the studio where we've been recording, and he says there's some problem with the master tapes." Allyn sighed. "I know we're not supposed to leave here, but it's important, you know. Do you think Harry might come up and bring Quinn the tapes?"

Taglia tried to weigh out the problems involved with some semblance of objectivity.

"Please." Allyn dropped his eyes. Long lashes dusted over his cheeks. "I, obviously, can't go. Quinn could drive himself, but surely it wouldn't be wise for him to go unprotected. Besides, I'd rather he stay. God knows why."

"It's more a question of whether anybody should come or go at all." Kincaid stepped out of the hall. Taglia blinked and sat back. He could feel a flush creeping up the back of his neck. *What the hell's the matter with me? It's not like I was doing something wrong...*

Kincaid continued, his gaze fixed on Allyn. "I don't think we should take the risk."

"Please." Allyn turned to Kincaid. "It won't take long. He can make the changes in the studio here. Harry will only be here moments."

"A shooting takes moments, too."

"He'll be coming to us."

"We don't know it matters much. It may be Derek they're after."

"That's absurd. It's my daughter they've snatched, innit?"

Taglia added, "He's got a point, Allyn. Quinn's the one with the enemies."

Kincaid flicked a sharp glance at Taglia before turning back to Allyn. "I'm not sure bringing Harry here is a good idea in any case, no matter how important those tapes are."

"What do you mean?"

"Has the matter of Harry Stuart and his fiancée completely slipped your mind? What if it's a trap?"

"Oh, that." The lines of worry which had been forming around Allyn's eyes vanished.

"The girl died. Stuart blamed Derek for her death."

"Megan did it to herself. Bad stuff. Quinn chose that night to reform, else we had lost him, too. He's always had impeccable timing, whatever else you may choose to say about him. Sick for days, in any case.

"Anyway, he's a fanatic for care where our tapes are concerned, and he has reason to be. He's the genius behind our livelihood. Which brings us back 'round to the matter at hand. He's got to get them up here or he'll fret. He's hard enough to live with as it is. I don't want the extra worry."

"If he isn't antsy now," Kincaid drawled, "I bet he will be." He crossed to the patio doors and looked out in silence. Finally, he shook his head. "Go on. Go tell him to call Harry and have the tapes brought up."

"So much for it, then." Allyn said and smiled.

A stilted silence settled on the room after the singer left. Taglia watched Kincaid, wondering what he could say to end the spell and heal the distance between them.

Kincaid turned away from the doors. When he spoke, his voice was quiet but icy. "Have you lost your mind?"

"What?"

"I can't believe you'd take any of his shit, Paul. I know you're a fan, but Christ! Are you so infatuated you haven't noticed Quinn's a junkie and Sterling's covering for him?"

Taglia clenched his teeth, too shocked to answer right away. Finally he managed to find his voice. "Who do you think you are to say that to me?"

"I'm the senior member of our team, and you damn well know it."

"You could be as 'senior' as Methuselah, and you still wouldn't have the right."

"I have every right! It's Quinn's drugs they're gonna bring in here, not any tapes. And you're too busy with Sterling to care."

"If that's the case, then don't forget who told him to go ahead..."

"He'll be out directly after he calls Harry," Allyn interrupted as he sauntered back into the room. His gaze took in both of them, but if he was aware of the argument or noticed the tension, he gave no sign. Instead, he crossed to the bar and poured himself a shot of whiskey. "Would either of you care for a drink?"

Bird of Paradise
G.J. Paterson

"No," Kincaid answered for them both.

Taglia looked from one blond man to the other, from Kincaid's dark rage to Allyn's golden brightness. *I can't stay here.*

"I'm going to go walk the perimeter," he said as he rose to his feet. "I'll be back."

Six

6

"Tell me something." Kincaid perched on a barstool. The hippie behind the bar was a millionaire several times over and the father of a kidnapped child. The idea that the two musicians might be jeopardizing Carys's recovery over Quinn's need for drugs disgusted him.

"What is it, then?" Allyn reached into the refrigerator behind the bar to pull out an ice tray.

"What is this guy actually bringing?"

"I beg your pardon?" Allyn seemed surprised by the question, but he didn't meet Kincaid's glance. "Exactly what he said, I should expect."

"This guy Harry is coming all the way from the studio to bring Derek some tapes."

"Really nice of him actually." Allyn met Kincaid's gaze this time.

"Bullshit. We both know there's nothing wrong with the tapes. If Derek did talk to him, it'll be on our tape recorder. *All* the calls are recorded, coming and going. Why don't we play the tape back and see?"

Kincaid punched the rewind button on the tape machine, untouched by the appeal in the singer's face. They listened to the whisper of the tape on the spools. He hit play.

"Hullo, Harry?" came Quinn's voice from the speaker.

"Yeah, hullo, Derek." Kincaid had no face to match the voice. It was male, young, and English.

"Everything going right?"

"Yes, sir." Stuart sounded as though the question puzzled him. "Everything's packed up and the masters are in the safe. You can pick them up any time. You've got your main strings up there, don't you?"

"Yes."

"Good, because Jackie was going to take another look at the pickups in the new Strat. He figured you had them, but he wasn't sure and I couldn't find them. It was a bit worrisome." There was relief, and rebuke, and a hint of resignation in Stuart's voice, as if his life rested on knowing where those guitars were.

"I've got them and some other things," Quinn said. "There should be odds and ends lying about. The double-neck, I think, and perhaps a mandolin, or an acoustic, and a few other bits. I don't try to keep it all straight."

"Yeah, it's all here, along with Gil's Alembic. I remember seeing the rest of it because I had to shift your lot to check the latch on his case. It was okay, you know, he just keeps closing it wrong."

"He's never become reconciled to the thing, although the Alembic bass is a wonder." Quinn laughed. "Listen, Harry, will you be there awhile yet?"

"A bit longer."

"Fine. I need you to make a pick-up for me, if you would."

There was a pause in which the windy hollowness of the open line and the faint hiss of the moving tape were the only sounds. Kincaid stared at Allyn. Stuart's voice came, slow and seemingly reluctant.

"Okay, Derek. The usual?"

"A bit more."

"I don't have much cash on me."

"Don't use your money. You can draw from petty cash. I'll square it later."

"All right. Do you want it up there?"

"Yes. We've got into a muddle. Can you be here in an hour? I'll explain when you get here. Bring the last mix with you. Leave the masters alone. Is that time enough?"

"Maybe a little longer, but I'll be there as fast as I can," Stuart said.

"Right." There was a click and then silence.

Kincaid pushed the stop button. He and Allyn stared at each other. Finally Kincaid said, "Well?"

"Well, what?" Allyn countered.

"The tape alone would hang him in any court in this country." The lie was cold and deliberate.

"I'm not at all good with abstracts." Allyn crossed over and sat down awkwardly in one of the chairs by the fireplace. "I don't pretend to understand the laws of my own country, much less this one. As it happens, I don't think some of the things Derek has done with his life are the best things he could have done. Still, I haven't the right to dictate what he does with the veins in his arms."

"Speaking of rights you don't have," Kincaid responded coldly, "how about what you've done to Paul?"

"Paul?" Allyn was plainly at a loss.

"Sergeant Taglia. Better known as Paul to his *friends*." Kincaid clenched his fists. He couldn't forget Taglia's expression when he'd looked at the Englishman. "My partner. Remember him? He's the cop who's going to serve time — along with me — if we get wrapped up

Bird of Paradise
G.J. Paterson

51

in this. Not to mention losing his career and everything else that ever mattered to him. Because he trusts you."

Kincaid hadn't realized how angry he was until it was reflected by the fear in Allyn's face. He had seen it before and had traded on it more than once. It was fear of his badge and the power it held.

"What else could I do? I can't let Derek get sick. Not on top of all else."

"You might have trusted us. You might have asked for help."

"How could we? You're cops. I'm supposed to tell you, 'Oh, by the way, Derek's an addict and we need to bring in some illicit drugs. You don't mind, do you?'"

"We're not your enemy." Kincaid's eyelids were gritty and his mouth tasted foul. "Who do you think is trying to get your daughter back, anyway? We could have gotten him medical attention."

"You are, of course, quite right." Allyn hunched his shoulders as though he were cold. His face was sober when he asked, "Where were you in nineteen-sixty-nine?"

"In Vietnam. Where were you?"

"In Manchester, maybe. Drunk on my arse, probably. Singing about peace, and sex, and girls in San Francisco putting flowers in rifle barrels." He held out his hands in what might have been a gesture of appeal. "How different we are. You frighten me, and I'm frightened already. I disturb you somehow, but you walked in here disturbed."

Disturbed? Kincaid remembered Taglia's face when he talked to Allyn. He remembered the confident, knowing expression in the singer's eyes. *I walked in here on a lie. I told him I didn't remember, and I lied. Allyn saw something he recognized.*

"Even if you bust Quinn when Harry walks through the door," Allyn went on, "it won't change anything. It isn't even me you're angry at. I'm only your albatross. The thing you can blame."

The thing I can blame. All right. Say it's jealousy. I know what jealousy feels like. I was jealous when I came in and Paul was sitting there mooning over Sterling. There's something between them. There must be.

Bird of Paradise
G.J. Paterson

"What are you going to do with the tape?" Allyn watched the blond man seated at the bar. The tape made them vulnerable. Fear of it burned his throat.

"What do you think I should do with it?"

"I can't think clearly. Between Carys gone and now this, I don't know anything. I don't want Derek to go to jail, of course, but Carys... Carys is...." He shook his head. Fear chilled him to the bone. "I don't know what to do. I can't ask you to involve yourself any further. I have presumed too far already."

"Can't argue with that." Kincaid's light blue eyes never wavered. "To answer your question, I haven't decided yet."

"How much ransom do they usually ask in something like this?"

"Depends on how much they think you have, and what their motives are in the first place. I wouldn't think it would matter too much to you."

"We're none of us as rich as you might think."

"I thought you rock stars were rolling in money."

"I'm on allowance." Allyn emptied his jeans' pockets onto the table before him. It was an interesting collection. There was a penknife, a gum wrapper, and an old business card which had been through the wash a couple of times and was too faded to read. There was also fifty-six cents in loose change, counting the English coins.

"Dead serious, you know." Allyn put his belongings back in his pockets. He picked up the business card and started to pocket it with the rest, then crumpled it and flipped it into an ashtray.

"Why?"

"Saves me going broke. I'm not like Derek. He and Miltie have been mates forever. Miltie doesn't sneeze without Derek knowing. Delegation of authority and all, but Derek's a rare one when it comes to money. Thing is, you see, in the early days there was no checking us. Me and Avery, anyway. Did the usual round of fast motors, mad pranks, and expensive women. Absolutely stunning the amount a woman can spend."

Bird of Paradise
G.J. Paterson
53

"Demetra?"

"Oh, yeah. Quinn never had much use for her, but I wouldn't listen. She was... is... beautiful, you see. She was the first flash bird I ever pulled. She seemed... I believed she truly loved me." Allyn sighed. Honesty compelled him to add, "She might have — as she understood it, anyway."

"What happened?"

"Carys, essentially." Allyn lifted his head, remembering the hysterics and the tears. "She was a high fashion model and didn't want children. I lived for the mere idea. She was pregnant before we married, actually. She wanted to marry me. I told her having the baby was the only way I would even consider it. What a switch, eh?"

Kincaid nodded. "I see what your manager was talking about."

"Fortunately, I did too before it was too late. I took Quinn's advice on investments, and all. Apart from buying my farm, which he never could understand."

"Tell me about your farm," Kincaid prompted him.

"I was born there. It'd been in my mother's family for time out of mind. She was the only child who survived, you see, and it came to her. My grandmother was still living when I was but a lad. I remember her. She spoke only Welsh and hissed at my dad when he called her ignorant."

"What did you think?"

"That it was my father who was ignorant. She knew when to plant by the phases of the moon, and when a ewe would drop her lamb. She could always tell the weather. By the aching of her joints, she said. She knew every bird and its habits, and every sort of animal would come to her hand, wild or not. Carys has that gift, too. We never had a doctor in while Gran was living. She gathered herbs and made tinctures and infusions and poultices. They tasted altogether foul but worked fine for man and beast. She had a Corgi which went everywhere she did. They worked the home flock without a word spoken. Even the old men in the village thought her uncanny that way.

"What little I knew of Welsh as a lad I learned from her. They didn't teach it in school when I was there, you see. In those days,

G.J. Paterson

54

you'd get a whipping for speaking it. It's all changed now, thanks to the Nationalist movement. Carys's learning it and me along with her, though she's much the better of the two of us."

"If it was your family's farm to begin with, why'd you have to buy it back?" Kincaid asked.

"My father's a drunkard and plays the ponies. It took years, because the farm was prosperous to begin with, but he managed to get heavily in debt. Gran died when I was six, and my mum two years later. He sold the farm not long after, and we moved to Cardiff. It broke my heart. I always swore I'd come back one day. The proudest day of my life, apart from Carys's birth, was the day I signed the deed and went out to take the place in hand. Quinn went with me, bless him, though he was a bit puzzled by it all. Gods, but it was a derelict and a wreck."

Kincaid nodded. "Is your father still alive?"

"Oh, yeah. He still doesn't understand how it is I have any money. He thinks I'm a gangster or something. It's the hair. Throws him off, I figure."

"You aren't close with your father, then?"

"No, we're not. I pay him to stay away, if you want the truth of it." Allyn sighed. "It's just easier that way."

"How about you and Quinn?"

After the briefest hesitation, Allyn said, "We were."

"What happened?"

"I dunno. Drifted off, I suppose."

"It didn't have anything to do with his drugs? Heroin, isn't it?"

"I... I..." Allyn stammered, paused to catch his breath. "I expect you should ask him."

"I'm asking you. Wasn't he a good enough friend to try to get him off the smack?"

The personal questions were bad enough. This going on about Quinn infuriated him. Who was Kincaid to ask this of him? Allyn's temper flared. Before he could constrain himself, he was on his feet, glaring at the cop. He whirled on his heel and strode from the den.

He went directly to the dresser in his room and opened the left hand top drawer. The box was there. He knew it would be. How long had he hated the sound of a phone ringing late in the night? How long had he been waiting for the call to come to tell him this time, this last time, the gambler had thrown and lost?

Allyn returned to the den. Without warning he tossed the plastic box to Kincaid. "G'wan," he said in a harsh, low voice. "Open it."

Kincaid unsnapped the lid and lifted it back on its hinges. It was a formidable array of medical technology — two small disposable syringes and needles, still sealed in their sterile plastic shields, a small packet of absorbent cotton, and a little, capped bottle of alcohol. The center of attraction was the tiny ampoules of colorless liquid.

"Recognize it?" Allyn demanded.

"No."

"It's Narcan." He spoke as calmly as he could past his anger. "I carry it with me as a matter of course, wherever I go. As do Miltie and Gil and Jackie. It's quite legal, you know. We all have prescriptions for them.

"Derek doesn't know we carry them, of course." Allyn stared down at the box in Kincaid's hands. "It seemed wise after we twice owed his life to the intervention of strangers. He's thirty-one and has been a habitual user of heroin for something like seven or eight years. He's been lucky. Luck will inevitably run out on him one of these days. I know it, and the others know it. He knows it, and he knows we know. We're all very knowing."

After a long moment Kincaid handed the box back to him and nodded. He pressed the rewind button.

Allyn sighed. The next call that came in would cover Quinn's frailty.

Seven

7

Quinn sat in a chair by the fireplace and gritted his teeth while Kincaid frisked Harry Stuart in the foyer. He smothered a sigh of relief when the roadie came into the den carrying a tape case.

Stuart was as homely as an old shoe, broad and muscular, with blue eyes and thinning dark red hair held back in a ponytail. He nodded to Quinn. "Hullo, Derek." He glanced over his shoulder toward the foyer. "What was that all about, then?"

"Have you talked to Jackie today?"

"No, sir. I went to the studio early this morning and haven't heard from Jackie or anyone all day. I was wondering why he didn't come by. Is something going on?"

"Let's talk in the booth, Harry." Quinn got to his feet and led the way through the kitchen to the small studio beyond it.

Stuart obediently followed him into the studio and waited while Quinn locked the door behind them and turned the lights on low in the control booth. The main room was dark.

"Carys's been kidnapped," Quinn said through tight lips. "Someone has taken her."

Stuart stared at him, slack-jawed. After a moment he seemed to gather his wits and said, "Who would do such a thing?"

"We don't know. We've no clue at this point. Do you have any ideas?

"About what, sir?" Stuart licked his lips.

"The kidnapping, Harry. Do you have any idea who might have done it?"

"No, Derek. No, sir." The red-haired man swallowed hard, shook his head jerkily. "How is Allyn handling it?"

"He's shattered. What would you expect?" Quinn sat down in one of the two chairs, turned on a small lamp beside the control board and leaned back. He wasn't surprised Stuart had nothing to add. The roadie wasn't always the most observant of men, even where the equipment was concerned. It had led to difficulties in the past. Still, Stuart was his. He had bound himself to Quinn after Megan's death with a combination of promises and a shrewd kind of fawning.

Stuart opened the tape case and handed Quinn a length of rubber tubing. He pulled out a small glassine envelope and poured some of the light brown powder into the spoon. "I tested it myself, just a little bump. It's good shit. I brought you enough for about three days. I hope that's enough."

"It'll do," Quinn said, watching closely as Stuart lit a candle and cooked the heroin with a bit of water. When the dose was ready, Stuart drew it into a syringe through a cotton ball while Quinn pulled down a sock and strapped his ankle, searching for a vein in his foot. The red-haired man started to pass the rig over.

"I'm too shaky," Quinn admitted irritably.

Stuart nodded and took Quinn's foot onto his lap. The quick familiar stab of the needle stung. When Stuart released the tourniquet,

Quinn sighed with relief. Liquid fire raced through his body. He settled back into the comfortable chair. He couldn't be bothered to speak a farewell as Stuart slipped out the door, locking it before shutting it behind himself.

He let the poppy's glamour overtake him. Take him down the ladder of dreams. Down to the place where old phantoms waited for his waking mind. Ten years fell away at once.

***

For a moment Quinn sat watching the young singer sleep. Privation and sickness had burnt all the dross out of his face, and the guitarist was worried. He gently began to wipe the dry skin with a cool, damp cloth. Under his touch, Allyn stirred and moaned, hovering on the edge of sleep like one drugged.

Quinn's mother had been a Nursing Sister in Manchester during the War, but he remembered only the clinical briskness of her care whenever he had been ill. He knew next to nothing about looking after the sick. He did remember dimly that those with fever should be kept quiet and plied with liquids to encourage the fever to break.

Avery's girlfriend, Nan, had been as much help as the doctor, apart from the prescriptions. Allyn had apparently been sick for some time.

"Where have you been living, and how?" Quinn asked softly. The other man made no answer. "Ah well, it's none of my business, now, is it?"

He went on wiping the younger man's face and paid no attention to his soft protests. "It's all going to come right," he murmured. Weakly, Allyn tried to turn his face away, crying out something Quinn couldn't follow. "Here now," Quinn admonished him. "Give over. You're burning up."

"No. Please don't," Allyn whispered. His eyes fluttered open. He pulled at Quinn's hands. There was a desperation in his actions that his strength couldn't match. His voice shook. "Please. Don't hurt me."

"Beg pardon?" Quinn searched his face, realizing with an unpleasant shock that Allyn was delirious and terrified. "Lord, dearie, no one's going to hurt you."

"Please." Allyn's gaze sought his face, but couldn't hold focus. "I'll do anything you want... just don't hurt me anymore."

"Allyn." Quinn took one thin, burning hand between both of his own, speaking as soothingly as he could manage. "Allyn, it's all right. No one is going to hurt you."

He could feel the singer's trembling, and see the distress on his face. Quinn's mind darted over the recent past as he tried to piece together a picture that made sense. He went on speaking, not caring what he said. He knew the content mattered less than the tone of his voice. "Lie down, Peacock," he murmured. "There, there, lad, you're safe here. I'm with you. There's no one will ever harm you while I am with you."

Allyn sighed and settled back down on the pillow. After awhile he fell into the same restless sleep, still clinging to Quinn's hand. His grip was surprisingly strong. Quinn didn't move. He sat holding the fine-boned hand, and he wondered many things.

Avery found him there when he came in. The drummer beat his arms across his chest to warm himself, hung up his jacket, and came over. Quinn gently unclasped the hand he held and laid it on Allyn's chest, stood, and glanced at Avery. "Have you considered, in the past few days, why Sammy let such a prize slip away?" he asked.

"No, only blessed our luck. You know I think he's bloody fantastic. It's too bad he got sick." Avery said. "If you don't mind, I'm for bed."

"Nah, go on then. I'll watch Sleeping Beauty."

"He is that."

Bird of Paradise
G.J. Paterson

"He's what we wanted."

"Damn right," Avery grinned. "Good night."

"Sleep well."

Quinn sat in a nearby chair and picked up a battered paperback copy of *Fellowship of the Ring* he had borrowed from a friend.

He never knew how much time passed, but the wise old man of the story was lost when a deep sigh and rustle from the couch attracted his attention. He glanced over at his charge. The younger man was drenched with sweat. Quinn checked and found the sheets were soaked, and Allyn's shoulder was moist and normal in temperature.

"Must get you out of there," he told the sleeper. "Don't want you catching pneumonia on top of the rest."

He pulled off the blankets and half-lifted Allyn to strip off the borrowed robe he was wearing. It fell from his shoulders and Quinn stared in shock. Welts crisscrossed Allyn's back. They were healed, but the scars were red and recent. Quinn pressed his lips together as he quickly finished his work.

Allyn moved restlessly in Quinn's hands. It was impossible to tell if he were struggling or trying to help. When he was settled back on his makeshift bed, dry now and warm, he sighed and fell into a more natural sleep.

Watching Allyn's sleeping face, Quinn was uneasy. He sat down in his chair again and ran callused fingertips over the threadbare upholstery, absently picking fragments of yellowed stuffing out of a seam. "What have you done to me, Sammy? That's what I wonder."

He hadn't seen Sammy Hayes in almost two years when the other guitarist dropped by to tell him about this fantastic singer who would be jamming with the Blues Works for a couple of nights. Quinn was skeptical. Word had gotten around Quinn was planning to put together a new band out of the wreckage left when he and Gerry Wiley had split White Mare right down the middle, halfway through their second American tour. It seemed every musician in England was either looking for a gig or knew someone who was.

He told himself he wasn't about to go listen to this guy based on Sammy's recommendation. Still, no one else they listened to had the right sound. It was worth a shot. He had gone down to the club, expecting nothing.

He remembered the moment Allyn's voice came howling out of the night. The spotlight hit the younger man and he seemed to turn to flame without burning.

Quinn jammed with the boy during one of the breaks. His voice swooped and soared, matching Quinn's guitar turn-for-turn through an intricate improvisation in "Mean Woman Blues." It left them both laughing, exhilarated.

He went back the next night, bringing Avery, Gil and Miltie with him. They took Allyn out to dinner afterwards to celebrate. Allyn hardly ate, although he seemed excited and eager to find out more about the new band and its prospects. It was clear he made a nice fit with Gil and Avery. At the end of the meal he rose with the rest of them to toast Leviathon and collapsed at Quinn's feet.

Quinn and Avery brought him to the little flat, setting up the couch for a bed, which led to him sitting there watching a sick man sleep.

"Sammy's no fool," he said aloud. "He did owe me something. Perhaps he owed you something, too."

There was no response. Quinn gazed at Allyn's sleeping face. At rest, it had an ethereal quality — like the elves of Middle-Earth, he supposed, heightened by whatever hardship the lad had been through. Despite the illness, it was a strong face. Quinn wondered what the fellow would be like once he was well. He was sure the gentle, almost passive aura would be burnt away. He sensed deep wells of fire in the sleeping man.

"Sammy's marred everything he ever touched," Quinn sighed. "Me for one, as far as it goes, and you as well, Peacock, but with no blows we'll ever see. It's not wise to tamper with a man's pride when that's all he's got. I suppose we shall never know."

He picked up his book again. The Companions made their way to the lost forest. Quinn strayed and wandered awhile in a land of trees like graceful pillars of silver as the wind sighed through their boughs amid a rustling roof of gold. Rippling music ran through the guitarist's mind. The fingers of his left hand twitched with the chord changes and runs he was building.

"Derek?" a soft voice intruded.

He glanced up quickly. Allyn was watching him with an alert but weary gaze. He held up the book to show Allyn the cover. "Sorry," he apologized. "I was a bit lost."

Allyn smiled and waved a hand in languid dismissal. "Never mind," he said. "I understand."

"You've read this, then?"

"At least a dozen times." He smiled. "I can read, you know. I'm not just another ignorant Taff. Where were you?"

"It's the first time for me. The part where Galadriel sings about leaving and going into the West, only she doesn't think she'll find a ship to take her."

Allyn chanted in a low voice,

"...Of Princesses and Queens, and Elves and dragon's rings
of sailing ships, enchanted harps, of battles and of kings
songs of good and evil intertwining in your mind.
In the secret gardens of the heart you find,
the bird of fire takes flight on golden wings
sweeping you to fields of light only magic brings..."

He let his voice fall away into silence, blushing a little.

Quinn stared at him, astonished. Finally he had the presence of mind to say, "You wrote that."

Bird of Paradise
G.J. Paterson
63

"Yes." The blush deepened.

"When?"

"Just now."

"Bloody brilliant." They looked at one another, neither speaking, holding to a moment of perfect understanding. Finally, something eased in Quinn that he hadn't realized was under tension. He stretched languorously, got up and walked to the kitchen. "Like some tea?"

"Yes, please." Allyn smiled. After a moment he shifted himself into a sitting position against the pillows. "I've been ill, haven't I?"

"Yes, for some time now."

"What day is it?"

"Wednesday." Quinn filled the kettle from the tap.

"Oh, it can't be. It should be Saturday at the latest."

"You've lost a few days, my lad. If your fever hadn't broken when it did, it would be to hospital with you."

"I *am* sorry for this." Quinn heard the worry in his voice. "We've got gigs coming up over the weekend. I'll be ready."

"You will not." Quinn turned from the stove and spoke emphatically. "You will stay right here until you're completely recovered. Can't have you breaking down halfway through the second leg of the tour. I've my investments to think of, after all."

"We've missed dates already."

"A few more won't sink us." Quinn lied, unwilling to burden Allyn with the whole truth.

Allyn sighed and lay back against the pillows. The silence stretched comfortably between them. He liked the feeling of someone in the room who understood things without the need of endless explanations.

He brought Allyn a steaming cup of tea and gestured at the record player. "Would you like to hear something?"

"Big Joe Williams," Allyn joked. "Or Muddy Waters."

"Right." Quinn nodded and headed for the disarrayed stacks of records piled on the floor.

"You actually have their stuff?"

"Yes." Quinn rummaged through the stack.

"Bill Broonzey?"

"In here somewhere. Django Reinhardt, too."

"I don't bloody well believe it." Allyn rose on his elbows. "I've hardly met anyone who liked that stuff, apart from me. Let alone had much."

"Neither have I, not in a long time. No singers, at least." Quinn turned to look at the younger man and couldn't keep from smiling. The records were treasures he seldom had an opportunity to share. "Now you know how I squandered my youth. What do you want to hear?"

"All of it."

"Yes, but what first?" Quinn laughed.

"Sorry." Allyn was laughing too, perhaps a trifle giddy from his illness. The rich sound was unsteady, but it pleased the ear. "I haven't listened to a record player with good music on it in months."

"Starving for hyacinths for the soul, eh? You've a treat coming. This is stereo. Not that it matters with these old recordings. Bought the system months ago, when I was flush from working steady sessions and money didn't much matter."

"You've spent it on the right gear."

Somehow Allyn's approval mattered, which surprised him. He realized he had been half-ashamed to flaunt something so expensive before someone who kept all he owned in one tattered suitcase. He shook his head. *Should have known. We have the same values. Music is the only true coin of our realm.* "What's it to be then, Peacock?"

"'Peacock'?" Allyn stared.

"Suits you." Quinn realized what he had said and smiled.

Allyn considered this for a moment, then grinned. "All right, then. A bird that makes a fool of itself when it turns around is all right by me."

They both laughed. Allyn said, "Play Broonzey first."

The vinyl was old and scratchy but somehow it seemed to enhance the music, as if it wouldn't be right for the pressing to be flawless. Quinn came back and sat down in his chair. He sipped his tea while Allyn lounged on the pillows.

The music flooded the room on a rising, dark and silty tide. Quinn listened as the warmth of the tea relaxed him. He was aware of the tenuous resonance building between himself and the stranger on the couch.

Quinn turned and found himself snared in Allyn's gaze. "*'The bird of fire takes flight on golden wings,'*" he said aloud and raised his cup in a toast to his fate.

Allyn smiled and raised his cup in answer. "Leviathon."

***

Quinn slipped further down into the warm and welcoming darkness until there weren't even dreams to trouble him. There, in the needle's temporary oblivion, he could rest at last.

Bird of Paradise
G.J. Paterson
66

Eight

8.

*T*he phone rang.

"Shall I answer it?" Allyn got to his feet, staring at the phone as though it were a coiled viper.

Kincaid picked up the headset. "Don't forget the call's being traced. Keep him talking if you can." The phone finished its second ring. "Go."

Allyn picked up the receiver convulsively. "Hullo?"

"Peacock?" A man's muffled voice came through the earphones.

"Who is this?"

"I left you a note. I've got your little girl."

The cop watched the singer's color drain away. He nodded encouragement and prayed Allyn could hold together through the next few minutes. His child's life hung in the balance, and there was nothing Kincaid could do to help. It all depended on her father now.

He frowned with frustration while Allyn took a deep, ragged breath and asked, "Is she all right?"

"Yeah, but if you want her back, you'll do what I tell you."

Kincaid concentrated on Allyn, trying to will him strength and calm. The voice was a monotone, cold with menace. It was muffled, as though the speaker was disguising his voice. The caller sounded American, probably white, probably from the south.

"Anything," Allyn breathed.

"Good. Two hundred fifty thousand, in small bills. You've got twenty-four hours to get the money together."

"I don't have that kind of money!"

"Don't give me that shit. Your last album's still on the charts, plus you got another one coming. It's bound to be a smash." The caller laughed. "You'll think of something. Or Quinn will. He's always done your thinking for you, anyway. Keep the cops out of this, Peacock. Any sign of cops and I'll kill her."

"Please," Allyn begged. "Don't hurt her."

Kincaid scribbled a note and pushed it across the table at Allyn. *Ask to speak to her.*

Allyn glanced at it and nodded. "I... I want to talk to Carys."

"You'll have to trust me," the kidnapper said. "There's your first lesson. Learn to trust what I tell you."

"My first lesson?"

"Trust me."

"I'll get the money somehow, but please, I must talk to my daughter."

"I'll call tomorrow and tell you where to bring the cash. You can talk to her then. Remember this — two hundred and fifty thousand, small bills, no cops. Peacock, you sure have a pretty little girl. Maybe I'm getting interested in how pretty. Think about that tonight."

"Wait. Please!" An electronic buzz was his only answer. He slammed down the receiver, picked up his glass and hurled it against the wall. The tumbler shattered into splinters and the whiskey trickled down. "She's only eight!"

Bird of Paradise
G.J. Paterson
68

"We're doing everything we possibly can."

"Bloody fucking hell! You can say we're rich and famous. What's the use of it? How many gold records does it take to replace my daughter's life?"

Kincaid made no reply. He watched Allyn pace.

"Rock and roll," Allyn stopped pacing and stood staring at the Christmas tree. "The whole thing's one long death trip anyway. I should have gotten out years ago. I knew it, but I didn't."

"Why didn't you?"

"Vanity and obligation." Allyn shook his head and poured himself another drink. "I'm bound by contract as though I'd sold my soul to the Devil himself. Damn Quinn anyway! It's my own fault. He knew the cards to play, but I'm the one who fell for his game. Obligations and contracts. I should have broken out somehow. If I had only known what would come of it…. They could lock me in the Scrubs for the rest of my natural life if only Carys was safe." He stared at Kincaid, his face haggard. "Where am I going to find the money?"

"Don't worry. Milton Ables strikes me as a man who will find the money. And my department will give him any help he needs."

Allyn sighed. "You're right, of course. It's just that I don't deal well with frustration."

The phone rang again. He set the new drink back on the countertop, untasted. "I don't think I can do this twice."

"It's probably one of our guys calling with the follow-up. Go ahead, pick it up," Kincaid said. Allyn picked up the receiver while Kincaid slipped his headset on again.

"Hullo?"

"Lieutenant Kincaid, please."

"You were right." Allyn handed over the phone.

Kincaid swapped the headphones for the receiver. "It's Rossington, Lieutenant. Sorry, the call wasn't long enough to get a trace."

"Yeah. I was afraid of that. Hang on a sec," Kincaid said. He glanced at Allyn. "I've got to take this. Can you give me a few minutes?"

Allyn gave him a penetrating look. After a moment he shook his head and headed for the hall. His bedroom door slammed.

"Okay. Tell Captain Ortiz the ransom is a quarter mil and that Milton Ables is the one to talk to about the money. He handles Sterling's finances."

"Hang on a minute while I run that by the Captain," Rossington said and then Kincaid was listening to the faint murmur of conversation from the squad room. A few minutes passed before he heard the sound of the receiver being picked up. "Got it done. The Captain's calling Ables right now."

"Okay, good. What've you found out?"

"We got the letters down to the lab," Rossington said. "We made copies, too. Did you get a chance to read them?"

"No, not enough time. What did you get out of them?"

"Most of them are just run-of-the-mill harassment. Some typed, some hand written. Two are a collage. Mrs. Calhoun must have kept them because they implied threats to Sterling — kind of a 'do this or else' sort of tone. There's only one or two letters per customer in that bunch."

Kincaid heard the snick of a key in the front door lock and automatically reached for his gun. "Hang on."

He took his hand off the weapon as Taglia walked in. A knot of tension he hadn't recognized loosened and he smiled at his partner with genuine relief. He waved Taglia over and offered him the headphones.

"Taglia's here too, Rossington, go ahead with what you were saying."

"Okay. The rest we call the 'Peacock Letters' and they all seem to come from the same person."

"*Peacock*?" He looked at Taglia. The puzzlement he felt was mirrored in his partner's eyes.

"That's right, Peacock. There are six of them, and the lab guys think they were all typed on the same machine. The tone sounds as

Bird of Paradise
C.J. Paterson

if he knows Sterling personally. No pictures, but the descriptions of what he wants to do will keep you up nights. You need to read them, Lieutenant. Have you got a fax machine up there?"

"Yeah, they installed one when they set up the phone system."

"Okay. I'll fax 'em to you."

"Well, I have my own set of experts on the band here." Kincaid said. Taglia grinned at him. "I'll research the bird stuff. Anything else?"

"So far we've cleared the drummer, Avery Pots, and three of the roadies. They were at a fight and have the ticket stubs. Gilbert McConathy, the bassist, was at a classical music concert downtown. We've left a message for Demetra Sterling. We're still working on everybody else.

"R&I sent up a shitload of criminal histories. Avery Potts and most of the roadies with the band have been picked up for misdemeanor drunk and disorderlies at one time or another. Same with Noel Moody, but he also has an assault, and an ADW here in L.A. No convictions. The only felony arrests were Sterling and Quinn. They were both arrested in San Francisco on one count of possession of heroin each. Charges were dropped against Sterling. Quinn got a big fine and probation."

"How about overseas?"

"Hayden called Interpol. They're going to do some checking and call back. That's it so far."

"Okay, let me or Taglia know if you hit anything of interest. You know where we'll be," Kincaid said and hung up.

Taglia said. "I gather the call came in. How bad was it?"

"Rough," Kincaid replied. "Allyn's in his room. He's taking it hard. Listen, about what I said before —"

"Forget it. You were right, I wasn't paying attention. It won't happen again." Taglia said.

"What's the deal about calling Allyn 'Peacock?'"

"I don't know. Maybe it's about their song 'Bird of Paradise.' Could be a nickname the band calls him."

"Yeah, could be." Kincaid said. He remembered the look on Taglia's face when he was talking to Allyn. He shook his head. Trust has to start somewhere. "Why don't you go get him?"

Kincaid tried to scan his notes but unwanted memories of waking up next to Paul kept intruding. His gut roiled in confusion. He closed his eyes, listening to the murmur of conversation down the hall. He looked up again as Taglia came back with Allyn trailing behind. The man looked dreadful.

"I have to know." Allyn's voice was choked. "Do you think he'll hurt her?"

"No," Kincaid said flatly, hoping he spoke the truth. "She's got to be able to talk to you tomorrow night. He knows it."

"That's some comfort. Or it should be, one would think. What about after he calls tomorrow? Will he hurt her then?"

"When he calls you demand he bring her to the drop off. He'll have to keep her alive if he wants his money." Kincaid hated the easy, assured way the words slipped off his tongue. It felt too much like lying.

Allyn stared at him. "There's no guarantee though, is there?"

"No. There's no guarantee."

Allyn gave a short, bitter laugh and shook his head. He went to the bar and picked up the whisky bottle. After a moment he put it back and sat down in a chair across from Kincaid. "I just don't know what to do. I wish Derek would come back. Sometimes I wish I'd never met the man, but I wish he were here now."

"I'm here now," Quinn said as he came through the arch from the kitchen. His gait was easy, loose and relaxed, but his pupils were pinpricks. "I take it that the bastard has called. I'd like to hear the tape," He stopped at Allyn's side and placed a hand on his shoulder.

Allyn gazed up at him, his expression desperate. The moment was almost too intimate and painful to watch. "He wants two hundred and fifty thousand dollars, Dee."

"Don't worry, old son. I'll ring up Miltie right now.

Kincaid cleared his throat and said, "You can call him later. Captain Ortiz is talking to him right now about the ransom. What we need is for you guys to listen to the tape."

"I don't think I care to hear it again," Allyn said.

"I know, but sometimes hearing the recording afterwards helps you pick up things you didn't have time to notice before."

"All right, then. Play it." Allyn leaned back in the chair and closed his eyes. He looked at ease, but his hands, balled into fists on the chair's arms, gave him away.

Kincaid rewound the tape and pushed the play button. Quinn took a seat on the couch, concentration clear on his face. When the call ended, he glanced at Allyn, frowning. "May I hear it again, please? Allyn, listen to this."

Kincaid ran the tape again. Allyn sat up, watching Quinn. Abruptly the guitarist said, "There. Did you hear it?"

"Hear what?" Allyn asked.

"What he said. He called you 'Peacock.'"

Kincaid felt his pulse race.

"What of it?" Allyn still seemed mystified.

Quinn shook back his long hair. "It's what I used to call you. How could he know? I haven't used that in more than two years."

"No." Allyn's eyes widened. "Not since..."

"...San Francisco," Quinn finished for him.

"When you guys got busted?" Taglia asked.

"Ah yes," Quinn said drily. "Our big publicity break last tour."

"It's a long story," Allyn said.

Taglia asked, "So who else would know about 'Peacock'?"

"No one," Quinn said. "It was a private joke in the band."

"Do you know who it is?" Kincaid interrupted.

Quinn's gaze never wavered off Allyn's face. "I'm... not certain. Possibly. I stopped calling you 'Peacock' because of him."

"Is it someone with the band?"

"No. None of our lot." Quinn glanced at Kincaid then back at Allyn. "At least not any more. Play it again."

This time, the musicians watched each other as it played. There was silence after it was through, filled only with the sound of the tape through the reels. After a moment Kincaid reached out and turned it off. Quinn leaned back against the couch cushions. "If it's who I think it is, he's trying to disguise his voice."

"The letter writer called you 'Peacock,' too," Taglia said.

"What?" Allyn turned to stare. "What letter writer?"

"Shit!" Quinn said, and Kincaid remembered Quinn knew about the letters, but Allyn didn't.

"Tell me," Allyn insisted. "What letters?"

Quinn sighed. "Harassing letters. Usually they're intercepted before they get to you. Normally Kate keeps them in London, but Lydia's been keeping them since you've been here."

"You think I'm a child who has to be protected from nasty mail? I want to see them."

"They're not here right now," Kincaid said. It was a lie of omission, but he didn't care. He could always show the singer the faxes if it seemed relevant. "They're at the station. I sent them down for fingerprinting."

"Allyn." Quinn's voice was rough. "You don't want to see them. Trust me."

"Trust you? That's what he said. 'Trust me.' Not much of an option any more, is it? How much do you know about them?"

"I've seen them."

"Why didn't you tell me?"

"To what purpose?"

"Have you read them?"

"Yes."

"You've obviously appointed yourself my minder, then."

"It does seem that way, I know." Quinn sighed and shook his head. After a moment he went on, "Inspectors, I have another point about the recording. How did the bastard know we've got an album coming out?"

"Wouldn't a lot of people know?" Taglia asked.

"You'd be surprised how few actually. Most all of them work for us in one way or another, and they're all sworn to secrecy. Non-disclosure agreements and all that."

"Let's focus on what matters here," Kincaid snapped. "Who the hell do you think is on the tape?"

"We don't know for sure," Allyn said.

"I don't care. Give me a name."

"Irons." Quinn's tone was ice. "Rick Irons."

Kincaid reached for the phone.

Nine

9

The phone rang as soon as Kincaid hung up. Allyn answered it with obvious reluctance, and then held out the receiver to Quinn. "It's Miltie."

Quinn juggled a cigarette to take the phone. "What is it?"

"I just got off the phone with the police. They want to know about the ransom."

"Yeah, it's a quarter million dollars."

"By mid-day tomorrow they told me. They want it early in case the sodding bastard does something dodgy." There was a long pause, then Ables sighed. "I called Eclectic as soon as I got back to the hotel. They've sent out Martin Cohen and Blaine Harris. I haven't talked to them yet but it looks like we may be able to work a deal with the company. If I do you might not like the terms."

"Do it." Quinn said. "They own us already, or like to think they do."

"This may cock-up your scheme."

"I don't care about that now. Just get us the money."

"Right," Ables said. "I'll ring you back when I've got news."

Quinn hung up. He was aware of Allyn's anxious, unrelenting gaze. He took a long drag on his cigarette.

"Miltie's got a plan working." Quinn said.

"What?" Allyn demanded

"He'll get back to us."

Taglia interrupted. "Talk to us about San Francisco. We need to know about this guy Irons. What did he do that made you stop calling Allyn 'Peacock?'

There was a long silence as the two musicians considered. Finally Quinn drawled, "Yes. Those are the things which might have a bearing here. All right, Allyn. Tell them."

"You tell them," Allyn retorted. "It was your dope. I want some tea."

"Right. Just hurry back," Quinn said. "I'll want help with the hard bits."

Allyn stood and looked down at him. "As always."

Quinn's gaze followed Allyn as he disappeared through the arch to the kitchen then he turned his attention to Taglia and Kincaid. "It was this like, you see. Before the last tour, I decided we had extended our studio sound to the point we needed more musicians to reproduce it. I'd been mucking about with over-dubbing tracks, and eventually there is a limit to what sheer volume can do." He flicked ashes in the general vicinity of an ashtray. "We argued about it all the way over. Allyn and Avery felt we should play the best way we could, while Gil and I thought we should give the customers the closest sound to the record we could manage. Eventually, of course, even I admitted we did much better, just the four of us. It's more to do with chemistry than sound."

"In a manner of speaking," Allyn said as he came back into the room. He sat down in the chair again.

Bird of Paradise
G.J. Paterson

"I'm getting to that," Quinn said. "Anyway, I carried the day, but by the time the dust settled we were here. We added a keyboardist for awhile. We didn't like the way it worked so we gave him the push early on.

"We picked up this guitarist, Rick Irons," Quinn said, seeing Kincaid was once again taking notes. "He came highly recommended, had been around, and was a known talent. At first it seemed it might work. Before long, though, Rick decided he didn't like playing rhythm to my lead. He wanted to do more.

"There was a certain tension between us, which came to a head in San Francisco. Anyway, word got back to me through the usual channels how Rick fancied himself over me on the strings. Sheer rubbish, of course. I should have ignored it, but it pricked me a bit."

Allyn said, "They wound up trading riffs at sound check one afternoon like schoolboys on a dare. Derek blew him off the stage, of course. And him with an injured hand."

"Silly thing for grown men to do," Quinn muttered. "It was only a whiskey-inspired impulse."

"We were late getting there, Quinn and me," Allyn said. "Made the others wait for us. We do know how to make an entrance. The whole arena was on edge."

"We walked up the backstage stairs." Quinn could almost feel the weight of his heavy guitar case in his right hand. "Ross was waiting for me with his guitar in his hands. I set the case down by my Marshall amps, flipped the latches, and lifted out my vintage Strat."

"She's still beautiful, you know," sighed the singer. "It was bold of you to try it with her, though. I know what Jackie thought of the wiring."

Quinn laughed derisively at Jackie's opinion, remembering how the face of the guitar with its faded sunburst finish glowed under the stage light like the hide of a living thing, battered but still strong. An errant spot caught the custom silver pickguard, highlighting the Art Deco-style engraving, "Sweet Fire." The feel of the guitar had been familiar and reassuring in his hands.

"It's funny, you know," Quinn turned his gaze to Kincaid. "I remember smiling as I slung the strap over my shoulder. Casual as may be, I plugged into my amp and flipped on the power. I took my time with the adjustments, checking my accuracy against the strobe-tuner. Wouldn't do to be out of tune. The whole time I was aware of Allyn talking with Gil, and of Irons standing across the stage, silent and waiting."

"Oh, he was cool, all right." Allyn laughed, a short, harsh sound. "Finally he turned around. Across the empty space their eyes met. There were daggers drawn on both sides, clearly. Derek strolled to the nearest mike. 'I hear you consider yourself a virtuoso,' he said, and didn't his voice ring out across the empty hall? Irons nodded with nary a word. 'Care to make a test of it?' Quinn asked and smiled ever-so-pleasant-like when Irons nodded again. Then out came Derek's lighter and cigarettes from his jacket pocket. He lit up, and after a couple of puffs wedged the burning cigarette under the strings on the head."

Surprise pricked Quinn, listening to the narrative. He hadn't realized Allyn had paid that much attention.

He remembered taking a spare pick out of his hip pocket and setting it firmly between his lips. He flexed his left hand. The deep cut he'd gotten three months ago had healed, but it had nicked a nerve. He'd gone on using it even though the doctors had advised him to wait. He'd known from the pain they were right, but the tour was set, and there had been no time to waste waiting for the flesh to heal.

"I was feeling a bit hesitant because of my injured hand and thinking how stupid it all was," Quinn recalled. "I knew there was no credit to be gained, no matter what the outcome. If I outplayed him, everyone would call me crass to use my talent to put a clearly lesser man down. If Rick should happen to outplay me, it would be so much the worse. The critics would be on me like sharks. Never mind my hurt hand."

There had been no more time for reflection. Irons was playing, and when he stopped Quinn repeated it, note for note, before building on to his own rebuttal. They would switch back and forth until one of them fell apart.

Bird of Paradise
G.J. Paterson

His world had narrowed down to the fiery notes.

"I have no idea how long the contest lasted," Quinn said. In the end it had come down to agony and the music's blazing fire. "When I came to myself again, Rick had stopped playing."

"Long since, actually," Allyn told the cops.

Quinn couldn't admit the first thing he was aware of was Allyn's face, laughing and laughing — not with Carys gone and things the way they were. He was a little ashamed of the memory and the warmth it produced in his bowels.

"I was falling about laughing." Allyn said. "I knew he'd win, I just didn't realize it would take him so long to notice. He swung his old guitar above his head, producing a storm of feedback, then brought it down and let the raging strings fall silent."

Quinn sighed at the memories. He had stood swaying, dripping with sweat, until he, too, began to laugh. Allyn had come to him then, and they leaned on one another like two shipwrecked survivors cast up on a beach, sharing the triumph.

"After a moment I realized the roadies and all were cheering." Telling it now, Quinn remembered waving to them and how he had savored the accolade, with his other arm around Allyn's waist. "I turned to shake Rick's hand. But he was gone."

Taglia leaned forward. "How many people witnessed the duel?"

"I dunno. Maybe a hundred people? Besides our roadies there were the promoter's staff and Eclectic Records' people. There were sound and lighting techs, too. And the inevitable handful or so of groupies. Looking back now I can see it was a stupid, childish thing for me to get involved in."

"You couldn't have known how he'd react because of it," Allyn protested. "He really couldn't stand that you were better."

"Rick *is* a good guitarist. I know too well how close it was. It wasn't just my hand, you know. He was younger and on fire to prove himself."

"Younger?" Allyn laughed. "Maybe, but he couldn't go the distance, could he? And it's not as if you were over the hill."

Bird of Paradise
G.J. Paterson

The fervency in Allyn's voice caught Quinn off-guard. He wanted see it in his face, but couldn't bring himself to take the chance. He lit another cigarette instead. "Some life in the old mare yet, eh? What a pleasant surprise."

In the kitchen, the kettle began to whistle.

Ten   *10*

"Let me get this straight." Taglia leaned forward to pick up his teacup. "I can understand that Irons hates you, Derek, because you humiliated him. What I don't see is how any of this gets you busted. Let alone how this could lead to him kidnapping Carys."

"I agree," Kincaid said. "And what does the guitar duel have to do with Allyn being called Peacock?"

"Shit!" Allyn snapped. "I don't have all the answers! But if that was Rick on the phone then this is where it starts." He paused for a moment, and the two musicians gazed at each other. "It's fucking hard, talking about this."

"I know it's hard, but we've got to tell what we can, old lad, or none of us will ever work it all out." Quinn told him. "It's not easy for me, either."

After a few moments of silence Allyn took a deep breath and began, "Derek and I went back to the hotel. We were sharing the Presidential suite or some such, and the band had the whole floor. I took a shower then went to Derek's room to talk over the show and see if he meant to go to the promoter's party."

The guitarist put his teacup and saucer on the coffee table and settled back in his chair again. The heroin still cushioned him. He was content to let Allyn tell the story while he moved among his memories.

***

The only light in the room came from a table lamp with a scarf draped over it and the candle on the little table before him. The flame dazzled as he sat watching the golden fire through his lashes. The view out the window beside him, a panorama of the lights of San Francisco, held little attraction for him.

A light rap on the door connecting his room to the rest of the suite broke his reverie. He contemplated the syringe and tourniquet and the rest of the paraphernalia on the table, then shrugged. "Come in," he called.

The door opened and Allyn strolled in, hair wet from his shower. He was naked except for a hotel towel tucked around his waist. "I wasn't sure you were still here," he said as he came up to the table.

"I was leaving."

"So I see." Allyn glanced at the rig on the dark green stone.

"Are you going to the party?" Quinn asked, ignoring the comment.

"No." Allyn sat sideways in the other chair, his bare legs over the arm. "It'll be the same old thing. Boring."

"Yeah."

"Gods, I am sick of this." Allyn nestled his head against the chair and rubbed his cheek on the velvet.

Quinn watched the casual gesture with a familiar, helpless fascination. *He's like a cat.* Something inside which seldom relaxed went soft watching him. Aloud he said, "It will be good getting home, won't it?"

"I swear you will never talk me into this again." Single strands of hair caught in the fine nap of the upholstery, shining like threads of spun gold, bright against the cool green.

"Until next time."

"Maybe." Allyn grinned and pushed a stray lock back from his face.

"Oh, you'll do it. You love it when the crowd goes wild for you. I've seen you too often, and I know you too well. You like the high. You're hooked, lad."

"Hah!" Allyn retorted. "You just like the joke of fucking across thirty feet of space in front of fifty thousand, and them all unknowing."

"You're the one who had best have a care, Peacock. You've no guitar to shield you."

"That's the come-on." Allyn gave him a sideways glance. "For me, I like having you a bit more to myself."

"What? In the dressing room?"

"It wouldn't be the first time, by far, would it? Nor the last, I daresay." A slow, confident smile gathered in the depths of Allyn's eyes. Quinn shivered, pulse racing. "Actually, I had something rather more immediate in mind."

There was a knock at the outer door. It was 1:00 am or a little after. There shouldn't be anyone coming around so late. Suspecting a persistent reporter or scrounging groupies, they waited in silence. After a moment the knock was repeated and a familiar voice called out, "Derek? It's me, Rick. Are you there?"

Bird of Paradise
G.J. Paterson

There was an odd note to Irons' voice. Quinn frowned and wondered what could bring Rick to his room this late. He sat straighter in his chair. "What do you want, Rick?"

"Police," a gruff American voice announced. "Open up!"

They jumped to their feet. "Oh gods," Allyn breathed, half laughing.

"Get out." Quinn said.

"And go where?"

"Back the way you came. Quick. Don't argue."

"I think I'll stay."

There was a crash as something heavy hit the door. Quinn snarled an obscenity while Allyn picked up the table and threw it through the window with a quick heave and surge of his powerful shoulders. The bright tinkle of breaking glass was counterpoint to a second crash as the bedroom door burst open. Police officers, some uniformed, some not, barged in with guns drawn.

The candle had fallen to the floor. Quinn snuffed the flame with his boot. There was no time to see what else might lie beside it.

Quinn raised his head and saw Irons standing in the doorway. The man's face was a study in shock. One of the cops walked up to Allyn, handcuffs out, and grabbed his wrist to force it behind him. Irons shot forward and grabbed Allyn's other arm as if to pull him out of the cop's grasp. Allyn shook Irons off without a glance. The man's face turned dark with anger.

It all seemed far away and came to Quinn in fragmented images — the fury on Irons' face, the light glinting off the badges of the officers when the main room lights were turned on, the wind through the shattered window. He didn't move as the cops swarmed over the room searching for evidence.

A cop walked up to Quinn. He noticed the chevrons on the man's uniform. The officer held out a paper. He took it but didn't look at it.

Bird of Paradise
G.J. Paterson

"Are you Derek Quinn?" the cop asked.

"I am." Everything seemed so distant, somehow.

"We have a search warrant."

Quinn watched one of the cops crouching by the window. The officer retrieved his little silver spoon with a rosewood handle and put it in a plastic bag. He went on searching, while another officer used a hand vacuum on the carpet by the broken window. Quinn admired their patience, but didn't think there would be much to find.

"Sergeant," one of the officers called out as he picked up a glassine envelope caught behind the curtain. It contained a smattering of white powder. The cop with the chevrons turned to look.

Distantly he heard another cop begin to read Allyn his rights.

"He has nothing to do with any of this," Quinn said as the Sergeant took handcuffs from his belt.

***

Allyn paused and poured himself a second cup of tea.

"Okay, let's jet back here a second," Kincaid said, scowling at his notes. "When did this happen? What was the date?"

"Oh, Lord," Allyn said. "I don't remember the precise date. When you're touring they get all mixed up — all you know is locations. 'If this is Dallas, it must be Tuesday' — you know? It was somewhere around August in seventy-six, but I probably don't even have the month right. Chris Derry would be able to tell you for sure. Or Miltie can tell us, too, if you need to know."

"Did Irons act any different than usual at the concert?" Taglia asked.

"No just the same. Stiff as ever, but somehow his presence put me on edge even more than normal. I don't know how to explain it. It was like he never stopped looking at me, or glaring at Quinn. Made me damn uncomfortable. It was a good concert, but not one of our best. No thanks to Irons."

"And what time did you get back to the hotel?"

"It would've been around midnight. Our concerts run about two hours. Enough time to shower, change clothes and relax a bit before the police arrived. Then they burst in and manacled us, like."

Quinn sighed, remembering the fear and the aching in his veins. He drifted back into the past.

***

The cold metal of the handcuffs pinched. *What a shame to be busted for something not yet done.*

Allyn turned and spoke quietly to the young cop who had arrested him. The officer blushed and fumbled to unlock the cuffs. Allyn and his escort went out the door into the main room of the suite.

He had to concentrate on using the last few moments available to him. "Rick!"

Rick stared at him, his jaws clenched with anger.

"Call Miltie," he said. "Tell him we've been taken down to the lock-up. You might mention I don't fancy a long stay."

Something changed in Rick's face. He flashed a toothy grin at Quinn. "You bet! I'll take care of it."

Two more cops set his guitar cases on the bed and opened them. Quinn resisted the almost overwhelming urge to move or speak as they lifted the instruments from their velvet nests. One cop yanked his favorite Strat from its case. With ignorant, simian curiosity, he peered at the silver plate and fiddled with the pots, switch and whammy bar, as if wondering what came off. Quinn watched its casual violation with a sinking heart, and willed the man to put it down.

After what seemed an eternity, the cop glanced through the compartment in the case then put the guitar back inside.

He closed the lid but didn't latch it. Quinn offered up a brief prayer that whoever found it on the bed would notice the latches weren't secure before picking it up.

Allyn came back wearing a t-shirt and jeans with no belt, and red sneakers without socks. His hands were behind him, already in cuffs. Their eyes met and Quinn saw the knowledge in Allyn's sober scrutiny. He would have turned away if he could, but there was no escaping the evidence in his own body, heralding the beginning nightmare.

***

"'Are you well?' I asked him as they herded us out the door," Allyn said. "'No,' he said with a shrug. 'No, it's gonna be a long night, old son. A long night indeed.'"

Kincaid was still taking the occasional note, while his partner lounged on the sofa sipping his tea. The casual pose didn't fool Quinn at all. The dark-haired cop's eyes were on Allyn, shrewd and considering.

For a moment there was silence. Allyn turned back to the detectives, "They rousted us down to the nearest jail. Which was a real circus, I must say. By the time we got there, someone had tipped the press. The place was swarming with reporters and paparazzi."

"Including the inevitable Chris Derry," Quinn added, cigarette between his lips.

Kincaid interrupted, "Who is he?"

"This fucking photographer," Quinn answered. "Follows us about whenever we're in California as if we were Jackie O. Can't take a piss without him peering over the next stall with his damn zoom lens. He's no Annie Lebowitz, but he gets his stuff in the magazines, all the same."

"Right." Allyn glanced at Quinn. "Derek wasn't in any shape to stay in jail all night. We both believed Rick would go straight to Miltie with the news. Miltie's attorneys would be there within the hour, and unpleasant as it might be, we'd be out in short order. Reporters or no reporters, we could stand the situation for a little while."

"I think it was our downfall," Quinn added. "They wrote up all the paperwork and asked a lot of questions at the first place, then put us in cells. I guess they didn't fancy all the fuss of the press yammering away in the lobby, so they shifted us. And we got lost in the process."

Eleven 11

"I need more tea. Anyone else? I'll be right back." Allyn leaned forward to pick up the tea tray. "Don't wait on me. I'll catch up."

He set the kettle on the stove and filled the tea ball with the loose, aromatic leaves. *If I had a choice, what would I do? Take Carys and go home on the next flight. Never leave her again — never give anyone else a chance to hurt her, either. In the name of the Lady, Rick, why do this?*

Every event of that night had rung along his nerves like the breeze through chimes. Years later, standing in a kitchen waiting for water to boil, the sounds of the police radio and the conversation of the cops in the front seat of the squad car filled his head.

***

The handcuffs pinched his wrists and the breeze through the driver's open window was cold in his damp hair. The cops talked American football and the prospects of various teams while the fog rolled in and formed halos around the streetlights.

At the station, he only glimpsed Quinn for a moment as they were brought in through the jail entrance. They were shuffled into separate rooms to be booked. Allyn reminded himself Miltie would be on his way. The same officer, who had watched him dress, sat down across the room's lone table and began to fill out a report. The procedure included innumerable questions — name, address, date and place of birth, occupation and more. Allyn answered dutifully, trying to ignore the voices of officers chatting in the hallway outside the door, talking about the musicians as if they weren't there. "The skinny guy's a pusher. They say he was caught with at least ten grams of heroin and God knows what else. The pretty boy over here threw the damn stuff outta the window and scattered shit everywhere. Don't know how much they were able to find, lost most of it, I'd guess. Can you believe it? When they arrested him, he was all but naked. God knows what they were doing before we got there."

Allyn blushed as the endless round of calculated humiliation dared him to speak. His booking officer searched him, patting him down from shoulders to ankles as he leaned on his hands against a wall. He was offered a phone call but declined. Miltie would be at the promoter's party and unreachable by phone. Rick knew they'd been arrested. He would track Miltie down and let him know. Surely he would. He had been really angry after the duel, though. How had he gotten involved with the cops back at the hotel? The thought of trusting Rick made him uneasy. With an effort he shook off the worry about things he didn't know and concentrated on the present moment.

Another cop arrived, dressed in blue jeans, t-shirt and leather jacket. He introduced himself and his manner was friendly and helpful. When he suggested the easiest way to avoid prosecution was to give evidence against Quinn, Allyn's cold detachment gave way before a sudden flood of rage.

He lunged to his feet, shoving his chair backwards. The detective was on his feet just as fast. Allyn stood where he was, staring at the plainclothes cop. "I have nothing to say to you." His already-stressed voice shredded under the rush of adrenaline. "I am a British citizen, but I understand I'm not required to answer your questions without a lawyer present. I have nothing to say until he gets here."

There was no getting around it. The detective smiled, but expression had nothing friendly in it. "I tried to help you. Oh well, hope you enjoy your stay."

The cell they put him in was narrow, cramped, and already occupied by four other prisoners. Quinn wasn't among them. He had stayed for Quinn's sake, but now he had no idea where the guitarist was or what was happening to him. He paced the cell and worried.

**

Voices in the next room brought him back to the kitchen, and he put the memories aside. He finished the tea preparations, placing the teapot on the tray and returned to the den. The conversation went on around him as he poured the tea and resumed his place.

"...put us in a van and moved us to the county jail," Quinn explained.

"You must've been pretty sick by then," Taglia said.

Quinn paused, stared at a point high on the far wall, not meeting anyone's eyes. "I was. Getting to the new jail didn't help at all. The deputies didn't give a damn."

One did, Allyn remembered. He went cold all over. *You were too sick to notice.* He glanced up to find Taglia watching him. Something like compassion settled in the depths of the detective's hazel eyes, and Allyn recoiled. *No, Paul. Don't look too close. You might not like what you find.*

Bird of Paradise
G.J. Paterson

The county jail had been a grim fortress of a building, reeking with the fetid smell of unwashed bodies, disinfectant, urine, and desperation. Allyn watched Quinn, pale and weedy under the lights. He knew why the guitarist kept his fists clenched, unwilling to show weakness before his enemies; it was the only way to keep his hands from trembling.

The officer who checked in their personal property was unimpressed. Their combined wealth consisted of a plain silver ring, three guitar picks, and twenty-three cents change. For one manic instant, Allyn considered telling him the band had made thirty million dollars in the last year, before taxes and expenses.

The night jailer — Roberts, his nameplate read — led them into the depths of the jail. Several other deputies awaited them, and they were ordered to strip.

Allyn was aware of Roberts' gaze on his body. The years dropped away as if they had never been, and he raised his eyes to the deputy's face, challenging. Anger shortened his breath. Something dark and deep inside mocked, *Maybe you never left the street. Everything else is a dream. See him looking? He knows what you are.*

He hated those small eyes in the doughy face watching him. Instincts honed on the streets told him Roberts was the power in the world he was about to enter.

They dressed in inmate jumpsuits, and the fat deputy walked them down the hall to their cell. Roberts caught the singer's gaze as he stepped past him. The man's smile said, *I'll see you again*, as the door clanged shut between them.

A bare bulb in a ceiling grate lit the tiny room. A thin young black man looked them over with disinterested appraisal from his bunk. "Cigarettes, man?"

Quinn shook his head. He stretched out on the opposite bunk and covered his eyes with one arm. Allyn stood staring down at him, confused and uncertain. For the first time that night he became afraid.

"No problem," the man said. "You a hype?"

Quinn didn't reply.

"Bad number, being busted." After a few moments he added philosophically, "Maybe somebody'll spring you before the shakes hit too hard."

The man transferred his scrutiny to Allyn. Before he could ask, Allyn explained, "I was in the wrong place at the wrong time."

"Happens." He seemed willing to let it go, then something changed on his face and he looked at them again. "You guys are, uh, English."

"Yeah." It didn't seem worth the bother to explain he was Welsh, not English.

"Don't I know you dudes from somewhere?"

Allyn was about to give in to recognition, but Quinn replied without moving, "I doubt it, mate. We're drifters. Just in and on our way out."

It's getting to him, Allyn realized. *His voice is gone back to Manchester. All the hooray is right out. He must be hurting.*

"Huh," the man said, then recognition flared in his eyes and with it came understanding. "Yeah, okay. My name's Leroy."

"Hullo, Leroy. I'm Allyn. This is Derek." Allyn realized how small and thin Quinn seemed, curled there on the pallet. The guitarist shivered, sweating as if he were under stage lights. Allyn pulled a scratchy green wool blanket from the top bunk and threw it across him. Quinn grunted his thanks and pulled it over his head.

"He a heavy shooter?" Leroy asked.

"I think so." Allyn sat on the end of Quinn's bunk. "I don't know much about it."

"You never been through this with him before?"

"No. I don't think he has, either."

"Huh. He's gonna be one sick dude come morning, unless he can score some shit. You got somebody outside?"

"Outside?"

"To get you out of this joint. Bail, baby."

"Yes, our mana — our friend will help us."

"That's good. That's real good, but late as it is, they won't set bail until the morning." Leroy frowned. "He'll get sleepy here directly and drop off. We get any luck and he's going to sleep all night. It'll be when he wakes up that it'll be bad news."

Allyn had been told enough horror stories to fill a book. He didn't know if any of them were true, but he couldn't bear to think of Quinn going through it. "Won't they let him see a doctor?"

"Now don't panic, man. Miracles have been known to happen." He smiled as if humoring a child. "It's just that in here, if you want a miracle, you're gonna have to make it yourself."

Allyn could think of no way to summon a miracle beyond Miltie. The minutes passed. He watched Quinn's huddled, motionless form, and visualized Milton Ables' arrival at the station to bail them out. The only sounds were the distant snores of prisoners in other cells up and down the block.

As Leroy predicted, Quinn's breathing evened out and deepened. Sleep was a shield against the relentless chemical changes in his body. Allyn got up and paced the narrow space before the bunks, stalking up and down behind the bars.

Leroy watched him as the minutes passed. At last he said, "Sit down. You remind me of some big lion going back and forth, back and forth, like you was in a cage at the zoo. Makes me crazy."

"Sorry." He perched again on the end of Quinn's bunk. "I hate feeling helpless, and there's nothing I can do."

"Now that depends." Leroy stared at him.

Allyn was aware of the measurement in his gaze. It wasn't a pleasant feeling. "What do you mean?"

"What your pal there needs is a little something. Most anything would do until he gets out. Dilaudid, if not the real stuff, but Talwin or even 'ludes would do it for him. Cheap thrills, but it should clear him up quick."

"I understand," Allyn agreed. "But if you don't mind me asking, where are we going to find anything with us behind bars and all?"

"They have plenty of stuff in the evidence room." Leroy's face was grim. "Of course we can't get near it, but a cop could. For you he might."

Allyn crossed his arms. "Do go on. I could listen for hours."

"I'm serious." Leroy gestured at the huddled form, "You want to help him or not?"

Down the cellblock, someone began to retch. Another voice cursed then subsided. Allyn raked his fingers through his hair.

"Yes," he whispered at last. "What do I have to do?"

"The fat ofay who put you in here? Sometimes he's known to do a favor. Not for free, understand."

Allyn met the other man's gaze measure for measure. *Not for free.* He understood. Bile rose in his throat, hot and sour.

The black man lay down again on his bunk, turning over to face the wall. Allyn ran his hand over and over the blanket's rough green fabric, watching the tiny threads bend under his fingers. He tried to keep his mind blank, but it was impossible. He couldn't shake the sound of Quinn's music from his mind. The memory of being on stage with him, the memory of what the music built between them.

I shouldn't do this. You won't thank me.

Move, the dark voice in his heart whispered. *Don't think about it. Don't ever think about it.* He stood, crossed to the cell door. He watched his fingers curl around the bars, white-knuckled. *See? You remember how this goes. It hasn't been so long, after all.*

Something inside rebelled, but he remembered the panic in Quinn's voice when the police had come. *"Get out,"* he had said. *"Back the way you came..."*

This is the way you came, his dark self breathed.

"Roberts!" he shouted.

After what seemed an eternity, a key grated in the cellblock door and someone entered. Allyn felt his face settle into the old familiar mask, tough but available, disdainful but inviting. It was the mask that spelled hustler as bright as neon.

The heavy-set guard stopped in front of the cell, and Allyn fixed him with a cold, flat stare. "What do you want?" Roberts asked.

"Help for my friend."

The wary, irritable face smoothed into lines of anticipation. He took a set of keys out of his pocket and unlocked the door, opening it long enough to let Allyn step out, then shutting and locking it once more. He seized Allyn's wrists from behind and snapped cold metal bands around his wrists.

Between fear and compulsion, it was suddenly hard to breathe. Roberts pushed him, indicating the way to go. Someone yelled raucous encouragement as they passed. Allyn moved without looking back.

They walked out of the cellblock and down a hallway lined with steel doors and around a corner.

"In here," Roberts said, thrust open a door and turned on the light.

Allyn stood on the threshold of a narrow green room with a table and three chairs under a picture window. A reel-to-reel tape machine sat on the table, along with an empty ashtray and a yellow legal pad. There was the reek of stale cigarette smoke. Dim light spilled through the window, and he realized he was seeing through a one-way mirror into an empty interrogation room next door. He swallowed hard, unable to make himself take the next step. He tried to think about Quinn, tried to conjure the vision of Quinn's face in the spotlight, laughing and playing, leaning back while his guitar blazed with music like fire. The image wouldn't hold.

Roberts shoved him into the room, and a key grated in the lock behind them.

He stood in the center of the space, filled with a strange, desperate passivity. Roberts unlocked the handcuffs and turned Allyn to face him. The man tilted his face up with clammy fingers. "You're pretty enough. Let's see all the rest again. Take it off."

Allyn stared at a spot on the man's forehead to make him think he was looking right at him. Slowly he unzipped the uniform and shrugged it off his shoulders. It pooled at his feet, and he stepped free of it.

"Get the stuff off that table and pull it out to the middle of the room." Roberts said, his right hand casually caressing the butt of his gun.

He obeyed, aware that the jailer was watching his every move with greedy eyes. He realized that his hands were shaking as he put the ashtray and note pad on top of the recorder. He picked up the tape machine and bent to sit it on the floor before pulling the table out. Task complete, he returned to his jailer.

Stepping closer, Roberts ran his hands across Allyn's chest, pausing to twist both nipples painfully. Watching Allyn's face for any hint of resistance, the man continued his conquest, hands slipping down to fondle him roughly. Apparently satisfied, the jailer turned him again, this time to face the narrow end of the table. Roberts seized his wrists from behind and clamped the cuffs on again, so tight that Allyn could feel his flesh tearing.

Roberts ran a hand between Allyn's buttocks, stopping to massage his anus with a thumb. After a moment he shoved his shoulders down onto the table. He kicked Allyn's feet apart and unzipped his own trousers.

The metal table was smooth against the singer's face as the other man groped him. The cold of it hardened his sore nipples. The man grunted as he shoved his penis hard against Allyn, not entering yet but taking possession, taking control. Allyn shook as repulsion and desire roiled in him. He was back out on the streets again, abandoning himself to a customer's demands, taking what pleasure he could find in it.

There was a pause. A tube of petroleum jelly and its lid were tossed down on the table inches from his face, a last bit of jelly protruding like a tongue. Prying fingers, slick with jelly, worked their way into him. Allyn had a moment to think of what it would feel like to pound his fists into the man's face.

There was a burst of pain and the jailer was in him, bucking him hard against the table. Whimpering, he moved as much as he could, but whether to escape or surrender he no longer knew.

Twelve

12

"Allyn?" Quinn asked, watching the focus come back to the singer's face.

"I..." Allyn shook his head. "Sorry, I was..."

"That night in jail. After I fell asleep," Quinn prompted.

"Oh, right." The singer's voice was hoarse. "Leroy and I sat up and talked for a long time. He warned me what to expect when Quinn woke up. Still, it was an awful night, and a worse morning, until Miltie arrived."

Taglia's eyes were fixed on Allyn. Quinn found the scrutiny disturbing. The cop's face wore a reaching expression as though he sensed the presence of a lie behind the careful story. There was a moment of silence and then Taglia cleared his throat. "Jeff, why don't we take a little break. I'm sure these guys are tired. Maybe it would be better if we took a breather."

Kincaid nodded agreement.

Allyn stood in one motion and walked toward his bedroom. After a moment Quinn heard the door open and close.

Taglia watched Allyn leave without comment. After a moment the cop rose, crossed to the glass doors and gazed at the sunlit yard beyond. The room was quiet except for the soft sound of pages flipping back and forth as Kincaid read his notes.

Quinn rested his head on the back of the chair, watching his cigarette smoke drift toward the ceiling. *The more we tell, the more secrets we keep. I know everything that happened that night but I can never admit it. And he will never tell me.*

***

He came awake by ugly stages, aching and barely able to breathe past the stuffiness in his head. Leroy dozed on his bunk.

Allyn was gone.

He sat up and stifled a groan as movement brought on another stomach cramp.

"How you feeling?" Leroy asked.

"Bloody awful."

"It won't kill you," Leroy said. "Though maybe you're gonna wish it would."

Quinn couldn't find anything to argue with in that. "Where's Allyn?"

"Fatso took him for a walk," Leroy replied, glancing away. "They'll be back."

After that there was nothing to do but wait. It seemed a long time. At last Allyn and the jailer came to the cell door. Quinn's breath caught in his throat. Even through a haze of wretched discomfort, he knew something was wrong. Allyn, eyes downcast and shoulders hunched, stood waiting for the man to open the door.

He looks old. He can't be. He's only twenty-five. Allyn is youth. Eternal golden youth like Adonis. He's the source of the secret, warming fire. Quinn searched the fine, drawn face and found no flame in it. *It is as though the sun went out when I wasn't looking.*

He had no idea what made the wrenching change, but anger rose out of his fear, feeding on the burning, chemical irritation wracking his veins. "Where have you been?"

"Out," Allyn said. "Getting this. For you." He walked to the bed and dropped two pills into Quinn's hand. His movements were awkward, his gait flat-footed and stiff. He sank down on the floor and rested his head against the blanketed pallet, his long legs folded beneath him.

Quinn knew without a glance what the pills must be. The desire in his veins was slow torture. He swallowed them dry. "How did you get this crap, anyway?"

Allyn's shoulders shifted as if he'd been struck across the back, but he said nothing.

Quinn sighed, "Oh, Peacock. You fool."

"Don't." Allyn's voice was quiet but sharp. "Don't ever call me that again."

***

Allyn returned after a few minutes and sat back down. "Miltie caught up with us about nine-thirty in the morning. He had two attorneys with him, and Jackie and Harry were waiting in a limousine outside in the parking lot. When they came for us, I had to all but carry Derek out." A muscle in Allyn's jaw worked as he looked over at Quinn. "We got him into the car. Thank gods for smoke-black windows. That's the only time I've ever seen him shoot up.

"Miltie had already sent everyone else on to the airport and had our hired jet standing by. He took us straight there and got us airborne in record time.

"The performance in Seattle that night was one of our worst ever. The next day we flew on to Los Angeles, where we could rest up for our Tuesday night concert. Monday afternoon, Jackie came 'round hinting he knew something, but he had to wait 'til the next day to be sure. He asked us to meet him at the arena before sound check."

Allyn pushed a stray lock of hair back over his shoulder. "We came in early, and he was there with two lads who work for the sound and light company we had taken on. They were a bit shy at first, as we don't muck about much with the lackeys, but they warmed up."

Taglia noticed Kincaid frown at Allyn's offhand arrogance.

"Jackie told us it was right at six a.m. when Rick tracked him down at the plane where he and the other roadies were finishing loading for the trip to Seattle." Allyn glanced at Quinn as he spoke. "He said he'd been looking for Miltie and told Jackie we'd been arrested. It wasn't until later, after Jackie found Miltie at the hotel, and Miltie called the station, he found out our arrests had been five hours earlier.

"Later in the day, Jackie heard rumors of Rick talking in his cups, bragging that now the audience would see the show they'd paid their money for. He did some investigating, and he tracked down these two roadies. They told us they were in a bar down the block from the hotel when Rick came in and had several drinks. He started boasting how he wouldn't have to carry a helpless, over-the-hill shooter, cover up his mistakes and such-like and drivel. Worst of all, this happened Sunday morning, *after* we were nicked, during the time Rick was supposed to be trying to track down Miltie."

"Someone tipped the press," Quinn added. "The exact rumor was that I was arrested for heroin possession. Not both of us — only me. Looking back now, it's plain Rick never mean for Allyn to be caught up in the bust. Otherwise, the media leak would have been both of us were arrested."

"Needless to say, it was enough for us," Allyn continued. "Came time for sound check, we were ready for him. As he came up on stage and plugged in, Quinn leaned into the mike and said, 'None of that, lad, you're out.' 'What do you mean?' Rick demanded. 'It's the old eighty-six,' Derek said. 'Take a hike.' 'You can't fire me, I've got a contract,' Rick said. 'Do you then?' Derek asked, all Mancunian of a sudden, which is a bad sign. Then he grabbed up Rick's prize old

Telecaster and gave it the grand heave through a Marshall stack. Smashed a six thousand dollar guitar to squealing flinders. Not to mention the Marshall. Townshend himself couldn't have done it better. They stood there glaring at one another until somebody had the sense to cut the power and kill the feedback. Then Derek said, quite cool, 'Can you play rhythm on a piece of paper?'"

Quinn shook his head. "Of course, he was livid. He meant to murder me, and he might have done it. Looked bad for me, save for Allyn here, who's a good one in a punch-up."

"Broke his nose for him. I'd have finished it, too, but Avery and Gil bound me with promises."

"Which is to say they'd have gone on sitting on you all day if that's what it took. Gil has always regretted that. After we told them the story, he and Avery were all for going out looking for the bastard."

Allyn laughed. "The gig in L.A. may have been Leviathon's finest hour. The audience was amazed. We did two encores, and they were still roaring thirty minutes later when the hall manager came to beg us to do another before they had the walls down."

"That was at the Forum." Taglia remembered the crowd, the smell of cigarette smoke and marijuana, the almost unbearable din of the music, and the beauty. *Odd to think of it now, knowing the story behind the spectacle. I wish Jeff had gone with me.* "I was there. You came back out and did fifteen minutes of some weird blues jam in the middle of 'Don't You Leave.'"

"Yet he swore he'd get even." Allyn gazed down at his hands.

"Yes he did, lad. Yes he did."

Kincaid pointed at the photograph album on the coffee table. "Do you have any pictures of the guy?"

"No. Why would we?" Quinn said. "Slimy wanker."

"Chris Derry might," Allyn suggested.

Quinn blinked in surprise, then shook his head with a rueful chuckle. "If anyone would."

"Do you have Derry's phone number?" Taglia asked.

"I think I might." Allyn got out of his chair and picked up the yellow card file by the telephone.

"You're amazing." Quinn burst into startled laughter. "Nice to everyone."

"Of course," Allyn agreed. "Man never knows when he might need a cup of flour. Besides, who else do we know who's bound to have a picture, like?"

Allyn flopped down on the couch with the card-file and phone in his hands, "Now, let me see... ah, yes, 'P'... here it is. Chris Derry."

"You have a man named Derry listed under 'P'?" Quinn wondered. "Whyever for?"

"For 'photographer,' of course."

"Of course," Quinn agreed. "Why not?"

Thirteen

13

Sitting at the bar near his partner, Kincaid hung up the receiver and spoke in a low voice. "I talked to Ortiz and told him Allyn left a message for Derry to call. He agreed we should bring the guy up here to interview."

Taglia glanced at the musicians who were talking quietly on the other side of the room. "I'm really hoping Derry will have pictures and maybe an address."

Kincaid met his eyes and for a moment the bond was back, but it didn't hold. The blond man looked away. "I don't want to get their hopes up too much on this," he said. "The guys downtown are digging as fast as they can, but it could still turn out Irons isn't the one. What'd you think about the San Francisco story?"

"Except for some judicious editing, it sounded pretty truthful."

"I thought so, too. I wondered about the editing, but I chalked it up to personal stuff. They strike me as pretty... close."

Close? Like partners? Like lovers? Like us? What are we? Taglia gulped at the idea. "Yeah, I think they must be. They've been partners for a long time."

"Yeah, they have." Kincaid's expression was thoughtful as he glanced out the patio's sliding glass doors. "I guess –"

The phone rang. Kincaid grabbed the headphones and nodded to Allyn who sprang for the receiver.

"Um, this is Chris Derry," a young man's voice, unmistakably Californian, came over the speaker. "There was a message on my machine. I'm returning Mr. Sterling's call?"

"Chris," Allyn sighed, lines of tension in his face easing. "This is Allyn."

Taglia watched Allyn and Kincaid as they stood side-by-side, looking at each other while they handled the call. Kincaid with his shorter, blown-dry hair, now-rumpled slacks and sport shirt matched against Allyn's unrestrained mane, blue jeans, peasant shirt, and silver jewelry. Taglia found himself fascinated by the illusion they were the same man, each staring into a mirror which revealed what might have been.

"Oh, hi, Mr. Sterling. What can I do for you?"

Derry sounds nervous, Taglia reflected. *Can't blame him. I'm sure this is the first time Derek and Allyn have ever gone looking for him.*

"Derek and I are here in town and we need some help from you, if you don't mind."

"Sure. What can I do?"

"It's about the last tour. We may need to refer to your notes on it, if you have any. Pictures too, of course."

"Oh." There was a slight pause while Derry digested the request. "Yeah, I have both. It won't take long for me to get them out of my files. Do you want all of them? You're asking about hundreds of shots."

"I'm afraid so, Chris," Allyn replied. "Everything you have on the tour."

"Okay. How soon do you want to see them?"

"How soon can you get them to us?"

"Are you still at the big stucco place on Oak Pass Drive?"

It was Allyn's turn to sound flustered. "Yeah, we're still here."

"Okay, Mr. Sterling. I can be there in an hour."

"Call me Allyn. Oh, and I almost forgot. Off the record, Chris. Everything is off the record."

"No problem. Off the record it is then."

Quinn stood, stretched, and started for the bedroom hallway. Allyn said, "Where are you going?"

"To fetch a guitar," Quinn replied as he walked to the door. "My fingers are getting twitchy."

Taglia glanced toward the patio doors. Dusk gathered beneath the trees. "I'm going out. I'll be back."

He flexed his shoulders to ease his tension and turned to glance back at the house. Already the windows had a welcoming yellow glow. The light from the sliding glass doors flickered as someone walked past inside. Taglia couldn't tell who from where he stood, but the person made an excellent target. He loosened the gun in his shoulder holster and stepped into the spreading twilight, every sense alert.

Sniper has all the advantages — sit tight and wait. Hunting the hunters, it's what Sung Ng called it back in 'Nam. Like hunting tigers by staking out a goat and waiting for the big cat to come.

A furtive rustling came to him out of the dark beyond the range of his vision. He froze and the sound stopped. *Something small and furry? A neighbor's cat on the prowl, maybe a coyote passing through? Or is it the hunter? I have never hunted tigers. It wasn't tigers Sung was after.* He stood, waiting. Steamy nights in a jungle far away rose around him, those nights when he had been alive and taking a chance on death. *What passes before your eyes when you die? It's the moments when you're alive right down to your toenails. For some it must go real quick.* He reflected on all those moments of life and death that had touched him and knew it would take him a long time to die.

He concentrated on the sounds of the night. *Could there be somebody out there?* He wanted to shout the question and end the waiting. Or was he being paranoid? He could barely keep straight the hunted from the hunters. The only victim he knew for sure was the child.

He resumed his slow prowl. *Irons hates them both, but it has to be Quinn he hated most. Then why steal Carys Sterling? Is her daddy Quinn's stalking-goat? What makes Allyn the thing Quinn would come after? The guy must believe taking Carys would give him a crack at both Allyn and Quinn.*

The wind rustled through the palm trees, and he watched their tops bend under its strength. He thought about Kincaid, safe inside, and himself, isolated out here. Yet, if anything went wrong, he admitted to himself, if somebody went for one of them, the other wouldn't stop, wouldn't rest until the matter was settled. Buddy system. New York, Vietnam, L.A., it didn't matter. It was still the same. The highest priority isn't even the law — it's your partner's life.

These guys. Shit, they're a couple of musicians. Lightweights. Allyn can come on as worldly as he likes, but he never sat in a stinking jungle and watched a buddy bleed to death, sliced to ribbons by a booby-trap. No one should have to. Once you go through such a thing, it changes the way you see the world. Changes it forever.

He hunched his shoulders against the chill night breeze and peered into the dark. Out in the night there was a faint, high-pitched squeak, and he froze again. A moment later, a small four-legged shape with something dangling from its jaws darted across a patch of moonlit grass. Taglia grinned as it disappeared into another patch of shadow. *There was another hunter out here, after all.* He prowled forward, knowing no matter how hard he searched, any number of concealed watchers might elude him.

Bird of Paradise
C.J. Paterson

He glanced at his watch, realizing to his surprise he'd already been outside longer than he'd meant to. He walked on, passing the tennis courts. He checked the bathhouse by the little swimming pool. It would be nice to go swimming under the night sky when the weather warmed. He remembered a night in 'Nam when some of them had gone swimming against the lieutenant's orders, and how his buddy had been ripped apart by one of those ingenious devices that spray a man with bamboo spears. Under the moonlight you couldn't see red, only how the blood turned the water dark.

He worked his way around the side of the house and checked to make sure the gate to the private garden off the master bedroom was still padlocked. The carport was clean. No sinister shadows lurked beside the Lotus, the Jaguar or the Trans Am. He slipped down the side of the house and soon found himself back where he had started, staring at the large, well-lit kitchen window and glass doors. A silhouette crossed the den, screened by the sheer curtains. Allyn, judging by his height. The figure crouched by the door, and a moment later the lights of the Christmas tree blossomed.

All his searching had revealed nothing, but he couldn't convince himself that meant there was nothing to find.

He sat down with his back to a tree and wished for a smoke, although he had given up the habit almost eight years before. Given it up on the boat back home, as he had given up so much in those days. Gave up smoking. Never touched another Lucky Strike. Never touched another joint, either, and never, ever touched another man.

Until Saturday night.

In the jungle, men used drugs for self-medication. Drugs became the only way they could find to cope with a world gone mad, the only way to endure children and women and cripples and old men screaming from their napalm hell. He didn't like the numbness of heroin, but he had seen no reason to turn down a joint's gift of blessed absurdity. It made the horror bearable. It kept him sane. For the same reason, he didn't turn down Sung Ng Lam, either, although running from such contact was what had made the Army seem like such a good idea in the first place.

Bird of Paradise
G.J. Paterson

He wondered what had become of Sung in all the years since he left. *Did he manage to escape the fall of Saigon? Is he dead somewhere in the jungle, or did he make it to the States after all? If he's alive, what does he look like now?* He tried to fit a gray three-piece suit on the lithe frame and smiled at the image.

Sung had been a member of the South Vietnamese Special Military Services, more savage than the beasts he hunted. In eighteen months, neither of them spoke a tender word which stretched beyond the moment. They both knew what they shared was for the duration and nothing more.

The bark pressed into his back, and he ached with longing, wishing he had said one thing, made one gesture to let Sung know the depth of his feelings. Orders came and he left. There had been time to leave a note. He had packed his things and gone.

Which is why we take chances, isn't it, Jeff? He almost laughed, waiting for a phantom enemy to come and take his mind off the ghosts. *Because moments of danger, moments of fear, are the moments we have. I walked away from Sung, but I can't walk away from you. First you pretend you don't remember, then you try to shove me away by pulling rank. I can still feel your kisses, and I don't believe you've forgotten either.*

Warm arms seemed to wrap around him, pulling him close. Shuddering desire crept along his limbs in response to the memories, and he suppressed a groan of frustration. Everybody wants that, somewhere along the line. *Everyone wants to be held in arms stronger than their own.* He remembered lying back in the hard-muscled embrace and knowing himself safe at last. At harbor, anchored in the only place he had ever worked to reach, and the only place he had feared to try for.

What can I do? If I push.... There are other alternatives to happily ever after.

Another memory came to him. *"Abomination,"* the Bishop's voice proclaimed in his head. *"This allegation is an abomination. No priest would do these things."* He was the victim then, although it was years before he realized it. At the time he'd paid the price and accepted the blame. He'd been sent from New York to his uncle's home in L.A. He swore to himself it would never, ever happen again. He would never bring such shame on his mother, on his father's grave, on himself, ever again. It didn't work, and two years later he was running into the Army and into the war where they would, by God, make a man of him.

He hadn't counted on the fear. He was a street-kid. Everybody knew Paul Taglia was one tough customer. He never guessed how the blossoming fire flowers would terrify him, how the wet jungle gloom would wear him down, how watching one comrade after another die would sap his courage and his strength. He would never have guessed how one murderous little bastard with skin like old ivory and a touch like silk, whose slender frame hid quick and deadly strength and whose smooth, impassive face masked a mind far quicker than his own, could make him feel so damn much better.

It was the Army. He leaned his head back against the tree trunk. *Hell, it was the war and you got through it however you could.*

Out of the Army and onto the force. Being a cop is one sure-fire way of proving once and for all you're a real man. They pick maybe seventy-five rookies out of six thousand applicants, and everybody knows there aren't any pansies on the LAPD.

Marriage hadn't helped either. His marriage to Maria Jimenez lasted three years. *No children, thank God. How could I have raised children to be good heterosexual citizens when I have to fight for it every day myself? I don't know what it all means.* After the divorce, he'd run up a record as a Casanova. He liked girls well enough to play the role. Still, he had never sat next to one of them all day, day after day, aching to reach across three feet of empty space and make some kind of real contact.

Hunters and hunted. It goes around and around. No war here to use as an excuse. Come out of the darkness, you scumbag, so this crazy old soldier can do more than wish for a cigarette and worry about what's gonna happen if his partner's allegedly lousy memory ever improves.

Bird of Paradise
G.J. Paterson

Nothing stirred out in the night. He sighed and got to his feet, stretching hard to loosen the tension between his shoulder blades. He yawned, scratched his chin and stood for a few moments, still watching for some sign of an intruder.

He was tired. The years alone had taken their toll. *I'm tired of running. We're both tired, whether you admit it or not, partner. We can't keep on running forever, can we? From each other? From ourselves?*

Fourteen

14

Chris Derry was younger than Kincaid expected. He may have been in his early twenties, but he had a pleasant, almost cherubic face that made him look like he was still in high school. His medium-length brown hair was parted on one side, and he had an amiable smile. His casual attire made an interesting contrast to the expensive-looking black leather portfolios and briefcase he'd brought into the den from his car.

Photographing rockers in bathroom stalls must make him a pretty penny, Kincaid thought as Derry started pulling file folders out of one of the portfolios.

"You said San Francisco on the phone," the young man said as he stacked folders on the coffee table in the center of the conversation pit. "But you didn't say exactly what you were looking for so I went ahead and brought photos from the whole tour. Just in case. Oh, thanks!" he added as Allyn handed him a soda and sat next to him on the couch with a can of his own.

"We really appreciate your help," Allyn replied.

Derry smiled, blushing faintly. Kincaid wondered how often the subjects of his photographs actually sat and talked with him.

"I have to confess, I'm curious," Derry said. "I promised you on the phone that this is off-the-record, and it is — anything you tell me won't go anywhere else. But I couldn't help but notice that the guy who opened the door to me has a gun. I'm guessing he's a plainclothes cop. Can you tell me what's going on?"

Allyn said tersely, "My daughter's been kidnapped."

Derry's expression turned to shock. "And you suspect Rick Irons, huh?

"There are reasons to suspect him.

"Because of San Francisco?"

"Yeah."

Derry's eyes narrowed. "What a piece of shit!"

Kincaid pulled up an ottoman and sat across from Derry. "I'm Lieutenant Kincaid. We'll need your pictures, and whatever information you have on Irons. Have you heard anything recent about him?

"I don't know" Derry pursed his lips and frowned. Kincaid thought immediately of a disgruntled duck and had to work at stifling a smile. "He sort of dropped out of sight earlier this year. I know he had an apartment in L.A. at one point. I have no idea if he still lives there. But I do know his agent works out of a Hollywood address."

"Do you have that address and phone number?

Derry nodded, pulled a battered address book out of his briefcase and leafed through it. "Yeah, here we are."

Kincaid wrote the information in his notebook. Taglia leaned over his shoulder and plucked the notebook out of his hand. "Be right back," he said, went to the bar, picked up the phone and began to dial.

"This is great stuff," Kincaid said. "Once we've been through these photos, Chris, could you take them down to the station? The rest of our team really needs to see them."

"Absolutely! Anything to help."

Kincaid glanced at Taglia, who nodded and gave him a thumbs up. Kincaid knew he would mention the photos to whichever detective answered the phone.

The room fell silent as Derry shuffled through folders. "Here they are," he said as he took out an envelope of prints and proof sheets and passed it over to Allyn. "San Francisco."

Quinn strolled back into the room with an acoustic guitar in his hands, as Allyn took the pictures. He sat down on the couch on Allyn's free side and began softly playing. Looking at him, Kincaid knew it hadn't taken an hour to get a guitar — even if he had to completely restring and tune the thing. It was obvious to him what detour Quinn had taken.

"Oh, this first one's misfiled. It should be L.A. Here, have a peek at this." Allyn held the photograph so Quinn could see it.

The guitarist said. "Wretched excess."

Allyn passed the picture over to Kincaid. "Derek Quinn caught in the middle of his Pete Townshend impersonation."

The color photo showed Quinn, moving fast. Only his face was in focus as he hurled a guitar into a Marshall cabinet amid a shower of sparks.

"Rick wasn't pleased, I can tell you," Quinn said.

"Would you be, if someone chucked Fire or The Lady through a speaker stack?"

"No. I'd carve the bloody bastard." The music he was playing took a martial turn.

"There you arc then." Allyn turned to the others. "These guitar wizards, like it or not, share a common thread. They think of their instruments as something like a third arm. No, it's more a mystic thing, like a place they keep their souls. They'd as soon be castrated as have something done to their axe."

Staring down at the picture, Kincaid nodded at the fanciful description. He transferred his gaze from the picture to the living man. In repose, Quinn's face was worn, a profound sadness graven on the handsome features. He was no wizard, only a man, weary and worried. Kincaid wondered if Quinn's use of heroin was his way of seeking relief from some unspecified grief in the way others might seek relief from chronic, debilitating pain.

"Ah," Allyn breathed out. He gave the picture he had been looking at to Kincaid.

There were five men on stage in a concert shot. Quinn and Allyn were in the foreground, leaning on one another, back-to-back, halfway to the boards. McConathy stood to one side, watching their antics with an amused smile. Potts, behind his enormous drum kit, was only visible as a blurred pair of hands and a wild mop of flying hair. The fifth man held his guitar in a classic pose, leaning back with abandon.

"You got a better picture of him?" Taglia said as he pulled up a chair to sit beside his partner.

"Here's a good one," Allyn said and laid the picture on the coffee table so that both cops could see it. It was a candid shot taken in a dressing room. The man standing near Allyn in the picture was much shorter than the singer, with crimped hair. His bleached blond dye job wasn't recent. Dark roots showed. He wore a hoop earring in his left ear and was dressed in a tie-dyed t-shirt and jeans

Quinn leaned forward to get a better look at the photo. "He doesn't seem comfortable standing there, does he?"

The singer nodded. "He wanted to be one of us, but we're a tight lot. I tried to be kind to him, but I always felt he was using me to further himself. Sort of, 'look at me, I'm with Allyn Sterling the famous rock star.' Made me bloody uncomfortable."

"Do you have any background on him, Chris?" asked Kincaid.

"Yeah, I do." Derry pulled a battered notebook out of his briefcase and flipped it open. "For example, he was born in Ruston, Louisiana, as Virgil Endicotte."

"As what?" Quinn stared at him, clearly astonished. He let the guitar fall silent, then leaned it against the couch beside him.

"Endicotte," repeated Derry, pausing to spell it as Kincaid picked up his notebook and pen. "He was in several groups back East in the sixties and early seventies. He changed his name around nineteen-seventy. Can't say I blame him. How many rockers have you ever met named Virgil? Truthfully, he never could get along. Bands were always kicking him out, or he was splitting on them or something."

"Chris, you amaze me. How do you know all this?" Quinn lit a cigarette and leaned back on the couch.

"Leviathon is a hobby of mine. You might be surprised at the stuff I know. I started researching him after you guys hired him on. I've always thought I might write a book someday.

"Anyway, Endicotte moved out here about five years ago. He tried to get into a couple of groups, but the word was already out that he had a big ego and wanted to run things his way. Nobody would touch him. He wound up doing session work."

"You don't have to get along with anyone to come in and lay down a track and split," Quinn pointed out. "Though it helps, of course. No one wants to work with someone unpleasant."

Derry nodded. "When he found out Leviathon was looking for a rhythm player, he got his agent to finagle him an audition. Derek signed him on."

"What happened to him after they kicked him out of Leviathon?" Taglia asked. Kincaid looked up from his notes and waited for the answer.

"Rick was angry. He went out threatening lawsuits and everything. I'm not sure why he didn't sue. I'm sure he could have gotten you guys for breach of contract or assault or something. Maybe his agent talked him out of it, or maybe he lost his nerve. *I* wouldn't want to take on Milton Ables.

"Anyway, he put out a press release claiming he had been betrayed and deceived by the band in general and you two in particular. Of course, he didn't say what you had done."

"I remember it," Allyn said.

"After the press release came out," Derry went on, "he kind of laid low for awhile. Late last year he tried to get a band of his own going. Clubs weren't much interested though, and he didn't want to do clubs anyway. He wanted to do the big venues. The record companies wouldn't touch him. My notes end this past April. As far as I can tell he's quit the business entirely."

Fifteen

15

The music from Quinn's guitar flowed through the room. Allyn was curled up on the couch, his long legs tucked under him, watching him play. Kincaid had never heard the song before and guessed it was something Quinn was making up as he went along. It was gentle, almost sweet, and had a Celtic flavor.

Kincaid glanced at his watch, surprised to find it had been more than an hour since Sergeant Fontinelli had called to let him know Derry had made it to Central Station. The soft, delicate sound of the guitar seemed to have suspended time, bringing a few minutes of relief from the tension that surrounded them all.

Quinn looked up at his movement and the music wound down to silence. "I'm sorry if I am boring you, Lieutenant."

"No. No, you weren't. It was really cool. Keep going if you feel like it."

"You know," Taglia said suddenly, "old Jeff here plays a mean guitar."

Quinn eyed the cop with renewed interest. "Does he?"

"A little," Kincaid temporized. "Country and Western and folk music, mostly. I have a Martin D-18 like yours at home."

"Do you?" Quinn held the guitar up for inspection. "I modified this one for an electric pick-up myself years ago. I've an old Martin D-45 in the other room. I have a marvelous guitar at home, made for me by a man in Kansas. I never take it anywhere because I used to have a fine old thing which got pinched from backstage on one of our early tours. I've never gotten over it. What do you say, Lieutenant, shall we give it a go?"

"I'm nowhere near your league," Kincaid said. It was one thing to play for Taglia. In song, he could say all the things he couldn't say in words. This was different.

Quinn shrugged, settling back on the couch and playing a fluid, mocking run down the strings. "Either you play, or you don't."

"Yeah, he plays," Taglia said. "Jeff is good, he's just shy. He's even teaching me, and I'm all thumbs."

"I do have a couple of picks on me." Kincaid pulled them out of his back pocket and held them up for Quinn to see.

Quinn smiled around his cigarette, took a long drag, and then set it in the ashtray on the coffee table. "How about you, Allyn? Shall we soothe the savage breast, and all that, like?"

"Perhaps."

"Which is it to be, then? Acoustics? Or dueling Strats at ten paces?"

"You'll have to be your own roadies, you know," Allyn observed.

"I've never played an electric before," Kincaid admitted.

"Acoustic it is, then," Quinn set his guitar aside and got to his feet. "Come along, Lieutenant, and get an axe."

Kincaid followed him into his bedroom. The room looked like it had been tossed by a professional. Clothing lay heaped on an armchair and seemed to creep out of the closet and the dresser drawers.

The single touch of order was the line of guitars on stands, neat as soldiers on review, with an old Fender speaker and amp combo behind them. Even the cords were coiled and tucked away under the stands. Two of the instruments were Fender Stratocasters. One had seen a lot of use. The lacquer was chipped and the pale wood of the neck was stained where the finish had worn off. The other seemed newer. Its black finish gleamed and the neck was pristine.

Kincaid said, "I don't know much about electric guitars, but these are real beauties." He went over and squatted in front of them for a better look but didn't attempt to touch. The standard plastic pick guards had been replaced with silver ones on both guitars. The plate on the battered guitar was engraved, "Sweet Fire." The other said, "Lady Release."

"Fire is my favorite guitar," Quinn said. "It's a '57 Stratocaster. I got it at a music store in London when I first came down to town back in the early spring of '61. It was the second electric guitar I had ever owned. My first one was nicked off the train. Took my last quid to buy this old girl, but when I saw her, I thought, 'I'm having that.' I've never regretted it. I slept in a park that night. I had my first session work the next day with a fellow named Sammy Hayes. I've lost track of the disc, but I pray it never comes back to haunt me."

"Bad?" Kincaid grinned up at him.

"Bloody awful. I did the vocals." Quinn laughed. He reached out one thin hand and touched the headstock of the guitar. "It paid for a week's lodging in an East End bed and breakfast, and a few meals into the bargain. It brought in more work. Weren't many guitarists, young and willing to work cheap in those days. There was Big Jim Sullivan, and Little Jim — Jimmy Page, of course — but they were high-dollar men by then. One thing led to another, and here we are."

"How did it get the name?"

Quinn shrugged a little, frowning, as if the memory pained him somehow. "A lady I once knew named it."

"What about the other one?"

"Allyn did that," Quinn said. "He had the plate done when I got the guitar, before the start of our last tour. Jackie put it on before I ever saw it. First time I opened up the case, there it was. Nearly killed myself, falling about laughing."

"It's beautiful."

"Isn't it? I don't think the sustain is as good, and I can't get used to the neck. My old guitar has the v-neck, you know."

"Right." Kincaid had no idea what he meant.

"Of course, Jackie keeps insisting I should retire the old girl. She's not up to stage work these days, he says." Quinn tipped his head to one side as if considering the idea. "It could do with a bit of work, I suppose. Some rewiring, maybe. I've never had any real trouble with her. Every piece of work of any importance I've ever done was done on this guitar. Now he's saying it's too dodgy. Still, she has 'the mouth of a bell and the heart of hell and the head of a gallows tree.'"

Kincaid glanced at Quinn. "Where's that from? It sounds familiar."

"Kipling," Quinn replied. "*The Ballad of East and West.*" The guitarist touched the tuning machines with his callused fingertips. Something in Quinn's gaze let Kincaid see past the chipped and faded tobacco finish to the essential form of the instrument. He could imagine what it had looked like all those years before, hanging behind the counter in the London guitar shop, and how it had seemed to a much younger man to be worth food or a place to sleep. Now it was getting old, the electronics were crotchety, the finish battered, and though Quinn could afford any guitar in the world, he wouldn't give it up. In a life without limits or boundaries, deep as the sea, this piece of wood was flotsam the Englishman found worth clinging to.

"Didn't someone once say, 'The older the grape, the sweeter the wine?'"

"Janis Joplin." Quinn met Kincaid's glance with a weary smile. "Newer doesn't always mean better. We'd better get back." He picked up the acoustic and handed it over.

Kincaid accepted the guitar carefully. He noticed at once the neck had been shaved to make it more like the thinner neck of an electric guitar. He was wondering what on earth Taglia had gotten him into when the phone rang, the sound muffled. Quinn walked to the bed and began burrowing in a pile of clothing beside the nightstand, pulling out a telephone. Before he had a chance to answer it, the phone stopped ringing.

"Allyn's got it," Kincaid said.

Allyn's voice called down the hall, "It's for you, Derek. It's Miltie. He wouldn't tell me anything except that it's boring details."

Quinn lifted the receiver. After a moment he said, "Okay, I've got it. You can hang up... Hullo, Miltie... You did? What did they say? All of it?" Quinn grinned and gave Kincaid the thumbs-up. "Allyn will be delighted... I beg your pardon?" His wide smile began to fade. He sank down on the edge of the bed as he listened to the report. "No... no, he won't care for that at all... Wasn't there any other way? He's sure to rip up at me about it... Oh, he'll never believe I'm innocent of collusion."

Quinn lay back, sending little ripples through the waterbed as he balanced the phone on his stomach. "All's fair, I suppose. Yes, but I do wish... no, it's only I had nearly convinced him. We've got the money and that's the main thing... Tell him? Why don't you? Coward. All right then... When? At the last possible moment. He'll have less time to think... Right... Ta. And Miltie, thanks."

He hung up but went on lying there, sprawled out on the bed, staring at the ceiling. Finally, as if the effort taxed him, he set the phone aside, hooked his fingers over the edge of the bed, and pulled himself upright. His eyes were shadowed.

"What is it?"

"Miltie did a deal. The label is going to pick up the tab. A couple of lads will be by with the cash before we need it."

"That's great, isn't it?" Nothing Kincaid had seen impressed him as much as the speed with which the record company had come to heel. *A quarter million is big bucks, even to a major corporation. These guys must have clout.*

Bird of Paradise
G.J. Paterson

"Oh, absolutely." Quinn stood. "I'm going to tell him as soon as I walk back in there. As for the rest..."

He looked improbably frail standing there. Kincaid realized Quinn was shorter than he had thought and thin almost to emaciation. "Can I help?"

"What?" Quinn cocked his head. "Oh, no. There's nothing you can do. Nothing for anyone to do. It's this time... I had hopes... Well, one does without hope, I suppose. We'll see. Thank you, but no, there's nothing you can do."

He glanced past Kincaid toward the bathroom. The detective understood the meaning of his look. He spoke quietly, making a peace offering of his comprehension. "I could go on back without you, if you want. You can come join us when you're ready."

Quinn stared at him until the warmth of a blush crept up the back of Kincaid's neck. "You've already gone against your own ethics and the law for me, Lieutenant Kincaid," the guitarist said finally. "Thank you for the offer, but enough is enough." He turned away toward the door.

Kincaid glanced back as they walked out. Light gleamed on the guitars' silver panels. Quinn brought his hand down on the switch and filled the room with darkness.

Sixteen 16

Sitting side by side on the couch, the guitarists began exploring for things they both knew. To Taglia, they couldn't have seemed more different, but he knew there would be common ground between them, bought with wood and metal strings.

"Do you know this one?" Kincaid asked as he strummed a few bars.

Quinn bent his head, listening, then nodded. "Yeah, I think I do. It's this, like." He played the phrase back, adding the lead line.

"You've got it."

"Close enough," Quinn agreed. "You take the break, though."

They played through the verse and chorus, feeling their way. Kincaid grinned and Quinn smiled back at him, obviously enjoying the discovery the cop really was a competent guitarist. Taglia took another sip of his soda and smiled benignly at the room in general.

They discovered more and more familiar ground. Allyn sang along on several obscure folk songs and spirituals and an aching version of "Amazing Grace," then they all slipped into "Oh, Happy Day" as if it had been rehearsed.

Allyn was on fire, his good spirits carrying even Quinn, who had come back to the room looking grim. The singing seemed to ease Allyn, erasing lines of worry and giving him back his spirit. There was a word for it. Vainly, Taglia tried to recall it. *Jeff would know.* He gave up with a shrug. *Who cares, if it works?*

"Okay, how about this one?" Kincaid suggested.

Quinn nodded, joining him for several bars. "I know it, but I don't remember from where."

"I do," Allyn spoke up.

"And the lyrics?"

"I know them."

"All right. Let's have it." Quinn gave the count and the two guitars swept into the rich Scottish ballad. On the beat, Allyn's voice rang in, flowing like warm honey, through the first verse of the song and into the second.

> *"Arise, arise, Mary Hamilton,"*
> *Arise and tell tae me..."*

He faltered then, but went on,

> *"...what thou hast done with thine own babe,*
> *That I saw and heard weep by thee?"*

He stopped as though a hand had closed on his throat. He seemed to force out the words, "I'd rather not sing the rest."

The guitars clanged discordantly and fell into ragged silence. Kincaid, stricken, whispered, "Oh, my God. I'm sorry. I like the tune. I never thought about the words."

"It's quite all right." Allyn said hoarsely. "There are no accidents, you know."

Catharsis. That's the word. Catharsis.

A rattling flamenco flourish from Quinn's guitar brought Taglia back to the moment. He resisted the urge to clamp his hands over his ears. Yet it wasn't the loudness, but some strange fury in the way Quinn's fingers flashed across the strings which made the burst of notes so biting.

The guitarist slapped his hand down on the strings, damping the sound into silence. He stared down at the guitar he held with disgust. "I can't do anything with this," he said. He stood and held out his hand to Kincaid. "Give me that damn thing."

Kincaid held out the guitar. Quinn took it and strode from the room. Allyn called his name, but he vanished down the hall. There was an awkward silence while Allyn scrubbed his eyes with the palms of his hands.

Quinn returned abruptly, his presence vigorous and commanding. In each hand he held an electric guitar. Taglia stared, amazed by the transformation. This was how he had always imagined Quinn — dynamic and compelling, the guitar-wizard of legend come to life.

"Oh, Derek, no." Allyn shook his head.

"Oh, Derek, yes," Quinn snapped. He handed the black guitar to Kincaid. "Come on, it's past time you learned something about an electric guitar."

"Where are we going?" Kincaid asked, getting to his feet.

"To the practice studio." Quinn walked across the room and into the kitchen. Everyone got up and trailed after him.

He opened the studio door and turned on the lights. Kincaid gave a low whistle of surprise. Taglia crowded in behind, eager to see whatever it was that Kincaid was admiring.

A multi-channel mixer dominated the electronics-filled room. Above it a wide glass window revealed the studio, which was easily the size of the living room. Quinn began flipping switches and sliding knobs on the mixer, balancing his guitar against one hip. Lights on the panel glowed red and green.

Satisfied, he led the way through the sound-proofed door into the studio. A drum kit — not fancy but serviceable — was in a plexiglass booth in the far corner. Three separate banks of amplifiers vied for space. Microphones were strung everywhere. An upright piano stood squarely against one wall.

Quinn put his instrument on a stand in front of a speaker stack. Kincaid set his on a matching stand and perched on the piano stool. He glanced at Taglia and grimaced wryly. "Bet this cost more than we make in a year, combined."

"No kidding," Taglia agreed.

"Do you play either drums or bass, Paul?" Quinn asked.

"Sorry, I don't. Playing the radio is about as far as I go."

"We'll manage with the drum machine then." He returned to the control room and sat down at the board. Taglia followed him in and watched with interest as Quinn adjusted a number of settings. "Lieutenant," he said into a microphone. "Play something while I get your volume set up."

Kincaid obeyed, playing a few bars of *Louie, Louie* while Quinn fiddled with a number of knobs and levers on the board. Satisfied, he interrupted, "That's fine. She hasn't been played in a few days. Take the strobe-tuner there and get her set up. Do you know how it works?"

Kincaid gave a thumbs-up and Quinn turned his gaze on Taglia. "It's as well you don't play drums, we need you for sound engineer. These slides are the volume controls for me, Allyn and the Lieutenant. If I ask you to take them down or up, they are the only ones to adjust. Don't forget where they're set now in case you need to take them back up. Okay?"

"Got it."

"Here's the microphone control for you. Press to talk, release to listen. Most important," Quinn pointed at the telephone near his left elbow. "You can tell it's ringing if the red light is blinking. If it rings, cut the board with this switch. The phone is our lifeline. The music is just to get us through the night."

Quinn stood, turning the chair over to Taglia, who took his place. He watched through the glass as the guitarist re-entered the studio, picked up his guitar from its stand and slung the thin leather strap over his shoulder. He plugged in the coiled cord and flipped the power switch. Immediately the room was filled with a low-cycle buzz.

"Ground hum," he said. "Flip your ground switch, Lieutenant. We had this problem the other day. Show him how, Allyn."

Allyn clipped the mike to its stand and went to help Kincaid. Between them, they got the proper switch thrown. The hum stopped. "Thanks, Allyn. And guys, call me Jeff."

Quinn nodded briskly and adjusted the settings on a small machine that started putting out a simple, steady rhythm. He listened, head cocked as he counted, made a minor adjustment then walked away.

"All right," he said at last. "Let's start with something easy, some rambling, twelve-bar blues sort of thing. Jeff, we'll run through it a couple of times without Allyn."

"Oh, here we go," Allyn said, perching himself on a tall stool before his mike stand. "Poor, innocent lad."

"Silence, knave," Quinn told him. "I'll get to you in the proper moment."

"You always have."

"Paul, would you please turn down the volume pot on Allyn's mike? I like feedback, but only when I control it."

Taglia did as asked then pressed the microphone switch. "You've got it."

The guitarist nodded, gave the count, and began to play a steady rhythm. Kincaid listened for a full twelve bars then, at Quinn's nod, joined in, sticking to the key's standard chord progression, following in the wake of the lead guitar.

Allyn unclipped the mike from the stand and held it up between his hands, appealingly, opening his eyes wide and speaking in a high, little-boy voice, "Please, sir, may I? Oh, please, sir? Give us a chance, sir."

Quinn continued with the rhythm, both guitars playing in unison. "Paul, take his volume up by half. Jeff, you got a feel for it? I'm going to lay down some lead work, then you come in."

At Kincaid's nod, Quinn threw back his head and began to play. Kincaid came in on the beat, and Taglia grinned as his playing flowed into the sound. He recognized the song at once: "Dead Shot Blues," from Leviathon's third album. It was one of his favorites.

Then, Allyn's voice came soaring in over the guitars and the electronic drums. There was something mocking about the way he sang.

"You say you're gonna sell your old guitar
You say you're gonna sell your old guitar
You say you're gonna buy a fancy car."

Allyn used the rough edges of his voice for all they were worth, playing with the bitter irony of the lyrics. He delivered the next two verses the same way, but after the bridge he sang with unembellished sadness:

"Say what you want, baby
You'll always be your daddy's son
You can say what you want
You'll always be your daddy's son
Say what you want
You're shooting with another man's gun."

Winding the song down, Allyn repeated the first verse and went on ad-libbing into a gradual fade-out, giving it over to the guitars. Kincaid dropped out of the song at Quinn's nod, leaving the lead guitar alone to end with a low, deep moan.

Allyn took a long, luxurious breath that sounded as if it were the first one in a long time that had not hurt. He smiled at Quinn. "Thank you," he said as he put the mike back on the clip.

"Don't mention it," Quinn replied off-handedly, adjusting the rhythm of the drum machine. "Don't get ready to quit yet, either."

"Oh, come on," Allyn said. "That was first-rate just now. We aren't going to do better if we play all night. Let's pack it in."

"What? Shall we disappoint Jeff, who I'll wager has never been to one of our concerts but who has heard *'Bird of Paradise'* and is dying to learn it?" He spoke lightly, but Taglia caught the glance he turned on Allyn as he lifted his head from the contemplation of his guitar strings. "Perish the thought."

Allyn met his gaze with a level, challenging stare, but the guitarist smiled back at him. After a moment, the singer shrugged and unclipped the mike. He coiled the cord in his hand and shook it out again restlessly.

Quinn turned to Kincaid to practice the chord progressions. They played through the verse and chorus a couple of times.

"All right, Jeff," Quinn said. "You've got the feel of it. This is the kind of song one must jump on hard from the beginning. Paul, be a good fellow and take Allyn's volume back up to the original setting, won't you? He'll need it for this."

"Let's give it something like the Stones might. I've never thought of it that way, but it might be interesting. Sort of a *'chucka chuck whacka chuck'* thing. This, like." He demonstrated on his guitar. After a moment, Kincaid joined in. They jammed for several measures then broke off, grinning. "You know, if you get tired of being a cop, maybe something could be done with you," Quinn said, and laughed. "You'd have to let your hair grow."

"Or dye it blue," Taglia added over the console's microphone. "Or shave your head."

Quinn paused to light a cigarette, take a puff, and wedge it under the strings at the pegboard. He closed his eyes as if waiting for cosmic confirmation for the right moment to start. Everybody room watched him tensely. Suddenly he lifted his head. "All right. Let's go!" he cried and called off the count.

The song broke into the room like an artillery barrage. Screaming feedback dropped off, and out of the fuzz of distortion came the clear notes heralding the vocal entrance.

"If I had a magic carpet..."

Quinn stopped playing. Kincaid stumbled on for a few chords and then halted, leaving the rhythm machine to thump on alone. Everyone stared at Quinn.

"Whaddya call that?" Quinn demanded.

"It's how the song starts," Allyn said.

"I know, but my old Aunt Tillie sings with more balls, and she's a Methodist. Let's have it again."

He gave the count, and once more the room threatened to shake apart. Allyn hadn't gotten two words out when Quinn broke off again, "No, goddamn it!"

"What is it?" Allyn asked, sounding weary.

"You were a full bloody beat late just now."

"I never was."

Quinn turned to him fully, eyes narrowed, his voice venomous. "Bollocks. That's bleeding buggery, and you know it."

"*Cnychu y bant,*" Allyn snarled back at him, the meaning clear even though Taglia could only guess the language was Welsh.

"Let's have it," Quinn said in the same tone and gave the count.

> *"If I had a magic carpet,*
> *I'd take you for a ride..."*

Quinn and Allyn stopped at the same moment and glared at each other. Finally Allyn asked, "What do you want of me?"

"All you have to give. But just now, I will settle for this song."

The room seemed to crackle with their anger, neither man willing to surrender. Then, unexpectedly, Allyn's defiance crumbled. "I... it isn't there," he said, sitting down on the stool. "I don't want to..." He carefully clipped the microphone onto the stand before him and ran his hands wearily through his hair.

"Or maybe you can't." Quinn's voice was a whip-crack. "Pick it up."

"No."

"I said: Pick. It. Up," Quinn demanded. "I once said I would have from you everything there was to get. I want it. I want it now. Now!" He whirled around to face his amp, deliberately doubling his cord. An ululating cry of feedback stormed through the room, wild as lightening in the mountains. The sound raged at the heart and set the teeth on edge. Out of the whirlwind of sound the opening notes came like daggers.

As though lifted outside himself by his fury, Allyn leapt up, snatched the mike from the stand and came in precisely on the beat.

Bird of Paradise
G.J. Paterson

"If I had a magic carpet,
I'd take you for a ride.
If I had a secret castle,
I'd lock you safe inside.
Don't trust my promises,
I am the Bird of Paradise."

In the relative shelter of the control booth, Taglia was hit by a wall of sound. He sat back involuntarily, driven into his chair, while Allyn, caught between laughter and rage, began to dance.

Seventeen

17

Quinn watched Allyn and smiled grimly, remembering the gig in Manchester back in 1969 — the night everything changed.

***

Movement in the shadows at the edge of the stage attracted Quinn's attention as he wrapped up the guitar solo in *"Mirror, Mirror."* Squinting against the lights, he saw Allyn staring at him from the wings. He was glad he wore his guitar slung low enough to hide his rising desire.

Quinn wound the lead line up to a screaming crescendo, breaking like a wave at the crest and leaving Avery the spotlight for his drums.

Allyn was heading down the stairs to the dressing room as he ducked offstage. He traded his guitar to Jackie for a towel and scrubbed his sweat-drenched hair. When he looked again, the singer had vanished from sight.

I've got to find out what's eating away at him. It's worth the chance. The way Avery's playing now, we probably have at least fifteen minutes before we have to be back. He ran down the stairs, following Allyn to the dressing room while the drum solo roared behind him.

The door was locked.

"Allyn?" He knocked firmly to be heard over the sound of the drums. "Are you in there?"

"Where the hell else would I be?" Allyn said through the door, and then louder, "No."

"It's Derek. Let me in."

"Bugger off." After a moment, the lock turned and the door swung open from the inside. Allyn walked away, a bottle of Jack held loosely in one hand.

Quinn glanced at the bottle as he relocked the door. "Bit early for that, innit?"

"Ah, here we have the immortal Derek Quinn," Allyn replied acidly. "Formerly noted session player, now lead guitarist, producer, tour manager, and nanny."

"You do need a minder, you know."

Allyn spun to face him, his fists clenched. "Do you think you're the man for it, then?"

"Could be." Quinn squared off then shook his head. "No, we'd only massacre each other. Something's got at you. What is it?"

"What bleeding business is it of yours?" Allyn sat down and deliberately took another drink.

"You silly arse." Quinn stalked forward and snatched the bottle away. "You fuck this tour, and you're finished. You know it, and so do I."

"I'd no notion you gave a damn."

"Who the bleeding hell said I did?" Quinn leaned over him, Mancunian to the bone now the temper was in him. "I've got my investments to think of, after all."

"That explains it."

"Come on. We've only got minutes."

Allyn looked away. "It's you. No, it's me, but it's you that does it. Do you follow?"

"Thousands wouldn't," Quinn said.

"You've got to lay off me on stage." Allyn glanced at him, then away. "Makes me nervous, all your prowling around and hanging off me."

"I've only the two hands, and both of them are on my guitar."

"You incite me. I want it stopped. Throws off my timing."

"Bollocks!" Quinn slammed the whiskey bottle down on the makeup bar.

Allyn shifted his seat, half-turning from Quinn. There was a moment of silence then his shoulders sagged. "Ah, that's it, then. I'll be shoving along, I guess."

" *What*? You *are* upset, aren't you?"

"I've been through this lot before. I don't want to do it again." Allyn held his gaze for a moment then got up unsteadily.

"Wait. No one wants you to go anywhere but back on stage."

"What about you?" Allyn looked slowly down the length of Quinn's body, pausing at his crotch. Quinn almost moved a hand to cover himself, embarrassed by his own desire. The younger man's face turned hard and cynical. "What do *you* want?"

Quinn took a step toward him, holding his hand out to stroke the blond man's face. Allyn lifted his chin and stepped back. Quinn sighed. "I don't want you to leave."

"I can see that." Allyn laughed harshly. "It's clear enough what you want now. But what about later? All that matters to me is the singing."

"That's guaranteed. We've signed a contract. We're bound together by that if by nothing else. No one can take that away from you." Quinn kept his voice quiet, aware of the swift flowing time.

Allyn smiled, but his expression was still cynical. He reached out his hand and said in a low, throaty voice, "Come here then."

Quinn slipped his hands under Allyn's thick, curly hair and started to pull him forward for a kiss. Allyn turned his head, and Quinn remembered hearing somewhere that hustlers didn't kiss. He dropped his hands, sliding them inside the singer's open shirt, letting them rest on the belt. He brushed the smooth, bare skin with his fingertips as he pressed closer, bringing their bodies together. Allyn's cock strained at the fabric of his faded jeans, pushing against his own hardness. "I know what Sammy is," Quinn said at last. "It won't be like that. Ever again. I promise you."

Allyn's voice was breathless as Quinn nuzzled against his throat. "How did you find out? Did Sammy tell you?"

"What? That you swing? I'd be blind to miss that. About what you were doing after Sammy gave you the toss? You told me."

"Me?"

"When you were sick. You were off your head there for a bit. You talked a little. You'd no notion what you were saying. I pieced it together. No one else knows. Don't forget, I know Sammy, too. And, yes, I can feel it on stage."

When the singer spoke, his voice was a whisper. "Do not dare tell me you care for me. Now, or ever."

Sammy taught you that, didn't he? "Lord, what an idea," Quinn lied. "Care for you? I seldom like you. Doesn't keep me from wanting you." Quinn caressed Allyn's crotch, feeling the outline of his erection through the worn fabric. "I'll take everything from you that you have to give. Not for love, you understand, but to feed my ambition. You're my golden goose, lad."

Quinn let his hands drift to the heavy pewter buckle. It came undone in his hands, and he reached for the snap on the jeans beneath it. His hands steadied as they did when he picked up a guitar on stage. This was a tune for which he knew the changes.

Allyn's flat abdomen was hard and taut beneath Quinn's fingers as he slipped his hands inside the waistband. The singer leaned back, bracing his wide shoulders against the wall. When he spoke again his voice was strained. "I don't know what I want."

"I've no idea what you want either," Quinn said as he eased the jeans down over narrow hips. "But trust me to know what you need."

***

Swirling and soaring, the guitar and the voice pursued each other like swallows tumbling through cloud and clean sky. Kincaid's rhythm guitar fell away, and the voice and Quinn's old guitar sailed on. At last the guitar swooped down to a gentle drone and silence, and the voice alone whispered the final lines of the song,

> *"I am the bird of paradise*
> *I take the eagle and the dove.*
> *I seldom fly alone, now momma,*
> *And I live on love."*

Taglia let his breath out in a long, long sigh. Somehow, even without the full band, Allyn and Quinn had managed to make it work.

The two Englishmen stared at one another without expression in the ringing silence. Both were breathing hard and sweating. Allyn gave a little shake of his head and smiled. "Did I get it right?"

Bird of Paradise
G.J. Paterson

Quinn unplugged his guitar cord and swung the guitar around on the strap to hang it behind him. He took the spare pick out of his mouth and put it in his pocket with the one he had been using. Then he smiled, too. "You're a sound one, that's certain."

Allyn lifted the mike he held.

Quinn laughed. "Hang it up, then. I'll let you off easy."

"The day I die." Allyn put the mike back on its clip.

Eighteen

18

"Well, that was a first." Kincaid paused to glance around the empty den. For the moment, they were alone. Quinn had gone to his room. Allyn was in the kitchen making coffee.

"What was?" Taglia asked.

"I've never had a chance to play guitar on the job before."

Taglia's smile was warm. "No, I guess not. Hey, you look beat. Why don't I make one more perimeter check then take the first watch?"

"Sure. All right."

"Okay." Taglia consulted his watch. "Why don't I wake you about three o'clock?"

"Sounds okay." Kincaid yawned, stretching. "Thanks."

"By the way, I liked the way you played tonight. You were terrific."

"It was fun." A tired smile pulled at his partner's lips. "A lot of it was the guitar Derek loaned me."

"Yeah. He must've known you'd treat it right."

"It's his new one," Jeff replied, a red flush creeping up his cheeks. "He doesn't like it as much as his old one. Not enough sustain."

"Sounded good to me."

"Thanks," Jeff said. "How about I give you twenty minutes? Then I'm heading for bed or falling asleep where I sit."

Taglia shrugged on his jacket. He went out the sliding door and his smile faded. He couldn't get the possibility of a lurking presence out of his mind. He turned up his collar against the chill and slipped into the darkness.

Nothing moved in the late night silence. The thin, cold wind couldn't kill the strong earthy smell of the rain-soaked ground. He took his time searching the area around the house, but found nothing unusual. There was no trace of the wildlife he'd seen and heard earlier, and no sign of trespassers.

Still paranoid, I guess, he decided at last and headed back for the house. He crossed the patio, his tennis shoes silent on the bricks. He could see through the glass doors that Kincaid had already left the den. He started to open the sliding glass door but stopped abruptly as the sound of voices reached him from the partly open window over the kitchen sink.

He took a step back so that he could see through the window. Quinn was closing the refrigerator door. Allyn sat at the table, leafing through the phone book.

"What are you looking for?" Quinn leaned over his shoulder.

"I thought I might go out," Allyn replied.

"Church?"

"What of it?"

"You've not been these ten years and more. You're Pagan on top of it. With your record it'll take more than one night to make an impression, I fear, old son."

"As wicked as that? What about salvation by grace?"

"Will you listen to him?" Quinn demanded. "Grace or works. Both assume salvation to be necessary *a priori*. Do you believe every bleedin' thing said to you, you silly arse? I only meant it's late in the game to change your style. Let's go dancing instead."

Allyn glanced up at him then smiled crookedly. "You idiot. They'll never let us go out, whether it's church or dancing. As if we would."

Quinn laughed and ruffled Allyn's hair good-naturedly. Allyn leaned back against him, and something changed in Quinn's face. He ran his fingers through the red-gold hair, untangling some of the strands he had mussed. "You do need something. A diversion, like. This hasn't been easy on you. Long way from the back streets of Cardiff, eh, lad?"

Allyn nodded but didn't speak, seeming content to accept the comfort of the moment. Quinn rested his hands on the wide shoulders before him. He began to massage them, tentatively at first but with increasing firmness. Allyn let his head fall back against Quinn's middle. "Mmm, that's nice," he said. "You have good hands."

Quinn chuckled and went on kneading the singer's shoulders, gazing down at him with tenderness softening the lines and angles of his gaunt face.

Standing unnoticed in the shadows, Taglia knew he should either withdraw or announce his presence. He had no right to stand there, silent witness to something that was none of his business, and he knew it. He couldn't move.

Allyn sat with his eyes closed, his lips parted, tension draining from his posture under the influence of Quinn's massage. He rubbed his cheek against one slim hand.

Quinn's other hand began to trace the tendons of the singer's neck, the line of his jaw, brushing his fingers over Allyn's mouth. Allyn nibbled at the fingertips resting on his lips.

The singer reached up, running his hands along Quinn's arms, across his chest, to his face. Quinn kissed the center of each palm raised to him then knelt beside the straight-backed chair. Taglia took a deep breath, his blood racing in anticipation of a kiss. Instead, Allyn wrapped his arms around Quinn and rested his head on his shoulder.

The guitarist's hand moved slowly up Allyn's thigh, "Perhaps I do know what you need, after all."

Allyn lifted his head and gazed at him. Finally he said, "Perhaps, but not tonight. My girl's gone, Dee. I can't think of anything else. I can't *feel* anything else. It's all fear inside me."

For several heartbeats they sat as if turned to stone. Watching them Taglia realized that it all made sense now. They had left something out of the story they told about San Francisco: they were lovers. Irons wasn't jealous of Quinn's playing. He was jealous of the bond between them.

Quinn said quietly. "No one knows what will happen."

"No one ever knows." Allyn moved out of his grasp and stood. Taglia stepped back further into the concealing night.

Allyn gazed down at Quinn. "Promise me something." He tipped his head to one side, holding out his hand to help him up.

"What?" Quinn took his hand but made no effort to rise.

"If things don't turn out as you might like," he pulled the guitarist to his feet, "don't do anything stupid."

Quinn balanced steadily on his feet, but for a moment he held Allyn's hand with both his own. Releasing it, he stepped back with a bland smile. "Of course not." He held the smile a moment then walked away.

Taglia deliberately rattled the door and entered as Quinn crossed the den. The guitarist gave him the briefest of glances and stalked from the room. Allyn came to the kitchen door, coffee cup in hand and watched Quinn go. Turning, he smiled at Taglia but the smile didn't reach his eyes.

"What's the matter with him?" Taglia asked, brushing the moisture from his jacket.

"Oh, it's nothing." Allyn shrugged. "I've managed to irritate him again. I shouldn't do it, I suppose. After all, he's the reason I've not had to go and get National Assistance. Still, I can't seem to help it."

"Yeah, everybody's tired and on edge. It's been a rough day." Taglia offered the platitude as an excuse they could both accept. "Maybe you ought to get some rest."

"You're right, of course. Nothing can be served by worrying, but I can't seem to help it." Allyn stared down at the empty fireplace, then glanced at the bar and shook his head.

"No, no more," he sighed. "It doesn't help, and I'd only regret it in the morning. I'm for bed then. Wake me if there are any calls, will you?"

"You know I will," Taglia replied.

As Allyn disappeared down the hall, an electric guitar began to play softly. Taglia recognized it as the tune Quinn had played that afternoon, more intricate than it had been, but still with an undercurrent of sadness.

Taglia went to the front door to check the locks then padded through the rest of the unoccupied rooms, checking windows and doors. He closed and locked the window in the kitchen. Security taken care of for the moment, he decided to go unpack his things.

As he passed through the den, he noticed the Christmas tree still glowing warmly in the corner. He smiled as he remembered his mother's eternal Christmastime nag — *"Turn off the tree if you leave the room and no one's there to watch it. You don't want it to catch fire."* He unplugged the tree and walked down the hall to the room he was staying in.

He rummaged through the meager supply of clothes he had brought, deciding what to keep out for tomorrow. Laying the clothes aside, he sat on the bed to listen.

The music became a strange mixture of blues, folk, and west coast raga. It wove a convoluted tapestry of sound, spacey and trippy like late '60s psychedelia, but the sorrow in it never faded. Taglia meant to listen just for a moment as he leaned back against the pillows.

Bird of Paradise
G.J. Paterson

Nineteen

19

Kincaid closed his bedroom door and sighed with relief. *Privacy, at last.* The stress of dealing with the kidnapping was bad enough. The tension he felt about Paul was worse.

He stripped off his clothes and walked into the bathroom. It was small, with a shower stall, a sink and a commode. He turned on the water in the shower and let it run. He leaned with both hands on the sink, looking at his reflection in the mirror without really seeing it.

I need time to think, but I can't get away from Paul. I can't get away from Quinn and Allyn, either. I think they're queer. But Allyn's married. Or at least he was. He has a kid. Are they... lovers? They must be. Why else is Quinn staying here instead of the hotel? But, if they are, why is Allyn spending so much time coming on to Paul? Does that mean Paul is queer, too? That the other night wasn't some kind of one-time fluke? Isn't that crossing a line?

He scrubbed a hand through his hair. *I've done some line-crossing lately myself. I let Quinn bring in a stash of heroin. What other lines have I crossed?*

The mirror began to steam up. Kincaid adjusted the temperature then stepped into the shower. He turned his back to let the hot water massage the stiffness out of his shoulders.

He had always considered himself a straight man. He liked women. He enjoyed the pleasure a woman could give. He had long told himself he was just too young to settle down and raise a family, but he was thirty-five and that excuse was wearing thin.

He had kept his need for sex with men in a tightly sealed box in his head. After all, it wasn't a constant thing. Once in awhile he'd take off on a weekend bender, disappearing into the darkness of a gay bar or the alley outside. Sometimes he'd go, even if he was in a relationship with some girl. He could see now it wasn't the women's fault. He kept them in a mental box, too. The relationship would last awhile, but he always found himself alone again, aching for what he believed was wrong.

Does that mean I am queer, too? I don't know who I am anymore. I sure as hell don't know what's right.

Kincaid shampooed his hair then picked up a new, fresh-scented bar of soap. The thick suds were soft against his skin as he washed.

Strangers in the dark. Men I pay for sex then never think about or see again. Except for you, Paul. You don't fit in any box at all. We're together all the time — on the job, after work, even on double dates. And no matter who I am with — I always want to be with you. I know we've crossed a line, Paul. God help me, I want to stay on your side of it. I just don't know how.

His skin was slick with soap, the water warm when he moved to let it pulsate against his ass. He began to massage his cock with a soap-lathered hand, thinking of Paul stroking him, touching him, evoking fire.

***

Bird of Paradise
G.J. Paterson
150

"Tha's a good party," Paul muttered as his partner maneuvered him up a short flight of steps. "Where're we goin' now?"

Jeff chuckled, struggling to guide the drunker man and get out his keys at the same time. "I'm taking you to your apartment before you pass out, Bucko."

"Good idea. Let's go home and get drunk."

"We're already drunk, Paul, and we're at your place. Weren't you paying attention?"

"We should'a brought home a couple of girls. I'm horny."

Jeff laughed bitterly. *Yeah, I'm horny too, partner, but not for girls.*

He wasn't certain if he were less drunk than Paul or only more determined they make it to the apartment. After a few moments of juggling keys, Jeff managed to get the door open, and they stumbled inside. He nudged the door shut with his foot and guided Paul across the studio apartment to the king-sized bed. He managed to yank back the covers just as Paul sat down on the edge of the bed.

"Now what?" Paul asked.

"It's time to go to bed. At least take your shoes off and lie down."

"Okay. Shoes it is." Paul kicked off the first one but had to bend down to untie the other, nearly falling off the bed in the process.

Jeff caught him by the shoulders and shoved him back onto the bed. Paul fell across the cream colored sheets and peered up at him owlishly.

"You're hopeless when you're drunk." Jeff shook his head and reached down to pull off Paul's other shoe.

"You're just now figuring that out?"

"Oh, just get some sleep. I'm going to crash. You need anything?"

"Yeah," Paul mumbled.

"What is it?"

"Don't go."

"No, I'm not leaving. I'm just going to sleep on the couch."

"I mean it," Paul said. "Don't go."

He looked at his partner. Jeff could barely breathe as Paul's suddenly all-too-sober eyes examined his face. Paul squirmed backwards on the bed, making room for him to lie down. As though in a spell, he found himself settling down by Paul's side. His partner closed the gap between them and their lips met. The kiss was rich and warm and tasted faintly of beer.

***

Kincaid shuddered as he came, spurting onto the floor of the shower. His erection shrank in his fist.

I left before you woke. I didn't want to see the look on your face when you knew what we'd done.

You want to talk about it. I can't. It was the best night of my life, and the worst. Ashamed, he finished washing, rinsed off, then shut down the water. He reached for a towel, burying his face in its soft, clean folds.

Thursday,

December 21, 1978

Twenty 20

*T*aglia woke with a start, the fabric of his dreams shredding irrevocably. He scrubbed his eyes with the heels of his palms then checked his watch. *Jeez! How long was I out? I can't believe I fell asleep. I'm falling apart on the job. Maybe something to eat or drink will help keep me awake.*

He got off the bed and went out of the room. The hall was dark, but a light was on in the kitchen. There was no sound. He slipped through the den and peered in.

Allyn sat at the table, wrapped in a robe of dark blue watered silk, a deck of cards spread out before him in a classic game of solitaire. He contemplated the cards for a long moment then dealt another card. He played it. Taglia stood watching while the long fingers tapped an irresolute rhythm on the stack of unplayed cards.

"You might as well come in." Allyn played another card.

Taglia didn't move. Allyn raised his head. "Did you want something?"

"I was having trouble staying awake."

Allyn's smile was crooked. "How odd. I couldn't go to sleep. Would you like me to get you something?"

"Got any milk?"

"Milk it is." The robe, only loosely belted at the waist, fell open as Allyn got up. He was naked beneath it. Paul glanced away, his breath catching in his throat, but the singer seemed unaware. Allyn took a glass from one of the cabinets then went to the refrigerator and opened the door. "Sorry, we're out of milk. I've got some lemonade. I made it yesterday morning for Carys. Or there is water"

"Water is just fine."

Allyn filled the glass with ice and water from a pitcher then brought it to Taglia. The light behind Allyn's hair flamed like a halo, but surely no angel ever looked like that.

The singer handed Taglia the glass, and perched on one corner of the table, watching him drink. The levelness in his gaze made Taglia take a large gulp. The warmth of Allyn's body was tangible, filling his nostrils with an elusive, spicy scent. Taglia was uneasy with the man's proximity — uneasy most of all with the knowledge that no safe distance lay between them, no conventions or bystanders. No one else ever need know.

He drank the rest of the water in two quick swallows and turned away.

Allyn reached out to take the glass. "Was there anything else?"

"No, thank you."

"One never knows." Allyn sighed and walked to the sink, turned on the tap and rinsed the glass.

"You should try to sleep," Taglia suggested. "You're under a lot of pressure."

"I gave it a go. I drank all this morning. I couldn't even get regularly pissed. I've given it up as a waste. I may give up sleeping, too."

Taglia saw the exhaustion in Allyn's face. "Don't you have a doctor? You know, somebody who could give you something to help you sleep?"

"I could get that from Derek, if I had a mind," Allyn said. He sat at the table again, pulling the cards toward him to shuffle.

"He'd give you anything you asked for."

"Is that what you think?"

"Why? Don't you?"

"It's no good romanticizing Quinn. He hasn't an ounce of better nature in him. Derek is here because he is convinced I'm a complete twit, I need watching, and he's better at it than anyone else because he won't indulge in any of my foolishness. He's always been careful of his investments. Besides, I've no taste for suicide. There has never been any pretense between us where drugs are concerned."

"I didn't mean to butt in. Would you like me to get you a doctor?"

"No, thanks."

Silence fell as Taglia compared Allyn's words to his own observations. The Derek Quinn he'd seen in the kitchen earlier seemed to be anything but the person Allyn described. "Allyn, why don't you trust people?"

"I used to. Then I grew up." He shrugged. "It's as much me as anything. I'm not easy to get on with. Carys's the one pure thing in my life. I love her completely."

"Oh, come on. There must be lots of people..." Taglia tried to keep his impatience from showing.

"Indeed. Thousands. But the good ones don't get through any more. Only the greedy ones. Listen. I've been in love, and it's never done a thing for me. I thought I fell in love with Demetra, and she's trying her level best to walk off with everything of value which isn't nailed down. In fact, if she thinks I care for something, she'll go after it too, nails or not. Offer me whatever you like — music, money, or sex. Those I understand. Don't offer me love. I don't believe in it. Not any more."

Taglia frowned, remembering Derek's face, suffused with caring as he stooped over Allyn. "I still think Quinn..."

"Let me tell you about Derek Quinn." Allyn stood. "Everything he does is calculated to a nicety in the scales of his ambition. He would sacrifice his own mum, not to mention me, to further his own ends. He is the most coldly calculating person you will ever meet. He is ruled by his ambitions. If you don't know it, then every dealing you have with him is fraught with peril. Because he is a dangerous man. All those with their sights on a treasure and the feeling they've nothing to lose are dangerous.

"He's honest about it," Allyn went on. "He repeats it over and over, even when not asked. No one ever believes it. He has such a nice smile, but it's the gods' own truth." He strolled to the door. "Believe me, Paul, the report Derek cared for anyone, now or ever, me or someone else, more than he cared for his own ends, would come as news to me."

Taglia followed him into the den.

Derek raised his head from silent contemplation of the low-burning flame in the fireplace as they emerged from the kitchen. Taglia wondered how long he'd been listening.

"You know me so well, old son," the guitarist drawled. "I have no secrets left."

"Nothing changes. You always have secrets." Allyn reached for his belt and unfastened it, tying it again more securely.

"Do you think so? Perhaps you are right. Our lives are lived between madness and secrets. Our secrets make us who we are." Quinn's smile was thin. "Art is not made by comfortable men."

Twenty-One

21

*T*he phone began to ring. Allyn moved across the room to answer it. The tension on his face as he picked up the receiver quickly turned to a frown. "We're fine, Jackie. Why?... Okay. Hold on then, let me get him for you." He turned to Quinn and held out the phone.

Quinn saw the dark-haired cop reach to turn on the speaker just as he took the phone.

"Okay, Jackie," he said. "What is it?"

"Something's up with Harry." Jackie's voice crackled into the room. "He says there's a problem and he must speak to you, direct, like. Face to face. He's drunk, but I think there might be something to it."

"Shit!" Kincaid said from the hall doorway. He was dressed in clean clothing and his hair was damp. "Didn't you explain the situation to Harry when he was here earlier?"

"Of course," Quinn said.

"Then why does he want to come back?"

"I've no more idea than you." Quinn gave him a flat look.

"What do we do?" Allyn asked.

The two detectives stared at each other as the voice came over the speaker again, "Quinn, he says it's urgent."

Kincaid sighed. "Bring them over. It must have some bearing on the case or Harry wouldn't be bothering you with it now."

"Right. Come on up, Jackie. But do try to be discreet about it though, all right?"

"My thought too, sir. We'll be up as fast as we can get there. Oh, and Derek?"

"Yes?"

"Be careful. Harry thinks you might be in danger."

"Don't worry. We've got our guardians, and we'll be careful."

"Right. We're on the way."

Taglia stopped the recorder, frowning.

Allyn stared at the machine, clearly bemused. After a long pause he ran a hand through his hair and said, "What do you think Harry's on about?"

"As I said," Quinn lifted his eyebrows, "I'm not omniscient."

Allyn stretched, arching his back and pushing the palms of his linked hands toward the ceiling, as if trying to shift some invisible weight. He walked to the unlit Christmas tree, knelt beside it and plugged in the lights, then sat back on his heels, watching the sparkle and glow. He reached out and touched a glittering, hand-blown carousel horse — a gentle brush of his fingertips, a gesture of tenderness and loss.

Derek sighed, thinking of the girl who had hung the ornament. There was nothing he could say or do. Allyn got up and stepped away from the tree, gazing at it as if he could run back time and recreate the hour and day, the laughter and warmth, and bring Carys home with the strength of his will alone.

There was a sound like a hammer blow hitting the opposite wall, simultaneous with the crackle of breaking glass. Allyn began to turn toward the sliding doors, reaching out as if to move the curtains aside.

Quinn's nerves and sinews reacted faster than his mind. He launched himself, a spring uncoiling, crashed into Allyn, and bore him to the floor among the Christmas packages. A second shot ripped the air above them. Only then did he hear the shouts of warning.

"What the bloody hell?" Allyn shouted, fighting to get out from under him.

"Gunshots!" Quinn hissed at him. "Be still. Someone's outside."

Allyn stopped struggling and they lay together, winded, hearts racing, staring into each other's eyes as knowledge of what had happened rushed in on them. Quinn was in some strange place beyond fear, in a kind of mad ecstasy where he kept repeating to himself, you are alive, you are alive — a prayer, a litany, a paean of thanksgiving.

Someone slapped the light switch, plunging the room into darkness lit by the fitful twinkle of the tree. "Anybody hit?" Kincaid asked in a low voice. "Allyn? Derek?"

"No. No, I'm all right," Allyn whispered back. "We both are."

There was a moment when all Quinn could hear was the wind coming through the broken glass door. Then he heard Taglia speak from near the bar, obviously on the phone, "Shots fired! We need back-up!"

"What about us?" Quinn whispered, rising up on his elbows. In the dim light, both detectives were darker silhouettes amid the shadows.

"Stay here," Kincaid said. "No, wait. Go into the studio. Lock the door. Don't come out till one of us comes for you. We'll knock — shave-and-a-haircut. Stay low. Go now. We'll cover you. Go!"

They scrambled to their feet behind the tree's shelter. Crouching low they ran across the den, through the kitchen, into the studio. Quinn slammed the door behind them, locking it before turning on the light.

Bird of Paradise
G.J. Paterson

Quinn reached up to touch Allyn's cheek, running his fingers over the unshaven contours of his jaw, the velvet lips, feeling the life flowing in and out over his fingertips. "You're alive."

"Yes, we both are, thanks to you." Allyn said and then pulled back. "But what of my girl?"

There was no answer he knew for that. They sank to the floor together. Quinn held the singer in his arms, swaying gently. Allyn sagged against him, and after a moment the warmth of the man's tears soaked through his thin cotton shirt. Quinn wrapped his arms more tightly around Allyn and went on rocking him silently, thinking of sex, and loss, and death.

Twenty-Two

22

"I caught the second muzzle-flash," Taglia said as he skirted the chairs near the fireplace, stopping beside the sliding door. He nudged the curtain to one side with the muzzle of his gun. The waxing moon, veiled and unveiled by flowing clouds, cast strange, uncertain shadows in the night. "He was by the fishpond. On the left, first line of bushes. See it? Nice little spot for a sniper. Nothing but lawn between him and the house, and the pond's down in a hollow. He can cover this door and both ends of the house at the same time."

Kincaid peered around the edge of the glass door. "Okay, I see where you mean. Is he still there?"

"Not if he's smart. I haven't seen him run. Damn it. I'm going out."

"We need to try to get him alive."

"That's the plan. I'm going out the front. If he decides to rush the house, you're going to have to stop him."

"Backup won't take long to get here. Take care." Kincaid's tone was grim.

The lights were out in the foyer. He unlocked the front door and eased it open. Close by, tires screamed as a car tore its way up the hill to the house. *Backup? Maybe they heard the shots.* The porch light was off. He flipped it on as a patrol car turned at the driveway, lights flashing, and rammed the gate open with its front bumper rolling toward the house.

Taglia stepped out of the door, badge in one hand, both hands in the air, as the patrol car came to a fast halt, its flashers extinguished. A single officer jumped out, his own gun drawn. "Freeze!" His voice sounded young and excited.

"I'm police. Sergeant Taglia."

"You reported a shooting?"

"The suspect is probably still on the grounds." Taglia lowered his voice, his gaze scanning the yard. "We need to search. You go south." He pointed with his badge. "I'll go north. My partner's in the house, by the back patio door. White male, thirties, tall, blond hair. He's watching, too, but he's staying inside to protect the targets. Stop anyone else you see."

The patrolman, hidden in the night by his dark hair and uniform, said, "Yes sir," and ran toward the bedroom wing of the house.

Taglia moved toward the carport by the studio. Distant sirens screamed as more backup units raced up the winding, narrow streets. A breeze shuffled fallen leaves across the driveway. He hoped the sounds would obscure his footsteps.

The carport was still empty. He crossed the open space as fast as he could, pausing at the shrubbery on the far side. He made his way to the end of the house and gazed out into the back yard. Nothing moved. Taglia started for the shelter of a large eucalyptus tree when three gunshots in quick succession broke the quiet.

He ran, zigzagging now as he crossed the open yard toward the koi pond. As he reached the shrubbery a dark-clad figure came running toward him from the south end of the house. Taglia stopped, gun aimed. He forced himself to breathe evenly, but his heart pounded and adrenaline flooded his system.

The figure was less than 20' away.

"Freeze!" he shouted. "Police! Drop the gun!"

The figure halted and raised both arms. Moonlight reflected from the silvery barrel of the gun in his right hand.

"I said, drop it!"

The gunman slowly lowered his right arm and tossed the gun to the ground in front of him.

Taglia circled behind the man, keeping his gun trained on him while pulling out handcuffs with his free hand. He got a cuff on one thick wrist.

The man's free elbow slammed him in the solar plexus, blasting the breath out of him. Doubled over, Taglia held onto his gun as the man spun out of his grasp. A big hand closed around his wrist, applying brutal pressure to try and force him to drop the gun.

Taglia gripped the gun with both hands and hung on. The gunman's beefy fist swung toward his face. He ducked far enough to turn it into a glancing blow. It still took him to his knees. The man used his trapped wrist to lever him back to his feet and yanked both their bodies together in a hideous parody of an embrace.

The bear-hug pinned Taglia's arms between their bodies, the gun trapped flat between them. His finger was caught in the trigger guard, and he couldn't release it. He struggled to free his hands, but the grip behind his back threatened to snap his spine.

He kicked at the other man's shin and made contact, but his tennis shoe softened the blow. The big man grunted but tightened his grip. Taglia struggled harder, praying the gun wouldn't go off. If it did, he was as likely to shoot himself as his opponent. His vision swam.

He arched his back, freeing the compression on his chest enough to catch a short breath. He shoved the butt of his gun with his right hand, pulled with his left. The gun shifted, away from him and into his opponent's chest.

Hoping he wasn't about to shoot himself, he pulled the trigger. The close-up roar of the gun was deafening and the recoil slammed against his ribs. Searing heat made him groan as the muzzle flash burnt his flesh. He clenched his teeth against the pain.

His attacker's grip fell away, and Taglia dropped to his knees. He sucked air in desperate gasps. He hurt. A voice in the back of his head screamed, *Get up! Get up!*

Then voices were shouting all around him. He couldn't make sense of what was being said. He tried to stand, but a hand gripped his shoulder. A surge of fear broke through his haze, and he grabbed at it, trying to pry the fingers free.

"Easy, Paul. I've got you," a familiar voice said, and the babble of other voices faded to the background.

Jeff.

Warm fingers tried to remove the gun from his still-clenched fist. He relaxed his grip and let it go.

"Where... where is he?" Taglia panted. He struggled to get up, succeeding with Kincaid's help.

"He's dead."

"No. Shit, no." In the distance, he could hear more police cars approaching. "We needed him."

"It's okay. You didn't have a choice. I would've taken him out myself if I could've gotten a clean shot at him."

Taglia sighed and bowed his head, leaning against Kincaid's chest. After a moment, he glanced up. "Who is he?"

"Noel Moody."

"Well, fuck! Any sign of Carys?"

"She's not here, or if she is, we haven't found her yet. Take it easy. There's a patrol officer down on the south side of the house. Moody shot him. Ambulances are on the way for both of you. Will you be okay for a minute?"

"Yeah."

Kincaid spoke to a nearby patrolman. "Get dispatch to cancel any more response units to this location. Call 'em. Don't use the radio."

Taglia closed his eyes. *Moody. I killed him. He was our link to Carys, and I killed him.*

Twenty-Three 23

Inside the house Taglia sat by himself in the leather conversation pit. The flash burn on his chest stung where the ambulance crew had cleaned and bandaged it. They had suggested he go to the hospital to be checked for broken ribs. He insisted on staying.

The sound of voices in the den was momentarily drowned out by the siren's wail as the other ambulance left to take the injured officer to the hospital. He listened as the sound faded into the distance.

Home. Maybe now I can go home and try to get my head on straight. He ran his hands over his face then brought them down to look at them. *At least the trembling has stopped. The adrenaline rush must be fading.*

He looked toward the bar, where Captain Ortiz and Kincaid were talking. *Jeff is still shook up or he wouldn't be so jittery.* He knew that having Kincaid as a direct eye-witness to the shooting would help him in the long run. Still, an investigation loomed before him.

Taglia noticed Allyn's spicy fragrance moments before the man joined him on the couch. He had dressed at some point, changing from his silk robe into blue jeans and a Beatles t-shirt.

"Are you all right?" the singer asked.

"No, Allyn. I killed a guy. I'm not fine." Taglia was surprised at the bitterness in his voice.

"I can't imagine. I never supposed it might come to this.... I'm sorry."

Quinn's voice broke in harshly. "Of all the sentimentalist's load of old cobblers." The guitarist stood over them, his face grim. "The soddin' bastard tried to do you. He wouldn't have spared a tear, mind. He has to have been in the mix somehow. The idea that there would be two plots running separately stretches the bounds of credulity too far. The gods only know what his involvement was."

"That's rather the point, isn't it? Us never knowing what it is he knew," Allyn retorted. "But the fact is, like him or not, there's a dead human being out there, not a bloody wildebeest."

Taglia wanted to shout at them both to shut up. He wanted to get far away from here. Thankfully, according to regulations, he soon could. "Officer Involved Shooting" the report would read. He'd be placed on administrative leave while the shooting was investigated. He could go home, sleep in his own bed, take time to do some thinking.

Damn. I wish I could have taken him without killing him. Now how will we find Carys? Moody could've told us where to find Irons. Or maybe we're on the wrong track. Maybe Irons isn't involved in this at all. Maybe it was all Moody.

Taglia glanced up when Quinn moved away. Two men in civilian clothes were being escorted into the house from the foyer. Two uniformed officers stood behind them. One of the officers was younger than Taglia, alert but edgy, his right hand resting on the butt of his pistol. The older man, a grim-faced veteran, stood squarely at ease, stolid and calm.

The civilians seemed as uncertain of their welcome as a pair of muddy dogs. Taglia recognized one of them as the red-haired road manager who had brought the tapes. He didn't recognize the other. He was about Taglia's height, but heavier, with sandy blond hair pulled back in a ponytail.

"Do you know these two, sir?" the young cop asked Quinn.

"Certainly, Officer," Quinn replied. "Harry Stuart and Jackie Carlisle. They're in our employ. We asked them here."

The older officer nodded and gestured them into the den. Carlisle joined Allyn and Taglia in the conversation pit. Stuart followed with a reluctant, shuffling gait.

Quinn crossed to the bar and poured a round of drinks. He handed them out, seeming surprised when Allyn declined his with a shake of his head. Quinn glanced at Taglia and offered the drink to him. Taglia accepted it, realized what he was doing and set it aside. *Alcohol makes you do stupid things.* More stupidity was the last thing he needed. Besides, until the captain said otherwise, he was still on duty.

Carlisle and Quinn sipped their drinks. Stuart guzzled his as if it were water. Taglia grimaced. He could smell the sour odor of sweat and alcohol on the man. He'd been drinking hard for some time.

There was an awkward silence. Quinn pulled out a barstool, set it across from Stuart and perched on it. He took a last puff of his cigarette, drew the smoke into his lungs and let it out slowly. "All right, Harry. What is this mysterious thing you have to tell us, face to face?"

Stuart shifted on the couch. His mouth worked for a moment but no words came out.

"It's about Noel, innit, Harry?" Carlisle prompted him.

"Hush now, Jackie, old son. It's Harry's story."

"When I introduced Noel to you, Allyn, I kind of lied about how I knew him. I told you Noel came to me looking for a job as bodyguard with plenty of references to show. It wasn't the truth."

Kincaid and Ortiz stopped talking, turning to listen to what Stuart had to say. Everyone except Quinn seemed to be holding their breaths.

"What is the truth, Harry?" Quinn asked.

"Well, I told Allyn I'd known him for a long time, but I only met him in October, after I got here to L.A. We met through Rick Irons. You remember him? Anyway, the first time I met Noel, he showed me a picture." Stuart brushed one coarse hand across his face. "I couldn't believe it. It was Megan."

"Megan?" Allyn echoed.

"My poor dead girl," Stuart whispered. The big man began to cry. "Megan McLafferty. He's her brother. Noel Moody is Megan's brother."

"How do you reckon that one out?" Jackie asked. "They don't have the same last names."

"It was a family thing," Stuart said. "Their parents divorced when they were kids. Noel's her elder brother. He told me how he'd come to America years before she died, with his father. The family name was Moody. Megan stayed with her mother, and her mum got both their names legally changed back to her maiden name. McLafferty."

Stuart wiped his eyes with the back of one huge hand. "I told him she never mentioned a brother. He said it was because they hadn't had any contact for years. He found out she'd died and had no money to go to the funeral."

"Did he know how Megan died?" Quinn asked.

"Yeah. We talked about it, but he already knew most of the story. That was the thing. He couldn't believe Megan had gotten addicted all on her own. I think he still remembered her as a little girl."

"Did he blame anyone in particular for her death?" The guitarist's voice was level and calm, but his eyes were hard as flint.

Stuart darted a glance at Quinn, then at Carlisle who nodded and motioned for him to go on. The big man ducked his head in a quick nod. "You, Derek," he whispered. "He blamed you for all of it."

"One doesn't feel surprised." Quinn stared at him coldly, a predator contemplating his prey.

Stuart seemed to shrink from within. His face was as lined and wrinkled as an old man's. "It wasn't my idea. Please." The words burst out. He turned to Allyn. "You've got to believe me. I didn't even know what they were planning until Derek told me about Carys this afternoon."

"'They?'" Jackie shook his head, his brow furrowed in confusion. "They who?"

"Weren't you listening? Noel of course. Noel and Rick." Stuart broke down, holding his head in his hands and sobbing.

Twenty-Four 24

aglia locked gazes with his partner. *We should shut him up. We should read him his rights. Stop him from saying anything else until he's in custody.* He could see the same thought in Kincaid's eyes.

They both turned to look at Ortiz. The Captain shook his head. Taglia suppressed a smile. *This isn't a police interrogation, it is Allyn's.* He returned his attention to the musicians.

Jackie slumped against the back of the couch, studying the ceiling. Quinn stared at Stuart, unblinking. Allyn's gaze was lost in some far distance.

Stuart's sobs subsided. Allyn's glance dropped to his face. "Where is she, Harry?"

"I don't know." Stuart rubbed his hands over his damp, reddened face.

Allyn lunged to his feet, kicking the coffee table out of his way. His strong, farmer's hands caught up handfuls of Stuart's t-shirt and hauled him to his feet. *"Where is she?"*

"I don't know!" Stuart wailed. "Rick has her! He moved her after we talked this afternoon. I don't know where she is now. Oh, God, Allyn, if I knew I'd tell you. I swear to you I would!"

Quinn laid a hand on the singer's shoulder. For a long, awful moment Allyn teetered on the brink of violence. He took a deep breath and flung Stuart away from him, throwing him back into the corner of the couch. "Your oath means nothing to me," he spat. "Only the truth will help you now. Where was she last you saw her?"

"Rick had her at the apartment where we met with him. She was fine. She even got mad at me because I wasn't there to bring her home. I swear...." Tears started down his cheeks again.

"Has he hurt her?" Quinn asked.

"No. When I saw her, Noel had given her something to make her sleep. She fell asleep while I was there. Noel told me how they got her out of the house last night without waking her. He drugged the milk, and she and Lydia drank some before bed, like always. It probably made Lydia sleepy, but it knocked Carys out. He handed her out the window to Rick. He said he threw the milk bottle away so no one would know."

"You said Rick moved her. Where to?" Allyn demanded.

"I dunno. I saw him out the back window as Noel and I were leaving in his car. He left the apartment right after we did, and he put her in the back seat of a car. She was still asleep."

"What kind of car?"

"I don't know."

"What color?"

"I don't remember..."

Allyn straightened, fists clenching.

"No! I really don't know. You know I don't know anything about cars, Allyn. I think it was blue. Blue... dark blue. It looked newish. American."

Bird of Paradise
G.J. Paterson
176

"How many doors?" Quinn asked.

"Doors? I don't know how many — wait, he put her in the back seat. Laid her down, like. It must've had four doors. I don't know anything else, I swear."

Jackie sat up and exchanged a glance with Quinn. "Yeah, you do, Harry. You know lots more. Just keep telling the truth."

"What happened when you met with Rick and Noel, Harry?" Quinn asked.

"I'm thirsty. Could I have another drink?"

"After you finish. Go on. What happened?"

"Noel was already there when I got there. I was all torn up about them taking Carys. I told them they shouldn't have done it. After that, it was like they didn't trust me anymore. Then Rick got mad because you'd fired Noel. He paid us, but Noel said he didn't want the money as much as he wanted to get at you. He said something about doing Allyn, to make you suffer. Carys started screaming at us so Rick slapped her, but he didn't really hurt her. She was already tied up so he gagged her. What with all that, Noel was still determined to come after you, Allyn."

Rivulets of sweat ran down Stuart's face. "I couldn't believe what he was saying. They'd promised me no one would get hurt. And they haven't hurt Carys. I know that for sure. As for killing Allyn... no, I couldn't. I said, 'Allyn hasn't done anything to you,' and Noel said, 'Megan didn't do anything to Quinn, either, but he killed her.'"

"What did Rick say?" Quinn asked.

"Rick got mad. He said something about Allyn belonging to him now. He said, 'I'll kill you if you touch him. Peacock is mine.'"

"What the fuck does that mean?" Allyn demanded.

"I don't know," Stuart moaned. "After that, Noel didn't say anything more about you. But I'm sure he's going to try to kill you. I needed to think about what to do so I had Noel drop me off at a bar. Then I called Jackie."

"You're too late, Harry," Quinn said. "Noel already tried to kill Allyn."

"What!" Stuart's face went from flushed to dead white.

"Noel is dead."

Stuart's mouth gaped and worked like a beached fish, but he made no sound. Allyn turned as if to walk away, then stopped and looked back, "Why, Harry? Why did you do this?"

"Megan was my girl," Stuart said and stood up. "We were *bleeding* engaged! Quinn stole her away from me. Quinn and his drugs. And it was Quinn and his drugs that killed her."

Quinn's eyes pinned the man with an unblinking, reptilian stare. When he spoke his voice was very soft. "Ah, Harry. We both know how Megan McLafferty really died, don't we?"

Twenty-Five 25

Three notes, so high on the keys that they were not really musical, were the only sounds in the room. Taglia watched as Allyn played them over and over. The singer's expression was thoughtful. Kincaid was looking at his notebook, flipping pages back and forth as he consulted what he had written and making notes for his report. Ortiz had left the room to take Stuart out to a waiting squadcar. Jackie Carlisle sat hunched forward, his face in his hands. Quinn leaned back against the bar, the front two legs of his stool off the ground, watching the rising smoke of his cigarette.

Finally, Allyn stopped playing and shook himself as if waking from a dream. "Derek, what did you mean?"

"About what, exactly?"

"When you said the two of you knew how Megan died. What did you mean?"

Quinn took a long drag off his cigarette, flipping ashes in the general direction of an ashtray. "There was strychnine in the junk the night she died. Meant for me."

"Yes, yes," Allyn said. "That's well known. What of it?"

"It was Harry who brought it."

"Damn it, Quinn, I know that too. Who put the strych..." Allyn choked in mid-word as understanding sank in.

Kincaid's head jerked up. "You mean you kept a man working for you after he tried to kill you?"

Taglia felt the same shock, "And you didn't tell us?"

"Derek," Allyn asked. "Whyever for?"

Kincaid's expression sharpened. "Wait. Mrs. Calhoun told me something about this. She said you kept Harry on for loyalty's sake."

"She wasn't wrong, so far as it goes." Quinn grimaced. "Harry never admitted to it, and I couldn't prove it — although I never let him know that. The French police weren't interested in the truth, and I wanted him where I could see him. But I never thought it would lead to something like this."

Allyn stared at him for a long, silent moment, fury gathering in his face. "So it does all come back around to you, doesn't it? This is your fault. You miserable bastard!"

He surged toward Quinn, but Taglia got between them. Jackie jumped to his feet and grabbed Quinn's arm, hauling him off the barstool and back out of harm's way. Thwarted, Allyn snarled, "If anything happens to her, I swear I will break you apart with my bare hands!"

"You!" Taglia shouted at Allyn, jabbing him hard in the chest with his hand. "Shut up!"

"Who the hell are you to tell me..."

"I said 'shut up!'" Taglia ordered. He glanced over his shoulder at Quinn and Jackie. The guitarist looked shaken, years younger, his dark eyes bruised, his skin so pale the blue of his veins shown through. "Get him out of here."

Quinn pulled his arm out of Jackie's grasp. Together they walked toward the hall, Jackie carefully keeping his body between the two musicians. Taglia waited until he heard a bedroom door open and close before he stepped away from Allyn.

"Sodding wanker! It's gone all wrong, hasn't it?" Allyn asked. "We aren't getting her back, are we?"

"You've got it backwards, Allyn," Kincaid said. "This information from Harry is huge. The department is still doing its damnedest to find Carys, and we're not going to stop. Don't give up."

"'Don't give up,'" Allyn mocked. "It sounds like the title of a cheesy rock anthem to me."

The front door opening and closing broke the stream of notes. Taglia looked up when Ortiz walked back into the room. The captain went to the far end of the bar and beckoned both cops to him.

"Taglia, your partner has already told us what happened from his point of view," Ortiz said. "We'll need a statement from you, but it can wait. Are you hurt?"

"I'll be fine, Captain."

"Good. Why don't you come by in the morning? We can get your statement recorded then. In the meantime, I'm sorry, but you know the regs."

I joined the department to help people, not kill them. God, tonight I killed a man. I want to go home.

"Who'll be conducting the investigation?" Kincaid asked.

"Internal Affairs hasn't told me yet."

"Oh, I'm sure all the boys at I.A. will give him a fair hearing. They go into investigations assuming you're guilty until proven innocent down there. This was justified, Captain. Moody was trying to kill him, not to mention shooting one of ours and taking potshots at Allyn."

"Stop," Ortiz ordered. "Your partner will get a fair hearing."

"Don't, Jeff. It's all right. It's what they have to do." Taglia gave his partner a lopsided smile. "I'll be okay."

After a moment, Kincaid nodded.

"I'm sorry, but I'll need your badge," Ortiz added.

Taglia removed his badge from his pocket. He glanced at it for a moment then handed it over.

Allyn called out, "Excuse me? Could someone please tell me what's going on?"

"It's routine after an officer-involved shooting, Mr. Sterling," Ortiz replied, turning to face the singer.

"What's routine?"

"He's not going to understand," Taglia muttered, then said aloud, "They've taken my gun as evidence in Noel's death, Allyn. There has to be an investigation into the shooting."

"Oh?" Allyn frowned. "Do they have to take your badge as evidence as well? Pull the other leg. It's got bells on."

"I'll be taking a leave of absence while the investigation is in progress."

"What does that mean?"

"It means I have to go now. I'm off duty until the investigation is concluded."

"I beg your pardon?"

"It's okay, Allyn. The department will send someone in to replace me, and Jeff will still be here. Don't worry. The new guy will be good, I promise. Better'n me, probably."

"That's not the point, is it?"

"It's regulations, Allyn."

Paul, don't you want to stay?" Allyn spread his hands in appeal.

"Uh, yeah, but..." Taglia scratched the back of his head.

"What's the problem then?"

"Sergeant Taglia killed a man," Ortiz said.

Allyn's expression became severe. "Sergeant Taglia killed a man who almost killed me."

"I understand. I'm sure he appreciates your gratitude, but the point is..."

Allyn slammed his fist into the keyboard, the piano making an ugly sound as if in protest. "I'll bloody well tell you what the point is! I didn't want you fucking cops in on this from the beginning. I knew you'd cock-up everything. I don't like cops, but I've come to trust these two. So the point is, either they both stay or you all go."

"Allyn, don't..." Taglia began.

Ortiz interrupted, "Now, Mr. Sterling, be reasonable."

"Reasonable? I'll give you bloody reason! My girl's gone, and I've little hope of getting her back. How will that look in the papers, eh? Los Angeles' finest fuck up getting my daughter back and pull the props out from under me, too. All because of a stupid regulation which means the cop who saved my life has to be suspended — excuse me, has to go 'on leave.' Think about that for a second, because it'll be all over every bit of newsprint come tomorrow morning. All it will take is one phone call. One call!"

"Mr. Sterling, will you please listen to me for a moment...."

"Right." Allyn walked over to the phone.

Taglia stifled a sigh.

"Mr. Sterling..."

"I feel certain Chris is home by now." Allyn picked up the receiver.

"Allyn, will you just shut the fuck up for a minute?" Taglia bellowed.

The singer stared and returned the receiver to its cradle. Taglia continued in a more measured tone, "You don't want to bring the press in on this, do you? Chris knows, sure, but he's already working with us and he's helping off-the record. Stop and think about what media coverage would do to Carys's chances."

"Paul." Pain and fear warred on Allyn's face. "I don't want anything to hurt Carys. The gods know that's the last thing I want! But why does this man have to treat you like some kind of criminal? He's taking you off the case because you did what you were left here to do — protect us."

"I'm not being taken off the force, Allyn. I'll be back as soon as the investigation is over. I killed a man tonight. Sure, Jeff and I say it was justified, but Captain Ortiz wasn't here to see what happened. Administrative leave gives me a chance to pull myself together. Despite what you may think, I don't enjoy shooting people."

"I know that," Allyn said. "It's one of the reasons I want you to stay."

"This is routine in a shooting, Mr. Sterling," Ortiz added.

"Is it? You see, Captain, I've never been involved in a shooting before. I don't know what the rules are, much less what's routine. Why does Sergeant Taglia have to be penalized for doing his job? Can't the investigation be conducted while he finishes his job here?"

"It's been the department's experience that it's in the officer's best interest to give him some time off after something like this."

"Is it?" The singer's gaze was back on him, searching for answers. "Paul, do you want the time off?"

Taglia discovered he was no longer certain what he wanted. "Jeff will still be here, Allyn, Captain Ortiz will send someone else to take my place."

"But Carys... How can I... " Allyn's gaze shifted from Taglia to Ortiz. After a moment, he shook his head. "Do what you have to. Carys's all that is important. Please, just get her back."

The room fell into a strained silence. After several seconds Ortiz spoke just loud enough for the cops to hear him. "What am I missing here, Taglia?"

"He's walking a thin line, Captain. He seems comfortable dealing with me."

"A thin line, eh? Somehow I'm not surprised." Ortiz studied the younger man for several seconds. "What about you?"

"Me?"

"Do you want the time off? You're entitled to it, you know. We can even pull Kincaid out, if you want him as your support officer."

Taglia glanced at Allyn. The singer's face was distorted by anguish. He weighed it against his own earlier desire for solitude and sleep, for peace and distance from the pressure of this case. *The scales never balance. Isn't this why you became a cop, Sergeant Taglia? In the hopes that, bit by bit, you can make the scales balance? You may have killed one man, but there's still a man and a child you can help.*

"No," he said at last. "I'd like Jeff as my support, but I can't take him away from here. And no, I don't want to leave either. But what about the regs? Aren't they carved in stone?"

Ortiz's lips curved into a grim smile. "You know the politics of this case. I doubt much of anything is carved into stone if it gets Carys Sterling back alive and keeps these guys alive, too."

"Then I'll stay. If I can."

Ortiz paused a moment. "I'm going to give you one more chance to think about it, Taglia. Are you sure?"

He glanced at Kincaid, "Yeah. If you can arrange it, I want to see this one through."

The captain nodded. "That's what I figured you'd say, and frankly I'm glad. This case is tearing up the mayor and he's tearing up the Chief. I don't think I'll have any problem convincing them this is the right way to handle things. Don't worry, I'll keep I.A. off your back until the case is over."

Taglia blinked in surprise as Ortiz handed back his badge. "You're going to let me stay on duty?"

"Follow me out to the car. I brought you a replacement gun. Just in case."

Twenty-Six

26

It was almost five a.m. when Taglia wandered into the kitchen to start a pot of coffee. Ortiz and most of the cops had left a couple of hours past, and Jackie had gone a little later. Except for the two officers guarding the crime scene outside, he had the place to himself. Despite his assurances to Ortiz, he was exhausted but restless. He wasn't sure he could sleep if he tried, which is why he had volunteered for the first watch. Coffee fit his mood.

He spent a few minutes watching the stream of dark liquid filling the pot. The coffee machine finished with a self-satisfied gurgle, and he poured himself a cup, sitting at the table to drink. It felt like the most normal thing that had happened all day. When he finished he got up to take a tour of the house.

At the entrance to the hallway he heard voices. Pausing, he cocked his head to listen. It sounded like...

Foghorn Leghorn?

The sound came from the master bedroom at the end of the hall. Allyn's room. The door was open a crack, and a faint light spilled out.

He eased it open a little wider and peered into a room lit by the flicker of a television screen. Allyn, wrapped once again in his blue silk robe, lay on the wide waterbed propped up by a pile of satin pillows. A sheepskin bedcover was pulled up to his waist.

"Come in," The singer said in an amused tone.

Taglia laughed, then pushed the door open and went in, closing it behind himself. "What are you doing? You should be asleep."

"Couldn't sleep. Getting shot at makes me uneasy."

"I understand the feeling. I made some coffee if you're interested." He glanced at the TV, fascinated. "Cartoons? What channel is that? I didn't know any station in L.A. played cartoons at this time of morning."

"They don't." Allyn pointed to a VCR underneath the TV set. "Got bored once I got here and I bought this treasure. It's helped me through many a long and tedious time, I can tell you."

"I've seen 'em in stores." Taglia sat down on the end of the bed, the better to examine the machine. "Can't afford one yet. Maybe by next summer the price will come down."

"How're you doing?"

"Me? I'm sore, but I'll survive. It's only bruises and a little burn."

Allyn smiled. "I never had the chance to thank you. It was a terrible risk you took going after Noel. Thank you for saving my life."

"Derek is the one who saved your life. He pushed you out of the way."

"He did, yes." Allyn reached forward, caught Taglia's right hand and ran warm fingers over the dusty-blue bruise forming on his wrist. "But you could've died."

"I'm pretty hard to kill." Taglia drew his arm back. He could still feel the tingle of Allyn's fingers on his skin. With an effort, he looked back to the TV set. "What movies do you have? Did you record them yourself?"

"Some of them." Allyn shifted, hauled a bulging duffle bag up from the floor and up-ended it on the bed, spilling black videocassette boxes all over the sheepskin throw. "Some I've bought here. Some of the best were given to me."

Paul picked up the nearest tape. "*The Great Dictator*? That's Chaplin."

"Yeah, I've got several of his, plus a whole tape of shorts. Keaton's *Steamboat Bill, Jr.*"

"Keystone Cops. Laurel and Hardy. The Stooges." Taglia gathered the tapes up in a pile and read the labels one by one. Several were animated movies.

"Carys loves cartoons. So do I." Allyn lay back against the pillows.

"Let's see. *La Boheme*?"

"Lillian Gish. Her eyes speak volumes. She's still beautiful, I'm told. Like a faded rose. I'd love to meet her."

Taglia paused and looked at him. "It seems weird, you having idols. People you'd like to meet."

"Does it?" Allyn considered it, then shook his head. "Everyone's got heroes, I expect. It's odd. I've no ambition to act, but I love those old films from the late twenties to, oh, I guess the mid-forties. They're all here. Garbo and Swanson, Gable and Bogart, Valentino and Theda Bara, Dietrich, Flynn, and Harlow. The issues were clearer then and the bad guys always took the fall."

"In *Wild Women of Wongo*?"

"What? Oh, that's Quinn's. He's got all those weird fifties sci-fi things."

"No kidding. *Plan 9 From Outer Space*. *Forbidden Planet*. *War of the Worlds*. This is terrific stuff."

"He sits for hours with the audio switched off and the color-tuning all cocked-up, playing an electric guitar through an amp stack and every sound distortion device known to man, glued to the set. Asked him once what he got out of it. He just said, 'Negative entropy, man. You know, Cosmic Energy,' and cranked up the volume on his guitar another notch to drown out further questions."

"Weird."

"I thought as much." Allyn handed Taglia another tape. "He's got everything Vincent Price ever did, back in England. I wouldn't let him buy them here. Didn't want my girl's brain warped. What he's bought here is bad enough."

Taglia read the label on the tape Allyn had given him. "*Casablanca!* Can we watch a little of it? That is, if you don't mind. It's my favorite film of all time."

"Mine, too." Allyn smiled. "Sure. Why not?"

Taglia perched awkwardly on the edge of the bed and swept the tapes into the bag. Allyn threw back the coverlet and the indigo blue satin sheets, got up and switched the cassettes in the machine. He punched a few buttons and climbed back into bed, settling in among the pillows. He smiled at Taglia and patted the space beside him. "Come on. Relax and get comfortable."

"I, uh..."

Titles rolled over Africa.

"Your arse will go to sleep if you sit there." Allyn laughed. "Get comfortable. I'll loan you some of my pillows."

"Yeah, you're right." Taglia shrugged. "Why suffer, huh?"

"Take that off first, though," Allyn said, pointing at Taglia's shoulder-holster with the borrowed pistol in it. Taglia shrugged out of the holster, wrapped it around the gun and put it on the nightstand beside him.

Allyn sighed and shifted on the bed to give Taglia plenty of room as the credits rolled by. "If you watch you'll see 'Songs by M. K. Jerome and Jack Scholl,' but the only one they actually wrote was 'Knock on Wood.' Even 'As Time Goes By' was written by Herman Hupfeld, not them. Doesn't seem right, does it?"

"Yeah, I guess. I never thought about it before." Taglia settled back gingerly among the pillows. "Too bad we don't have popcorn."

"Oh, I'm such a pig." Allyn leaned over his side of the bed and brought up a huge bowl of popcorn.

"Terrific." Taglia put a handful into his mouth. "Yechh! What is this stuff?"

"Popcorn."

"It's sweet."

"Of course. It's got a glaze on. Don't you like it that way?"

"Is this how you eat popcorn at the movies in England?"

"Yes, and in Wales, too."

"No wonder Monty Python is so screwy."

"I'm sorry."

"It's okay. It'll take some getting used to, that's all. I haven't had caramel corn since I went to the circus as a kid."

There was silence while the globe turned and the escape route traced its way across Europe to Casablanca, then Allyn said, "There's the one continuity mistake in the entire film."

"What is?" Taglia took a smaller, more tentative bite of popcorn.

"What are Macaws doing in a Moroccan bazaar? They're South American parrots, not African."

"Maybe they imported them."

"Oh, yes. Hadn't thought of that."

There was another long pause while the usual suspects were rounded up, and the weasel stole the guy with the bizarre tie's wallet, and Allyn quoted in perfect synch, "'...Vultures. Vultures everywhere.'"

"Shh..." Taglia poked him in the ribs.

"Sorry. Didn't mean to upset you."

"No. It's, uh, Jeff talks back to movies. Drives me nuts. How many times have you seen this one, anyway?"

"I haven't a clue. Lots. I'll be good. Not a peep more shall you hear."

The promise held through Conrad Veidt's arrival. It even held up through Dooley Wilson singing "It Had to be You," and "Knock

On Wood," although Peter Lorre's entrance was a near thing. Taglia began to relax and enjoy the movie. He decided he didn't mind the peculiar popcorn after all.

Allyn hummed along to "Baby Face," but since it was such a short bit of song Taglia didn't complain.

Then Lorre was grabbing at Rick's lapels, whimpering, and neither one of them could resist reciting with the movie.

"Shh..." Allyn stifled a giggle.

"Shush, yourself. You started it."

The film began to exert its spell over the two watchers at last. Then it was Bogart and Bergman in Paris, driving down the Champs Elysee, driving through the country, and standing by the window, young and beautiful, both of them.

Taglia shifted a little on the waterbed and reached for the popcorn. His hand met Allyn's in the bowl. He turned to find the singer gazing at him. A flush crept up the back of his neck.

Allyn sighed and turned toward him, his hair spilling forward over his shoulders. Taglia took a deep breath, intoxicated by the scent of him. Rick stood at the train station, reading the note in the rain.

Allyn nuzzled against him, leaving a trail of nibbles from his ear to the hollow of his throat, murmuring something too soft to make out.

"What?" Taglia managed to say.

"The popcorn. We've spilled it."

Taglia smothered a laugh. "Never mind the popcorn." He slipped his hands inside the robe, running them over Allyn's chest. "You could do something about the bowl."

Nimble fingers were unbuttoning his shirt, pulling it loose from his waistband. "What do you suggest I do about it?" Allyn breathed in his ear.

"I don't know," he said when he could. "Who cares? Get rid of it."

Allyn sat up and reached for the bowl. The blue silk robe slipped from his shoulders as he turned to put the bowl on the floor. Taglia saw scars, long since healed, crisscrossing his back. Taglia began to speak and then thought better of it as Allyn hastily pulled the robe back up to his shoulders.

There was a dull thump as the bowl hit the carpet. Allyn lay down again, facing him. Like an artist unveiling a masterpiece, he untied the robe and laid it back from the body beneath.

"Oh, God," Taglia whispered, "I used to have dreams about you."

"I'm real. I'm here," Allyn answered him. "Touch me."

Taglia reached out, stroking down the broad chest muscles, the flat stomach, to a soft flank, coming to rest on the velvet warmth of an inner thigh near Allyn's thickening uncircumcised cock. His own filled at the sight of it. "The Germans never did figure out how to outlaw miracles."

"No, they didn't." Allyn smiled as Taglia kicked off his sneakers. The dark-haired man sighed as Allyn pulled him close, his touch vital but delicate. Allyn's hand, strong and gentle, wandered over Taglia's flesh, hesitating when his fingertips touched the bandage over the burn on his stomach. "I don't want to hurt you."

"I'm not hurting," Taglia said. Allyn's hand resumed its wandering, warming him, encouraging him to make explorations of his own. The singer sighed and murmured his pleasure, the sounds low and thrilling to the ear. His fingers worked their way down the black thatch on Taglia's chest and across his belly. He unbuttoned the fly on Taglia's jeans and ran the zipper down. His fingers slipped under the elastic on the cop's briefs, and froze.

Taglia felt the hesitation. "Allyn?"

"We can't do this." Allyn pulled away from him, swung his bare legs across the edge of the bed and sat up. "I can't do this."

"Uh... what?" Taglia propped himself up on his elbows.

"My girl's gone. I've neither reason nor right to forget. Not for a second. Not for one single second. Besides..."

"Besides?"

"Besides there's Jeff." Allyn said. "That's more than a simple release of tension is worth."

"It was more than that," he protested as his partner's name went through him like a knife.

"Was it? Ah well, yes it was. Or it could have been. It was nice, and I thank you. As for you, it might be good with me, mind you, but it would be better with Jeff. He's the one you want, isn't he?"

He finished re-buttoning his shirt and scooted to the edge of the bed as if nothing had changed, but nothing would ever be the same and he knew it. If Allyn could see it others could too. He couldn't resist saying, "And then there's Derek."

"Whatever the fuck that means," Allyn said. "But we'll always have L.A."

Taglia mustered a small laugh as he picked up his shoulder holster and shoes, and opened the door. He paused, hand on the doorknob, and glanced back. "'Here's looking at you, kid.'"

Twenty-Seven   *27*

A small movement in the dark startled Taglia as he shut the door behind himself. It was Quinn, leaning against his bedroom door, still dressed, with his arms crossed.

"I see you gave him what he wouldn't take from me." Quinn's voice was cold.

"What?" Taglia asked. "Oh, no. We watched a movie. It was nothing like that."

"Like what, officer?"

"We didn't. I mean, you know. We didn't do anything."

Quinn gave a sharp laugh. "Then why are you carrying your shoes and your gun? No need to cover for him. I know what he is. I've always known."

"I guess it's no surprise he doesn't trust you." Taglia felt his anger rise. "You don't trust him."

The door to Allyn's bedroom crashed open. "What the hell's going on out here?"

"You know better than I," Quinn replied.

"What's that mean, then?" Allyn said.

"How was the movie?"

"We watched *Casablanca*," Allyn replied. "Not that you've any right to ask."

"Ah. That explains the Bogart, doesn't it?"

"That's all that happened," Taglia interjected.

Quinn flipped the light switch outside his door. The hall lit up. Allyn stood in his untied robe, staring fixedly at Quinn. Taglia glanced at Allyn and blushed.

The guitarist looked at both of them and laughed. Allyn's face flushed red, whether from anger or embarrassment Taglia couldn't tell.

"There are no words for you!" Allyn's voice rose. "You and your secrets have all but handed Irons my daughter. Maybe you are mad! You've no right to a claim on me. You never have had."

Quinn arched one sardonic eyebrow. "Which you have always made abundantly clear. Did you make it clear to the dear sergeant here as well?"

"Guys," Taglia said. "Let's dial it back a notch why don't we? It's not a big deal. It was just a movie."

Slowly, deliberately, Allyn wrapped the robe around himself and tied the sash. His gaze never left Quinn's face. When he spoke again his voice was quiet, "Are you calling me a whore, then?"

"Am I? You would know that better than I," Quinn said. "And you and I are still bound together by contract, just as we have always been."

"I'll give you your bloody fucking contract!" Allyn took a step toward Quinn, arms coming up, fists clenched. Quinn didn't react.

Kincaid charged around the corner. He caught Allyn by one arm, wrenching it into a hammer-lock. The singer gasped at the pain, struggling against the restraint.

"Calm down, Sterling!" Kincaid snapped. "Stop fighting and I'll let you go." After a moment Allyn quit resisting and Kincaid eased his grip. "Everybody just chill out. Paul, what's going on here?"

"Well, uh, I just came out of Allyn's room. We'd been watching an old movie on his VCR. Derek was here in the hall. I think he had the wrong idea about what we were doing."

"Did I?" Quinn asked. "That's certainly possible, I suppose."

"Cnychu y bant," Allyn snarled, but he didn't move.

Kincaid released him and stepped between them. "Look, you two fighting like this is only serving Irons' purpose. It doesn't matter what you're fighting about — emotions run high at a time like this. The most stable people turn on each other when this kind of thing happens. They start blaming each other and it can destroy them. And it can destroy any chance to get the victim home. You've got to keep your wits and hold it together. For Carys, okay?"

Quinn straightened, laying a hand on the doorknob to his room. "I see your point, Lieutenant, and I apologize if I was wrong."

"How about you, Sterling?" Kincaid asked.

Allyn grimaced. "Yeah, yeah, I'm good."

"So are we cool now?"

Allyn nodded, rubbing his shoulder as Quinn returned to his room, closing the door firmly behind him. Allyn watched him go; then, after a quick glance at Taglia, he went to his own room and closed the door as well.

"Jeez, what a pair," Kincaid muttered once both doors were shut. He shook his head and looked at Taglia with narrowed eyes. "Let's get some coffee. I want to talk to you."

Now he wants to talk. This isn't going to go well.

"Sure," Taglia agreed. "I made some awhile ago."

He dropped his sneakers by the kitchen door and shrugged into his shoulder holster while Kincaid sat down at the table. He got cups from a cabinet and poured coffee for them both.

They drank without speaking. Taglia sat staring at the steam rising from his cup between sips. The silence began to weigh on him.

He glanced up and saw his partner studying him. He had always thought of blue as a cool color, but now, looking into Kincaid's eyes, he remembered that it is blue where the flame is hottest.

"What were you doing in Sterling's room, Paul?" Kincaid asked at last.

Taglia felt a flush creep up his neck. "Just what I said. We were watching a movie."

"Quinn seems to think there was something else going on."

"Quinn apologized."

"He said he apologized *if* he was wrong. Not the same thing."

Taglia sighed. "Okay. We watched *Casablanca*. We ate some caramel popcorn. We fooled around a little. Nothing came of it."

Kincaid stared at him. "Have you lost your mind? I never thought you would be that stupid."

"Oh, come on! I wasn't in there an hour. And we *were* watching the damn movie."

"An *hour*? In an hour Irons could have broken in. In an hour he could have burned the house down around us. You were supposed to be on guard!"

"I was guarding our victim's father. We watched a movie, damn it! What business is of yours, anyway?"

"I'm your supervisor. I should write you up," Kincaid said. "You have a job here, Sergeant. Right now you're looking at dereliction of duty and fraternization."

"Fraternization?"

"With a civilian!" Kincaid glared at him.

"Oh, I thought maybe your lousy memory had suddenly improved."

Kincaid stiffened. "I was drunk. So were you. Things happened. I barely remember. Anyway, last Saturday night was a mistake."

"It didn't seem like one to me," Taglia said quietly.

"Are you telling me you're queer?" Kincaid demanded. His face was white around the eyes. "Or that you think I am?"

Queer.

The word stood between them, stark and appalling. "What am I supposed to think?"

"Not that, that's for sure!"

Taglia sat back in his chair and took a deep breath. He spoke in a softer tone. "People are saying 'gay' these days, Jeff. I'm not accusing you of anything. Can't we just talk about this like two rational adults?"

"There's nothing to talk about. Whatever happened last Saturday was a one-time deal." Kincaid stood up.

"Well then, so was tonight. It won't happen again, Lieutenant." Taglia got to his feet as well.

"Okay, well that's settled." He turned and walked into the den.

Taglia looked down at his shoes, still sitting beside the door. "Not really," he said softly. "Not between us. Nothing is settled at all."

Twenty-Eight 28

"Check and mate," Quinn said with satisfaction. Kincaid had turned out to be a very good player. They had played three games so far, two now for Quinn and one for Kincaid. "Shall we have another?"

"I don't know how long we have until the captain gets here." The cop glanced at his watch. "It's after ten and they're on their way."

A sigh and a murmur came from Allyn, who had fallen asleep on the couch during the second game. Quinn glanced at him. Despite everything last night, he felt a familiar, bemused tenderness well up inside. The slight dose he had taken that morning was no defense, being only enough to tide him over until the next one.

Taglia caught his eye as he walked over to the sliding door and stood looking at the fair day outside. Quinn would have welcomed a storm and driving rain to suit his mood. It didn't seem right that the day was lovely and life all around them was going on unhindered and unaffected, while inside the house he could feel Allyn's life falling apart around him.

"You never know how long you have for anything," Quinn mused, then turned his attention back to the board and began to reset the pieces.

Apparently restless, the dark-haired cop strolled over to the bar and turned the radio on low. Even though the sound was soft, Quinn could make out Jagger's familiar voice singing about honky-tonk women.

The door bell rang its tinny version of Big Ben's chimes, drowning out the radio. Kincaid started to get up but Taglia was already headed to the front door, gun suddenly in hand. Quinn went on setting up the game, carefully putting the pawns in their places. He heard Allyn yawn and sit up. A glance showed him how tired the singer was and that he badly needed a shave. For all of that, his face was that of a pre-Raphaelite angel — beautiful, inaccessible, and full of sorrow.

He heard the sound of the front door closing, and Captain Ortiz entered the room, followed by the record company men. Taglia trailed behind them.

From the sublime to the ridiculous without pause. Quinn refrained from shaking his head. At least they had sent Martin Cohen, who was as close to a friend as Quinn had at Eclectic. That didn't make up for Blaine Harris, who dressed as if he was heading for a discotheque as soon as he wrapped up their business. His wide-lapelled jacket opened to show his shirt, unbuttoned half way to his waist so that the two heavy gold chains, one of them sporting a heavy gold peace symbol, bounced against his pudgy chest. Martin looked more the New York entertainment agent with his gray wool coat and jaunty fedora. Martin was older as well, a wiry man somewhere in his fifties, with keen and clever eyes peering out through horn-rim glasses.

"Hey, Blaine," Quinn said. "Martin, it's good to see you."

Harris, grinning, extended his right hand. Quinn stood up and shook it, using the elaborate street-style handshake the other man offered. Harris made it seem like the ritual greeting of a secret fraternity. Quinn was more focused on the leather briefcase handcuffed to Harris's left wrist.

Harris and Cohen sat down in the conversation pit. Quinn followed them and sat down on the couch a little way from Allyn. Harris unlocked the handcuffs and set the briefcase on the coffee table. There was a dry click at the turn of a key and Harris lifted the lid.

Quinn looked at the money for a long time. "It's funny, you know. There's enough here to topple small nations, one would think, and it's going to ransom the daughter of a docker's son from Cardiff." He lit a cigarette.

"All I ever wanted was to sing the blues and make enough to avoid a day gig." Allyn leaned forward for a better look at the cash. "I don't know how to thank you for this."

"Oh, I'm sure Blaine will think of something," Quinn replied. *I wish there were any other way.*

Harris cleared his throat. "I guess maybe we have. Or didn't Milton tell you?"

"Tell me what?" Allyn gazed at the man. "I've not talked to Miltie since yesterday."

Harris grimaced, as though unwilling to be the bearer of bad news. "Umm... we thought if everything goes right, you would, you know, rethink your position about the tour."

There was an electric silence. Quinn studied the end of his cigarette.

Allyn sighed. "In other words, Miltie signed a tour agreement in exchange for the ransom money."

Harris cleared his throat, then took another glance at Allyn's face. He swallowed hard. "Er, yes. I guess you can figure it that way."

The singer gazed at Quinn. "You knew, didn't you?"

Quinn shrugged, nodded.

"Wheels within wheels," Allyn said. "You never could tell me anything straight, could you? Ah, it's to be expected, I suppose. Yes.

Yes, I'll tour. I'll spend the rest of my bloody life on the road if that's what it takes to get Carys back. Small enough price to pay."

Allyn met Taglia's glance as if they were alone in the room. "What is the best way to take this to that monster?"

"We'll have to wait and see what Irons says when he calls back," Kinkaid beat Taglia to the answer. "The details will take some planning."

Harris cleared his throat again.

"What now?" Allyn asked, his glance darting to the man.

"Delivery of the ransom was part of the agreement, too." Harris fidgeted. "We want you to let the police handle the drop."

Allyn stood up and took one slow step forward, his eyes hot blue slits. Harris shrank back in alarm. The singer caught himself. At last he spoke in a low, harsh voice. "This is blackmail, Blaine, old sod. I won't forget."

"Now, Allyn..." Cohen began.

"Martin. Don't start with me. I know this isn't your style. It still comes down to the same thing, doesn't it? Leviathon owes you two more albums. This new one is the first. After the second, it's our ball again. You may consider this a threat, if you like."

"Let's not be hasty," Quinn said.

"Whose bleeding side are you on?" Allyn wheeled to face the guitarist.

"My own." Quinn met Allyn's gaze without flinching. "As always, of course."

"Of course. I should have thought. Did you know about this deal?"

"Does it matter?"

"You miserable bastard." After a moment Allyn took a deep breath. When he spoke again, his voice was level. "You have all conspired to leave me no choice. I almost hope the bastard manages to get the money and kill me as well. It would be what you deserve."

"I daresay," Quinn said. "It was dirty pool, old chum, but waltzing makes my feet hurt."

Bird of Paradise
G.J. Paterson

"You cold and bloody swine. Of all the filthy tricks..." Allyn stared at Quinn with unmistakable fury in his eyes. Quinn was aware that the two cops were tensed in response to the menace in the singer's shoulders.

Quinn's left hand closed on the chair arm, knuckles white with the effort of control. "I knew nothing about the last part of the agreement."

"Do you expect to be believed?" Allyn glared around at them all. "You can all go to hell." He whirled and strode out of the room, leaving an embarrassed silence behind him. Down the hall, a door slammed.

Twenty-Nine 29

Quinn let his head fall back on the cushioned headrest. Sorrow washed over him against the backdrop of his morning's dose of ennui. He sighed. He should feel a bit of triumph at this point. He'd got all he wanted, after all.

All I ever said I wanted.

All I ever said. And if you're angry now, it's all right. The proper things will be accomplished, and you will still be safe.

He was surprised at the upwelling of bitterness. He'd always prided himself on his tolerance. He'd always been patient. He'd always hoped Allyn would come to truly see him as he was. Knowing Allyn had sought comfort in another man's arms just last night burned.

He remembered the last time he and Allyn had taken a trip together. It was 1969, and they'd wound up hiking in Maroon Bells Park above Aspen. It was the summer before the singer's wedding.

They stood in the last shade of the forest. "Everything is beautiful here," Allyn said, "and fresh. As if we were the first ever to see it. It doesn't seem real, somehow. Even the Brecons seem dim in comparison."

Quinn stared out at the sunlit meadow, thinking of the dark, gray cities left behind in England. "It's vast. As if we have stepped through some barrier and found ourselves in Middle Earth."

"I half expect to come 'round a bend and find myself face to face with elves or a company of traveling dwarves."

"So long as there are no orcs. Shall we camp here, do you think?"

Allyn walked out into the meadow. "Not here. The little stand of trees over there will be better. It's close to the water. Besides, if I'm right in my map-reading, it's a regular campsite, and we can have a fire tonight."

That's cheering, at least. Quinn followed Allyn across the flower-strewn meadow. *Almost makes up for having no guitar.*

The map was right. There was an iron fire-ring under the trees. They sat their packs beside the ring. Allyn went to gather some fallen wood while Quinn carried their two collapsible buckets to the stream. Trudging back, watching the ground to avoid stumbling, he was almost overset by the soccer ball zipping at him from camp.

"You bloody maniac!" he shouted. "Do you never give up?"

"I'm sorry," Allyn called back with an irrepressible laugh.

"Sorry?" Quinn set the buckets down and went back to retrieve the ball. "Sorry is it? You'll soon be sorrier yet. You've been looking for this for ages. It's time you got what you deserve."

"Idle threats are never impressive."

"Idle threats, eh?" Quinn put his hands on his hips. "If it's football you want, then that's what you shall have. I warn you, m'lad. I hail from Manchester, where we play a man's game. No coal-country Taffy ever born could come toppers over me in a fair contest."

"I'd best change my shoes then." Allyn sat by his pack and unlaced his boots. After a moment Quinn walked over and joined him. Pulling off his boots, he fished a pair of tennis shoes out of his pack.

"You don't have cleats."

"That's all right." Quinn tied his laces and stood. "It gives you an advantage. You're going to need it."

He walked to the ball and stood staring down at it. He hadn't played football in years. Team sports had never been his strong point. Allyn, on the other hand, brought a ball to recording sessions and chased it up and down the halls at breaks. He played every chance he got with a team in the Welsh village he had made his home. Quinn was in reasonable shape, but he knew Allyn was in excellent condition. Still, he meant to win this contest.

He glanced up and down the meadow. It was flat except for the tussocks of grass which might make the footing uncertain and the flight of the ball erratic. A cluster of boulders at this end would make a good enough goal. A fallen tree at the far end would do for the other side.

He herded the ball down the field. He was halfway to the fallen tree when Allyn shouted behind him. "Are you going to play or try to hatch the bleedin' thing?"

He whirled and drove hard back up the field, his unbuttoned shirt flapping in the breeze. Allyn was caught off guard, and he whipped the ball past him while the singer stood flat-footed. It was a momentary success. Before he was halfway to the goal, Allyn popped up before him as if transported by magic.

From then on, the game resolved into a grueling drive to keep up with Allyn. The mountain sun was mild, but in minutes both men were sweating. Quinn struggled to catch a breath against the burning pain in his side as he ran. His sole reward was the harsh sound of Allyn's breathing as he too struggled for air.

Calling on reserves he hadn't known he possessed, Quinn made a deft steal, whipped around and drove toward the goal. Allyn was at his side, but in his single-minded intensity, the singer failed to see a rock hidden in the grass, stumbled, and almost went down. Quinn streaked for the goal, hearing rapid footfalls behind, growing louder.

A shove sent him off balance. As he fell, his legs tripped Allyn. They collapsed together in a heap with the singer half across him. Quick rage balled his fists, and he pushed Allyn away, setting himself for a stiff punch.

Allyn lay on his back with one arm thrown across his face, gasping for air. Quinn sat up and pulled the singer's arm away, peering down at the contorted face. "Are you all right?"

Allyn nodded, unable to speak. Quinn lay back, propping himself on his elbows. In a few moments, Allyn caught a shuddering breath and groaned.

Quinn laughed. "Serves you right! That little trick would have had the crowd on the field from Aberdeen to Zanzibar."

"You're better than I thought," Allyn gasped.

Quinn laughed again, pleased. "Are you sure you're all right?"

"Yeah. Winded."

Now that he wasn't moving, Quinn was aware of the aching in his body. He wanted to lay there until his heartbeat calmed.

Across the valley, the afternoon sun set the peaks on fire. The gentle wind was cool. He shivered as it trickled over his sweaty chest. He sat up and pulled his shirt off, mopping his face, arms and torso, replacing the unpleasant chilliness with a refreshing tingle.

Allyn still lay on his back, spread-eagled on the grass. His eyes were closed, his hair spread like a halo around his face. His tanned skin was slick with sweat.

Quinn leaned over and began toweling the singer's chest with the shirt. He dried the arm nearest him, rising to his knees to reach the other. He wiped the beads of moisture from forehead and cheeks, down over the throat where the pulse beat in the hollow. The cloth brushed across Allyn's nipples. He paused a moment to dry the patch of hair growing in a diamond around the navel and disappearing beneath the waistband of the shorts.

He had to move down a bit to reach the thighs. As he started to shift, a hand on his belt stopped him. He glanced back. Allyn still lay with his eyes closed, but his right hand was clenched on the belt. Quinn yielded to the pull, allowing himself to be drawn back. He lay down beside Allyn, who let go of his belt and reached out for him.

Allyn's hands wandered over his body, strong and certain yet inexpressibly tender. The guitarist found himself shivering in the rising heat of his desire. He ran his hands across the wide shoulders, tracing the delicate structure of the throat turned up to him. Under his fingers he could feel the racing pulse. He bent to kiss it, while Allyn ran his fingers through his damp hair.

Allyn pushed against him, his strong golden body warm and solid in Quinn's arms. Taking his time, he moved up the throat, making Allyn wait, catching his impatient hands and pinning them over his head. He held them down with his right hand, while his left was free to make its own explorations. Allyn writhed to some music he alone could hear.

"There's no need to hurry." Quinn breathed the words into Allyn's ear. He discovered it was the one with the silver stud, took the earring between his teeth and tugged gently. He brushed a kiss across the fine high cheekbones. He paused and looked down at the other man, reveling in his beauty and his desire.

Bird of Paradise
G.J. Paterson

Allyn opened his eyes and stared up at him. "Are you worried about the orcs?"

"Not in the least." Quinn forestalled further comment by unfastening Allyn's belt buckle one-handed and running the zipper down. Allyn drew up his knees and lifted his hips off the ground as Quinn tugged down his shorts. He kicked off his shoes and lay naked on the green earth, like a golden offering spread on an altar.

Allyn's face was suffused with a ferocious, innocent sensuality. The mountains and trees and rocks came to a point in him. To Quinn, he had become Shiva, focus of the world's desire.

Allyn's mouth parted, and his tongue ran over his glistening lips. Quinn trailed his hand down the length of chest, over nipples standing like bosses on a shield at the touch of his fingertips. He paused below the navel, skirting along the lean flanks and stroking down the powerful thighs as far as he could reach.

Allyn's cock stood out rose-dark against the cream of his thigh. Quinn slid one leg over Allyn's, pressing them together. He slipped his hand over to cup Allyn's balls, making the movement a tender caress.

Allyn shuddered, and Quinn retraced the route, drawing his fingertips over the glowing flesh.

"Please..." Allyn groaned.

"Please what?"

"Don't make me wait."

"Greedy," Quinn admonished him. "Patience is a cardinal virtue."

"I'm a born sinner," Allyn whispered. "Do it."

Stringing it out, Quinn shifted his position. At the last moment he released Allyn's hands, then bent to kiss the thick, swollen shaft before him. Allyn moaned a half-sob of pleasure as Quinn took him in. At first he ignored Allyn's impatient upward thrusts, intent on a rhythm of his own.

He felt his own jeans yield to insistent hands. He moved to help as much as he could without breaking the beat. Suddenly, hot and wet, Allyn's mouth was around him. He caught his breath as lizards of fire slithered across his belly.

Allyn was too close to his own climax to keep it up. He pressed his face against Quinn's thighs, muffling his passionate gasps, clutching the guitarist's hips with painful intensity.

Quinn slowed down to spin it out. His delicate sense of timing and intimate knowledge of the man beneath him let him dictate Allyn's spiral toward release. In his head he could hear the surging rhythms of the driving electric blues they both loved. He played Allyn as he did his music.

He returned to the faster tempo, Allyn's particular trigger for release. He took Allyn in, as much as he could, swallowing as though dying of thirst. The musty, salty taste reminded him, as always, of the sea.

They lay together for several moments while Allyn recovered. The singer stirred, reached to pull Quinn down into his embrace, but the guitarist resisted, squirming instead to remove the rest of his own clothes.

He shifted positions, crouching across Allyn's chest. Allyn's hands caught his hips, trying to pull him forward, to draw Quinn's cock into his open, eager mouth. Quinn teased them both, holding himself back while Allyn sought to reach him with his tongue. Then a gaze which burned like blue flame caught him, held him.

Movement was difficult. All Quinn wanted was to feel. Allyn's tongue teased his cock and balls. Then it wasn't possible to wait any longer. Quinn flung back his head and plunged down into the alchemical furnace which sought to envelop him.

His fingers tightened in Allyn's hair, his back arched, as he gave himself over to sensation, the final act of trust.

Bird of Paradise
G.J. Paterson

The singer was caught up in it too, sucking a sweet, relentless rhythm. Quinn watched himself, glistening, slip in and out of Allyn's mouth. Groaning, he pulled the singer's head closer burying his lips in the dark tangle of hair forested around the base of his cock. Passion filled him with a pulsing, draining cadence while heat suffused his body and mind. He was swept away on the deep river rushing through him. Thought and memory were lost, leaving him drifting egoless on a broad sea of light.

His body swayed with sudden weariness, a weighted, leaden thing. Somehow, he managed to lie down alongside Allyn without collapsing. He must have dozed because a bit later he became aware of the singer covering him with a blanket. He tried to ask him what he was doing but lacked the energy to do anything but mumble.

"Shh," Allyn whispered as he lay down again at Quinn's side. He slipped his arm under Quinn's head and cradled it on his shoulder. "I don't want you to scorch."

Quinn smiled and reached up to stroke Allyn's cheek with his fingertips. He inhaled the scent of him, sweat and sex and an underlying whiff of pine from the wood he had gathered for the fire. He had a sudden flash of gratitude to whatever deity had taken him out of a cold London winter to a land of sun-drenched beaches, big cars, more money than he had ever dreamt possible, and an army of fans. Now came this last, ultimate peace on a meadow of late summer flowers. He was surrounded by silent grandeur and domed by deep blue, and for once he felt utterly content.

They had come so far from that first night below the stage in Manchester when Allyn had dictated the terms for both of them. But the singer must be aware that what was between them was more than chance, opportunity, and casual desire. The one thing left to make his life complete was to put aside the silence and the sham and speak.

Tonight I will find the words, somehow.

Bird of Paradise
G.J. Paterson

After supper they sat before the fire, wrapped in the same blanket, their arms companionably around each other's waists.

Quinn spoke softly, reluctant to break the silence. "We could've had music if you'd let me bring a guitar."

"Wasn't room."

"You found room for a football."

"It's hanging in a bag from my pack. Besides, it's less delicate."

"There is that."

There was another long silence. Allyn stared into the flames as if reading some mystery in the fire's red heart. Quinn disengaged himself, got up and went to his pack. He rummaged through a side pocket and found what he sought by feel. He brought the little package to the fire and dropped it into Allyn's lap.

"What's this then?"

"It's the fourth of August. Did you think I'd forgotten?" Quinn sat down again.

"My birthday. Thank you."

"Open it, then thank me."

Quinn drew the blanket around his shoulders as Allyn tore the paper off the package and threw the pieces onto the fire. The box was palm-sized and heavier than it looked. He held it in his hand for a moment then took off the lid.

Red firelight reflected in the gleaming silver of the large, square buckle. It was set with turquoise and coral, a masterpiece of American Indian art.

Allyn lifted it out and held it up to catch the light. "How could you know this was the very thing I wanted when I never imagined it existed?"

"I found it in Santa Fe," Quinn said. "It's called Navaho sand casting."

"It's magnificent!" Allyn struggled with the snap on his belt, trying to remove his old buckle.

Quinn leaned over to help and between them they got the new buckle attached. He let his fingers linger on the smooth stones. It was already growing warm from the heat of the body behind it. "It does look good on you. I thought it would when I bought it."

"We've been out in the wilderness so long I'd forgotten the date. Which reminds me, I've a confession to make." Allyn took Quinn's hand and squeezed it. "I'm a bit ashamed I haven't said anything before. You're the best friend I've ever had, Dee, and you deserve better from me."

"I've been content." Quinn kept his voice steady, but the unexpectedness of Allyn's words had his heart racing.

Allyn smiled at him. "You're good to say that. Anyway, do you remember Demetra Poppadoupolis?"

"The fashion model?" Quinn couldn't imagine what on earth she had to do with anything. She'd hung around the band and had come after him first, but something about her repelled him. She was beautiful but cold, reminding him of a diamond merchant toting up the value of every facet. "The one you were dating in London? The one that flew over to New York to see our gig at the Garden?"

"Yeah, her. Although she came to see me more than the band. And she had a shoot there, anyway."

Quinn drew back a little, reclaiming his hand and frowning. "What about her?"

"It's still a secret." Allyn's tone was happy. "But I wanted you to be the first to know. We're engaged, since New York. We're to be married next month. Soon as I get back to London."

Quinn stared at him as he felt the blood drain from his face, leaving him cold and empty. He forced the words out. "Do you care so much for her then?"

Bird of Paradise
G.J. Paterson
216

"Of course. Else why would I marry her? I know it's a bit sudden, but we decided not to put it off. We'd like you to be best man. Will you do it?"

Quinn caught a laugh at the back of his throat, strangling it unborn. Bitterness beat at him in rising black waves. There was a roaring in his ears, or perhaps it was the sound of the stream out in the dark. From an impossible distance he heard his voice say, "I don't know. I shall have to think."

The moon was slipping behind the mountains as Quinn sat beside the dying embers. Beyond the fire's faint glow, he could make out the dark outline of Allyn in his sleeping bag.

He was writing a song. Lyrics were not his forté, but these lyrics came so fast he could barely get them written down. He knew he might live the rest of his life without writing another song to match it. *I would as soon never have written this one.* Still, he could imagine how it would sound, sung in Allyn's raw, hungry style,

I am the Bird of Paradise,
I take the eagle and the dove.
I seldom fly alone, now momma,
And I live on love.

Thirty 30

The sound of the stream in Colorado became the sound of voices pulling him back to the present. He didn't open his eyes, pretending to still be on the nod. Behind the façade he struggled with an epiphany like Jacob wrestling the angel. He couldn't hide from the source of his anger and bitterness any longer. Now it had a name and that name was fear.

I let you go without a word because I was frightened. Frightened of loving you, and frightened of losing what I already had. I was sure you would never give me more.

"Derek! Wake up, buddy," Harris demanded. "We have to know — will he go along with the agreement?"

Quinn opened his eyes.

"He'll have to," Kincaid interrupted. "It's the only way. Captain Ortiz and I have a plan."

"Yeah." Taglia caught his drift. "With the right wig and clothes, you'd be a dead ringer for Allyn. At least from a distance...."

"I sure hate to upset him like this, though." Harris said. "Will you talk to him for us, Derek?"

"I doubt it will do much good," Quinn murmured.

"Please try. Tell him we want to help."

Quinn stretched then got to his feet. The place in him that had been full of fear was replaced with stillness and a sense of light. "Perhaps it is time we had a bit of a chat, after all."

Quinn tried to turn the doorknob of Allyn's room. It was locked. "Allyn? It's me."

There was no answer.

"Open it, or I'll kick it down."

After a pause, the door opened. Quinn walked in and closed it, locking it behind him.

The two men stared at one another, and Quinn was uncertain whether they would fight or talk. He never let his gaze waver from Allyn's face. If it came down to a fight, he would need every break he could get.

"What in the name of bleeding hell have I done to deserve this betrayal?" Allyn demanded at last.

"I'm not betraying you. Can't you see that?" Quinn held back a sigh. *So it'll be talk.*

"All I can see is a frigging *madman* has my little girl and has *demanded* I bring the money for her release!"

"We don't know what Rick wants. He may kill you."

"*He* will *kill her.*" Allyn's voice shook with suppressed emotion.

"He may do that in any case. There's no need to hand him your life into the bargain."

"Oh, yeah, that would put a crimp in your precious touring plans, wouldn't it?" Allyn crossed the room, then spun on his heel to face him. "Still, look on the bright side. Think of all the free publicity you'd get. I'm certain Blaine could tell you how much you could make off of it just in record sales."

"Can't you grant I might be thinking of you?"

"I can grant you might be thinking of your investments. It may mean nothing to you, but she is my daughter!" Allyn strode forward. "I'm going to take the money to save her."

Quinn folded his arms, standing between the singer and the door. "I think not."

"How the fuck do you think to stop me?"

Ten years of denial blazed up in Quinn. He backhanded Allyn with all the force he had. The blow rocked the singer off balance. He reeled, stumbled and almost went down, catching himself at the last moment against a table, sending a lamp crashing to the floor. A drop of blood glistened at one corner of his mouth.

The two men glared at each other. Neither moved. At last Allyn straightened, using the table for a brace. The red mark from Quinn's blow was plain on his face. He started to speak then looked away.

Quinn's lips twitched, in spite of himself. "If you say, 'thanks, I needed that,' I'll do it again."

"Oh, no. I don't think that's at all necessary."

"Now, will you sit down and listen to me?"

Allyn nodded and sank into a chair, resting his elbows on his knees. Quinn remained standing, looking down at him. At last he drew a deep breath. "This may not be the proper time for it, but I've a confession to make."

Quinn wasn't able to keep a tremor out of his voice. "Rick means to kidnap you if he can, Allyn. I can't face it if something happens to you without you knowing what I have to say. And I know damn well you will find a way to do what you please about the money, so I may not get another chance."

"For gods' sake, Dee..."

"Keep still. This doesn't come easy for me. I lied to you, a long time ago, and I've been lying to both of us ever since. Ten years ago you told me not to say I cared for you. And I told you I didn't. I've gone on like that ever since. It was a lie then, and it's a lie now. I do care. I care very much."

He turned to the door where he paused, hand on the doorknob, shoulders tensed for a blow to fall "Do whatever you like. I just thought you should know."

He closed his eyes when Allyn's warm tenor tore at his heart,

"I've got a heart of stone
I'll break yours, if you love me,
It's in my bones."

The guitarist turned around as Allyn said softly, "I am the Bird of Paradise, Dee. But I never knew yours was the heart I broke."

For a moment Quinn was silent, not trusting himself to speak. He walked back and reached out to stroke Allyn's reddened cheek with his callused fingertips. "I'm sorry I hit you."

"It's all right."

"For ten years I've watched you beat yourself against the glass, like a butterfly in a jar. All because I hadn't the courage to stand up to you in the beginning."

"More like I hadn't the courage to let you speak," Allyn replied.

"No. My mistake was I thought, given time, you would get over your past and come to trust me. Then along came Demetra, and you married her instead."

"Ah, yes. One of my more famous mistakes." Allyn ran his hands through his hair.

Quinn smiled. "Not all of it was a mistake. There is Carys, after all."

"Yeah," Allyn said and then frowned. "You began the junkie thing after the wedding. Funny I never made the connection before."

Allyn's unexpected insight was too close, too new, and hurt too much for Quinn to accept. He shook his head, but he couldn't meet Allyn's sober glance. "I was no innocent schoolboy when we met. I wouldn't take too much burden onto your shoulders over it."

"Still, it's a heavy thing."

"You know, I've been thinking of giving it up. It's rather a bother."

"Clearly we have a lot to discuss later."

"Will there be a later?" Quinn asked, surprised at his own shyness.

"I don't know." Allyn's voice was soft, and Quinn lifted his head at last, meeting the singer's gaze. "You must believe I hope so."

Thirty-One
31

Sun streamed through the good side of the patio doors as Taglia came into the den to find Allyn alone with his photo album open on his lap. When he came closer he could see that he had been looking at pictures of his daughter. Allyn shut the book abruptly.

"Where is everybody?" Taglia asked.

"Quinn's in the studio noodling up a new tune idea that has just come to him. The red light's on above the door, which means he doesn't want to be interrupted. Your partner was here but went to his room to take a call that came in from your station."

"I thought I heard the phone. Maybe I had better go see what's up." He turned to go.

"Paul, wait," Allyn said. Taglia turned back to look at him. "Have you ever wondered, what it would have been like if you had been someone else? I mean if you had been born in a different place and time? It's rather odd, isn't it? Here I am, son of a docker, raised in Cardiff, born in a tiny village in Wales. Seems odd I'd end up a rock star, now doesn't it?"

"It's what you wanted to be," Taglia replied.

"Ah, but is it, now? I don't remember. It's not what my old Dad wanted."

"Yeah? What did he want you to be?"

"A mechanic," Allyn said, his voice taking on a bit of a lilt, a storytelling quality. Taglia recognized the music in it and knew enough about the singer to be wary. "After me Mum died, you know, he wanted more than anything that his son not work the docks or go to sea. Even arranged an apprenticeship for me."

"How did you wind up in a rock band?" Taglia's own father had wanted him to be a cop, and he had indeed become one. Fathers' wishes for their sons were their own wishes made flesh, and often enough they came true. He wondered where the mechanic lived on in Allyn Sterling. Maybe in the car under wraps in the carport.

"The normal way, I expect." Allyn shrugged and sat on a gray stone bench beside the path. He moved to one end, making room for Taglia. A gust of rain-washed wind tugged at the detective's flannel shirt. He pulled it tight around himself and continued to stand.

"My poor dad. I didn't want to be a mechanic. I ran away as soon as I could. I was on the streets at fifteen. Doing the odd job, sleeping where I could. I knew, even then, that I wanted to sing. I drifted to London and joined the blues crowd. I was too young to be a customer in any of the clubs, but I kept on getting in with the bands.

"Then I met Sammy Hayes. He was older than me... about twenty-three then, I should think. He had this band called Blues Works. I started singing with him when I was about sixteen. We gigged around London, then hit the road. I was with them about eight months."

His voice slowed. "Then Quinn, who was trying to hold together his old group, came in. He jammed with us one evening, and later asked me to come with him. I did, and here we are."

"Allyn. Did you start this just to lie to me?"

The singer jerked his head up to meet Taglia's steady gaze. "I've told the same story a million times these last ten years, and no reporter has ever had the balls to tell me I'm editing."

"Editing?" Taglia asked. "Not quite lying?"

"That's not the same as volunteering anything, now, is it?"

Taglia shrugged.

"I've never talked to anyone about those early days," Allyn said. The music faded out of his voice, the surety and the ease. Taglia heard to it go and knew he was listening to the truth at last. "I never talk to strangers. Except now I'm frightened, and words are somehow like fire to keep back the dark."

"'Bless me, Father, for I have sinned?'"

"I dunno," Allyn admitted. "I'm not Christian. I don't believe in heaven or hell, besides the ones we make for ourselves. Will you talk to me? And let me talk? Please? I'm a stranger here, and frightened, and without friends."

"Derek..."

"No." The answer was quick, sharp and definite. He paused for a moment then shook his head. "No, this is something I can never talk about with Derek."

"I'm here." Taglia sat beside him on the couch at last, close but not touching.

The singer glanced away, as if permission had taken away his desire. After a moment he began to speak. "Sammy Hayes... ah, Sammy. He was the lead guitarist. Good, not up to Quinn's level, but good all the same. Friends with all the right people." Allyn shook his head and gazed down at his hands, loosely clasped between his knees. "A handsome fellow, too."

There was another pause. When Allyn spoke again, his voice was quieter. "I was young, you see, and confused. It was swinging London in the twilight of the sixties, and everybody did everything with anybody. Anyway, I was always careful of the ratios, careful how many men to women. Then there was Sammy.

"When we were in London there was no problem. There was this bird I was staying with most of the time. On the road... that was another story. I realized I, of all things possible, was in love with this man. It was then I started to drink a lot." He cleared his throat. "We were all drinking, of course, but I got royally pissed almost every night. As I only did it after the gig, no one said anything."

There was a long silence. Taglia had almost decided Allyn wouldn't resume his story when the singer said, "It was in Birmingham, I think. We were there for a four-day gig, which was good for us in those days. I was drunk by the time we got to the hotel. We were doing well enough by then to afford them once in awhile. At any rate, when we got there I found I was to share a room, which meant a bed, with Sammy. My common sense told me it was stupid, but I was too drunk to protest. And truth be told, I'm not sure now how much I really wanted to protest.

"Once we were in the room I hopped into bed straight away, turned my face to the wall and ordered my shattered nerves to go to sleep. I couldn't, of course." Allyn's fingers were clenched together. "I don't know how long I lay there until he sat down at the edge of the bed. He said, 'Allyn, are you sleeping?' I didn't say anything. I thought even then things would be all right, but he reached over and touched me."

"I think I see where this is going," Taglia whispered. He wondered if that was how Jeff had felt — tasting the sourness of too much liquor, the slippery confusion of conflicting desires, the ultimate surrender to a rightness that would seem all-too-wrong in morning's light.

"There wasn't another word spoken between us for the remainder of the evening." Allyn's voice had gone harsh and low. "All was done in silence. There was no tenderness, not even that which sometimes happens between strangers. Next morning, before I could speak, he said, *'Lord, was I pissed last night. I can't remember a bloody thing. Can you?'* I, gods help me, looked him straight in the eye and said, *'No, neither can I.'* I was sick inside."

"People do it all the time," Taglia said, feeling the irony. "I've heard it called it the *'Christ-was-I-drunk-last-night syndrome.'* They always call God into it somehow. I don't know why."

Bird of Paradise
G.J. Paterson
228

Allyn nodded, his voice grim. "The next night was the same, except my performance was a little more frantic than usual. Sammy pushed me on stage, and we were all over each other. I got drunker than ever, if it's possible. The third night I made up my mind. It was tearing me up, and I decided nothing could be worse. At a moment that seemed right to me, I told him I loved him.

"He didn't say a word." Allyn stood, as if the stress of remaining seated was more than he could bear. He moved several paces, stopping beside the wet bar. His posture was stiff with anger. "The next day he said to me, 'You'll be leaving the band, then. You needn't bother with tonight. I've brought in a replacement.'

"I was stunned. I said, *'Why?'* and he said — I can scarcely believe it, even now — he said, *'We don't want your sort in the band.'* *'My sort?'* I said. *'How are we different?'* I might have been drunk, but I hadn't forgot who touched whom first. He thought it was too sordid to discuss, and I was hopelessly working class anyway, ignorant Taff that I am. Yet he stooped to tell me, *'The body has its needs, but one doesn't have to be slave to them.'*"

He stroked the gleaming teak of the bar, then turned and leaned his hip against it. "He said, *'I've no intention of discussing the matter further with you. I took the liberty of telling the others you're leaving for personal reasons.'* It occurred to me I hadn't any money and no way home. I was frightened. I begged him to let me finish out the gig. At least I would have my share of the take to get home on. He was adamant. He gave me enough for a ticket.

"I got back to London without the price of a pint on me. I had nothing but what was in my little bag. The bird I was staying with had another man by then. I was out on the streets."

A fleeting expression crossed his face. Taglia couldn't tell if it was disgust or sadness, or a strange wry humor. "However, there are ways of getting on in London, if you don't want a regular job. There aren't too many who will hire a musician anyway. I daresay it is the same in any large city. But you can always manage, if you're young, and reasonably good-looking, and hungry enough."

The last three words revealed a vision to Taglia of a much younger Allyn Sterling, standing on a street corner in the raw London night, dressed in his gaudy, tattered stage clothing. Watching as a stranger approached and hoping the man might be good for a meal and a place to spend the night. Hoping too, that he wasn't with the vice-squad and his tastes weren't too odd.

"How long?"

"I don't really know any more." Allyn hesitated as if in thought, biting his lower lip. Taglia read his expression as a lie. *He knows. I wonder if he's lying to me or to himself?*

"It seemed an eternity," he went on at last. "It was winter — I remember there was snow. One night as I was discussing matters with..." he paused and Taglia watched him search for a word, give up and go on brutally, "...with a client, who should stroll by but Sammy Hayes himself. It was St. James' Park. We both knew what the other was doing there."

Allyn laughed. The sound wasn't pleasant. "Right enough, a few days later, I saw him again. This time he came straight up. *'I've been expecting you,'* I said. *'I don't go for nothing these days. You'll have to pay.'* Of course, I was hoping for a fight. I'd gotten over my confusion — or I thought as much at the time.

"*'This is nothing like that,'* he said. At least he had the grace to look embarrassed. *'Our singer's ill, and we'd like you to fill in for a couple of nights. I thought perhaps you could use the money.'*

"*'I do all right,'* I said. I can't resist saying it, but he knew he was spot-on with me. I was sick of life. I felt I should never get back my pride. What of it, after all? Whoring is whoring, after all. So I said, *'All right. I'll do it.'*

"When I got to the gig, it was as though I'd never been away. They all seemed glad to see me, but nobody asked a question. I had no idea at the time when I might get on stage again. None of the auditions I went to were successful. My confidence was shattered, you know. I wanted to make the best of it. In the first set there were a couple of good, bluesy numbers, the kind of thing I can do well. I really put my heart into it. I still don't think I have often topped that night. I was wailing out into the dark, and I meant it.

"How was I to know the dark was listening? At the end of the first set, the waitress brought a note 'round to the stage, scratched on a matchbook cover. Sammy read it and passed it over. It said, *'Derek Quinn.'* Just that. I borrowed a nub of a pencil from the barmaid, signed my name and sent it back."

Allyn glanced at Taglia. "You must understand. Derek was already something of a celebrity. A genuine contender, mind you. Noted session player and lead guitar in White Mare, a group which might have caught the Who if it had stayed together. They played the Marquee Club and the Crawdaddy and those places, right after the Stones and The Who. Album out and all. Single charted in the top ten. Serious stuff, this. But White Mare had these terrible internal problems and split up in the middle of a tour. Quinn was trying to keep the remaining tour dates by looking for people to fill in.

"I wasn't thinking about that. I was pleased that what might be my last performance would be one to remember. He came up on stage, all quick and eager. He had his guitar with him. Sweet Fire, same one he still uses."

Taglia watched him gaze into those dark eyes for the first time. He knew how it must have been, like the pause before the thunder, the sense of expectancy, the silent yes coming from deep within. You make the little gestures to brush it aside, both of you talk about trivialities to make it smaller. Still the yes hangs between you, binds you together in the pause before the thunder comes.

"He plugged in, talking all the while, trying to find out what we all knew in common." Allyn gave a small smile and shook his head, hair swinging away from his jawline and back again. "Some things cannot be escaped or hidden from. The moment we began, I knew it was magic. Derek's playing pushed me far beyond anything Sammy had ever done. It was years later when the critics began calling him *'The Master of Time and Space,'* but it was true that night if never before or since.

"I have no idea how long we played. We found ourselves out in the street with the sun coming up. He asked me how he could get in touch with me later. I hadn't a clue what to tell him. Then I remembered I was to sing with Sammy again that night.

"He was at the club again that night. He and Avery and Gil came up and jammed during a break. Miltie was there too. They invited me out to breakfast. Over my third cup of tea, they asked me to join their group. All I can remember saying is I didn't have a place to stay. Derek didn't seem to think it odd. He told me I could stay at his place, with him and Avery. They had room.

"I said, *'Yes, I'll come in with you.'* And I rewarded him by falling deathly ill. I was sick for almost two weeks, and all the while he nursed me like a brother. Never said a word about the tour dates we were missing." Allyn sighed. "I got better at length. We went out. By the tour's end, we had a recording contract of our own. The rest I think you know. Anyway, you can read it in any rock history and listen to ten years' worth of recordings."

"I'm sorry, Allyn. I wish there was something I could say."

"It was all quite long ago."

"Do you think Sammy set up the thing with Derek?" Taglia asked.

"Got me sort of an audition, you mean? I dunno if it's true, but I've wondered. Sort of a way to make amends? Yeah, maybe. Derek's never said a word about it in ten years. Of course, Sammy can't."

"Why? Where is he now?"

"Sammy?" Allyn shrugged. "He's dead. Some few years ago. Another flaming crash from the fast lane."

Taglia nodded without speaking. Allyn grew quiet. In the silence, the flesh prickled along Taglia's arms — the heaviness in the air that was years of thunder in the moment before it falls.

Thirty-Two   *32*

"So, what happens now?" Quinn set his empty glass down at the bar and glanced at his watch. It was well after noon. Allyn lay stretched out on the couch, one arm draped across his eyes, although Quinn knew he was wide awake and listening to the conversation.

Kincaid answered. "Ortiz had a team search Irons' apartment, which they located thanks to Chris' information. They found some papers that showed Irons got an inheritance a few years back, some land about two hours north of here. There's a team out there now. They'll be stopping by to meet with us when they get back."

"In the meantime," Taglia added, "we wait."

"I'm tired of waiting," Allyn announced. He sat up and stretched. "And I'm hungry. We're running low on edibles. I don't suppose we could send out for pizza?"

Taglia laughed. "Nope. It'll be sandwiches again, sorry. Unless you want to cook."

"I'll see what's left. Maybe I can whip up something."

The phone rang. Quinn stared at it, startled. Allyn was on his feet and across the room in three long strides. At Kincaid's nod, he took a deep breath and picked up the receiver.

"Peacock?"

At the sound of the voice, Allyn sank to the floor as if the strength had left his legs. "Rick." Though his face was contorted with fear, his voice was perfectly normal.

"I hope you're able to come up with the scratch, Peacock, because today's the day. Here's how I want you to handle this..."

"Carys," Allyn interrupted. "You said I could speak with her."

"Oh. I did, didn't I?" Irons sounded tinny over the speaker. Traffic noise surged and faded in the background. "Well, that's another lesson for you. I'm in charge, Allyn. If you want something from me, you have to ask nicely. Maybe if you beg..."

"Please, Rick. Please let me speak to her."

"Good! You're learning." The voice sounded pleased. "To reward you, you have my permission to speak to your daughter."

After a moment, a young, shaky voice came on the line "Daddy! Is it you?"

"Carys!" Allyn leaned forward. "My angel — are you all right?"

"Yes, Daddy." Tears filled her voice. "I want to come home, but I'm so scared. He wants to hurt you and Uncle Derek."

"I know, little love, I know. We're safe, but I'm coming to get you."

"Be caref — No! I'm not done yet! Daddy, be careful!" Her last word was a shriek.

"Carys!" The anguish in Allyn's voice was a whip-lash across Quinn's heart. He bent to grip Allyn's shoulder tightly.

Irons' voice was back. "Bring the money and meet me at the Greek Theater, one o'clock tomorrow morning. And Peacock, come alone. I mean it. You bring cops and your 'little love' dies."

Bird of Paradise
G.J. Paterson
234

The line went dead before Allyn could reply. He stared blankly at the receiver clenched in his fist until Quinn took it from him and placed it back on the hook. Kincaid shut off the recorder.

Allyn looked up at Quinn with unshed tears glistening in the corners of his eyes. He held up a hand, a mute gesture of appeal. Quinn took it in both of his own and pulled the singer to his feet.

"Lady love her," Allyn whispered. "She's the one in danger and she's telling me to be careful."

"It doesn't surprise me," Quinn told him. "She knows you well enough."

Allyn began to laugh but the sound turned to sobs. Quinn wrapped an arm around his waist and led him to the couch. They sat down close together and Allyn turned to bury his face in Quinn's shoulder.

It was four thirty by Quinn's watch when the doorbell rang. Allyn flinched at the sound in his sleep. *How is it that I am always the one keeping watch over you, my elven princeling?* Gently he shook Allyn's shoulder. The singer sat up and stretched his cramped frame.

Taglia went to answer the door with his hand on his gun. There was a murmur of voices, and then Taglia was back with two newcomers in tow. Kincaid got up to meet them.

"We need to talk to these guys without the two of you," Kincaid said to Allyn. "We'll all be back in a few minutes. I'll introduce everybody then."

The four detectives went back into the foyer and into the front room. Quinn could hear the sound of the pocket doors closing.

Allyn was on his feet at once, pacing across the den from the Christmas tree to the archway into the kitchen and back again. Finally he paused to watch the blinking lights on the Christmas tree.

"She'll get to see it again," Quinn said.

"I don't know if I want to bring her back to this place."

"I understand."

Allyn sighed and turned away from the tree. "You know they're going to insist that Jeff take my place tonight."

"And you still want to do it yourself."

"She's my daughter. It's my responsibility and my right."

"We don't live in a feudal barony, my lord." Quinn said as he got up from the couch and went to the bar. "Maybe you can still talk them into seeing things your way. They're not bound by Eclectic's contract, just you. And if you decide to break the contract..." Quinn shrugged and took a bottle down from a shelf behind the bar. "Care for a drink?"

Allyn shook his head. "None for me, thanks. How about some tea? You make it better than I do."

"No, you just like it when I serve." He put the bottle back. "Tea it is."

They were drinking their second cup of the rich, fragrant brew when the four detectives joined them in the den. The cops declined the offer of tea but took seats in the conversation pit. Kincaid introduced them. The tall, dapper, Black man was Detective Rossington and the other, a strongly built white fellow, who was built to play rugby, was Detective Babcock.

"I understand why you want to take the money to Irons, Allyn," Kincaid began. "But you need to know that we now have evidence that indicates you are Irons' target not your daughter."

"She's the bait," Babcock said. "The only safe way to make the exchange is for Lieutenant Kincaid to go in, dressed as you."

Allyn grimaced and shook his head. "I don't care about the danger to me. Rick knows me, and he'll recognize a ringer. I'd gladly trade myself for Carys if that's what it takes to keep her safe."

"We don't know it will, Allyn." Kincaid said. "He may plan to keep you both, so he can use her as a hostage to force your obedience."

"Obedience!" Allyn spat the word as though it was too bitter to swallow. Quinn watched the sound of it shudder through Allyn, although he doubted the other men could see it. The singer's face grew grim. "In that case, just tell me — do you have any leads on where she is?"

Taglia said, "We found her fingerprints at Irons' apartment here in town, but not at the ranch he owns up north. She's probably still with him, wherever he is now."

"I'd say this afternoon's phone call rather proves that," Quinn agreed drily.

"The other information that's come in today is that Demetra is in Majorca, so that rules her out. We've ruled out everyone else in Leviathon as well, so it looks Harry was right: it was a three-way conspiracy between him, Moody and Irons."

Allyn sighed. "That's a relief, anyway, that no one else is in it. What kind of evidence do you have that makes you think he's after me?"

"It looks like Irons has been planning this for quite awhile." Rossington said. "He was working security at the Hollywood Bowl, but he gave his resignation, saying he had a new band and was going on the road.

"Babcock and I went to take a look at the ranch. It's a pretty big spread, way off the beaten track, so there're no neighbors around to see anything," Rossington's voice was warm and rich, in bizarre contrast with the news he was giving. "No one was around. There's a house and barn and several outbuildings. In the house, in one of the bedrooms, we found..." he grimaced, "...I guess you'd call it a shrine. Two of the walls are covered with pictures — newspaper photos, magazine pictures, even snapshots. Of you, Mr. Sterling. Hundreds of them."

"*Me?*" Allyn caught his breath.

Rossington pulled a briefcase up onto his lap and removed a manila envelope. He sorted through a thick stack of instant photos, handing select ones to the singer, keeping others to himself.

The pictures overlapped one another on the walls, mostly shots of the band on stage with himself front and center. There were three poster-size blowups of photos that Allyn recognized. Two had originally been pictures of himself and Quinn. In one, Irons had replaced Quinn's face with an oversized shot of his own. In another, Quinn's face was simply blacked out. The third poster was a picture of him and Rick Irons. They were backstage at a concert, in the dressing room. Irons had his arm flung over Allyn's shoulder and was grinning broadly.

Allyn glanced at Quinn. "What does it mean?" he breathed. "I didn't know... I swear to you..."

"There's more you need to know," Babcock said. "We found diaries. The oldest was from seventy-two or -three. He doesn't mention you or Leviathon until around seventy-four. His writing starts out sounding like something a teenager would write, but his ramblings get weirder as time went on. He talks about freeing you from what he calls *'Quinn's mind control.'* When he found out you and Carys had come to California last summer, he started writing about using Carys to draw you to him. Then the diaries stop."

"At about the same time the Peacock letters stopped," Kincaid added.

Allyn stared at Kincaid. For several uncomfortable seconds, no one spoke.

Kincaid said, "It's too dangerous for you to take the money to Irons tonight at The Greek, Allyn. Please. Let me handle it."

Allyn shook his head at last. "But Carys.... I can't. I have to be there for her."

Quinn saw Taglia close his eyes, lowering his head in resignation. Kincaid's expression hardened. "Okay, Rossington. Show him the rest."

The detective handed over the rest of the photographs, half to Allyn, the other half to Quinn. "Irons has made some special renovations to the barn. The doors and windows are barred. The interior is split into a number of rooms. All of them are barred, too. It looks like a jail. Or a dungeon."

Quinn's stomach clenched when he saw the first photograph. A long table, with chains and shackles at all four corners, occupied the foreground. Behind it was a heavy, barred door with a jail-cell lock. The second picture showed racks of whips, chain collars, handcuffs, gags, masks, and other paraphernalia. The third displayed a wall with shackles at ankle and shoulder height, and a leather full-head mask. Quinn looked at Allyn. The singer's face had turned pale. The photos fell from his trembling hands.

Rossington was still talking. "...It looks like he's set the barn up as a sexual torture chamber. We think he planned it for you, Mr. Sterling, because all of the... equipment... seems to be designed for an adult, not a child."

Quinn saw Allyn lose focus on the words being spoken. He was breathing harshly. Taglia started to rise to help, but Allyn shook his head. Quinn knew he wouldn't tolerate anyone's touch, not now.

Allyn lunged to his feet and fled the room.

Thirty-Three 33

"I'm sorry," Rossington said. "I know that was rough."

Taglia watched Quinn turn his attention to the detective. He was sure the guitarist would rather go after Allyn than stay and listen.

"He needs to know what we're up against," Babcock pressed. "If Irons managed to kidnap him then discovered we've already found his ranch, he could take them both and disappear — or he could just kill them."

"Of course," Quinn said, trapped in the conversation, "But..."

Taglia stood. He met Kincaid's questioning glance. "I'm gonna go talk to Allyn."

Quinn looked at him too. He opened his mouth as if to speak then stopped, pressed his lips together. He nodded once at Taglia then turned his attention back to Babcock.

The door to Allyn's room was open a crack. Taglia pushed it further and stuck his head inside. The darkened room was empty. A light was on in the bathroom.

"Allyn?" When he didn't get an answer, he went further into the room, shutting the door behind himself. He stopped at the bathroom door.

Allyn sat on the white tile floor, his back against the tub, eyes closed. His left arm was draped across the toilet bowl. An acrid scent lingered in the air. Taglia took one glance at his pale, sweat-streaked face and went to the sink, turned on the cold water and reached for a washcloth. He wrung it out, squatted down in front of the other man and gently wiped his face. Allyn opened his eyes, took the washcloth and pressed it to his mouth. After a moment he sighed, "Thank you. Where's Derek?"

"He wanted to be with you but he couldn't get away, so I'm here. You want me to go get him for you?"

"No!" Allyn shook his head weakly. "Oh, gods, no. I could never talk to him about this."

Taglia sat on the floor. The tile was cold through his thin jeans. "Do you want to talk to me?"

"I don't know if I can." Allyn's voice had something broken in it. "I didn't tell you everything before. It's so... I can't...."

"Yeah, I get it." Taglia said as kindly as he could. "You ready to get out of here? We can sit in your room."

After a moment, Allyn nodded. Taglia clambered to his feet and stuck out his hand. The singer shook his head and got up on his own. As soon as he was able they walked into the bedroom.

Taglia switched on the lamp beside the bed. The warm glow suffused the room, pooling against the midnight blue satin pillows and creamy white fleece. It glistened in Allyn's hair but did nothing to brighten the darkness in his eyes.

Allyn sank onto the bed, curling his legs beneath him and pulled the sheepskin throw around his shoulders. "I'm so cold. I don't think I'll ever be able to get warm again."

Taglia sat on the edge of the bed, careful not to touch him. He was guessing that Allyn had seen some rough trade during his homeless days. "I'm here, Allyn. If you need anything, let me know."

The singer was silent for several minutes. He clutched a pillow to his chest, fingers clenching and unclenching. "I've never said anything about this to anyone," he whispered hoarsely at last. "It happened a few weeks before Sammy came to find me. I was desperate. I was living in alleys and abandoned buildings with some of the other fellows, when we could get in. The weather was terrible, and I was so hungry. There were these men. They kept coming 'round St. James Park. Some of the others in the Park had warned me about them, so when I saw them I'd walk away.

"One night, they saw me before I saw them. They told me I could go with them for a few days and that they paid well. They'd take care of me. They said they had a nice place, where I could rest. Where I could have a bite to eat. Where it was warm."

He fell silent again and drew the sheepskin close. It was awhile before he continued. "I'd already gotten to the point where I sometimes wished I could fall asleep and just not wake up again, but I didn't have the nerve for suicide. When these men told me about their place, I didn't really believe them, but I just wanted out to so badly...

"I'd turned seventeen in August. I thought I was pretty jaded. I had no idea what I'd gotten myself into. The others had been right. The men were porn filmmakers, and they were into all those same things as Irons. I was kept locked up, and it was still cold. They took my clothes. They beat me when I tried to get away. And they filmed me. Sex or pain, they filmed me."

"The scars on your back." Taglia kept a firm grip on the helpless anger inside

Allyn nodded bleakly. "I was hoping you hadn't seen them. Yeah, they gave me the scars. I could barely move for days." He closed his eyes briefly, and Taglia saw the dampness in the corners. "It wasn't really S&M, of course. Friends of mine play with bondage and S&M.

I guess they enjoy the restraint, when there are safe words to stop the pain or humiliation. There were no safe words for me."

Taglia remained silent. Nothing he could say, nothing he could do would remedy Allyn's anguish. Nothing would help but acceptance.

"I had to be obedient." Allyn laughed, the sound was soft but bitter. "I was a slave. I had no choice. In the end I did what they wanted. With them or anyone else they brought in. Between filming sessions, they left me alone in the cold."

Allyn fell silent as he stared into his own past. A tear broke free from his lashes and slid along his nose. He shifted enough to wipe it away then pressed his face against the sheepskin.

When it became apparent the singer was not going to continue, Taglia prompted, "Did you escape, or did they let you go?"

"I don't think they ever meant me to leave." Allyn's fingers bunched in the soft, combed fleece. "I could hear them talking sometimes. I think they planned to kill me when they got tired of me. And they'd have filmed that, too, I'm sure."

"How'd you get away?"

"After awhile I quit fighting, quit resisting at all. I was their good, obedient boy. They became less careful in how they watched me. One day they got careless enough for me to get loose. I found a shirt and pants. I thought about waiting for them and killing them, but I was afraid I wouldn't be able to do it. In the end I ran until I couldn't run any more, then I hid. It took me almost a day to get back to the building I'd been living in before I went with them. My suitcase was still there, and I was able to change clothes, but it was two more days before I had the nerve to go out in public. I left only because I was too hungry to keep hiding any longer. I had to go back to St. James Park to survive, but I was ready to run again if I saw them."

"You got away. And you survived. Allyn, that's amazing!"

Allyn shuddered. "I survived thanks to Quinn. He got me out of that game. I really do owe him my life, but he can't ever know. Because of him, I've managed to let go of most of the horror. I used to always be afraid that it might come back to haunt me. Blackmail, especially after Leviathon became famous. But nothing ever happened, and over the years I've managed to... not think about it so much anymore. Now there's this, with Rick. He must know about it somehow. How could he have found out, Paul? What on earth am I going to do?"

"Hey, I don't think Irons knows anything about any of this. He's the kind of guy who can't pass up a weapon. If he thought he could put the screws to you directly he wouldn't have bothered with Carys."

Allyn's expression turned thoughtful. After a few moments he asked, "But why me? All I've ever wanted was a band to sing with. Both those bastards back in London and Rick wanted to trap me in their sick fantasies. There has to be something that tells them I could be used like that."

"Haven't you ever looked in the mirror, Allyn? Those guys in London saw something all right. They saw a good-looking kid. A runaway no one knew about, hungry, cold and naïve — no matter how jaded you thought you were. As for Rick, he's crazy. He could have targeted anyone. You just happened to be the one he picked."

Allyn started to shake his head, and for a moment Taglia wondered if he was going to argue the point. Instead Allyn frowned and remained silent. Taglia considered a dozen things he might say but just sat there, letting the singer have the space to think.

After several minutes, Allyn shifted restlessly. "I'm a coward," he said. "I have to face Irons, but I don't know how I can."

"Oh come on, Allyn! You're being threatened by a maniac who's holding your daughter for ransom and wants to lock you in a dungeon! You've seen the pictures, and you've already been there once — no wonder you're afraid. Hell, I'd be afraid! It doesn't make you a coward. Besides, you're forgetting you don't have to face Irons at all. That's why Jeff and I are here."

"I don't understand why you would," Allyn said. "Even now, knowing everything, you are planning to let Jeff go to the Greek dressed like me. I know you care for him. I see it in your face and you as much as told me last night. But if things go wrong, he could be hurt, even killed. In my world nothing comes for free. Everything is a trade-off. I just don't get why you would do this for me without asking something from me in return."

Taglia laughed softly. "Okay, here's my request for you: cooperate with us. Help me protect Jeff tonight.

"Look, we're cops. We help people. It's what we've done together for seven years. When he made Lieutenant a couple of years back, he could have chosen anyone as his partner. He chose to stay with me." He hesitated before continuing, "This thing between us — it's new. It's so new, I don't know what it means, and he sure as hell doesn't. I can't worry about both of you. I need you to stay here, Allyn. Please. Let us do our job. We'll bring Carys back to you."

For several seconds, Taglia wasn't sure what Allyn was going to do. At last, the singer tossed the throw aside and stood, a smile beginning to curve the corners of his mouth. "Deal, then!" he said, offering his hand. "That's a trade I can accept. Give me a few minutes, and I'll be out to do everything I can to see Jeff looks my part. Then I'll get out of your way. With help from the Lady, we'll all live to see tomorrow."

They shook on it.

Thirty-Four 34

Allyn rejoined Quinn and the cops in the conversation pit. He settled on the couch next to Quinn and reached for his now-cold tea, took a sip, grimaced and put it back down. "Okay, what did I miss? And how can I help?"

Taglia leaned forward. "We didn't miss much. Just tying up loose ends. It mainly boils down to Jeff and me leaving the house at the same time but in separate cars. I'll take my own. Quinn's offered to let Jeff drive the Jaguar."

"That would work. Irons would believe I was driving an XJS, and you won't have to deal with the Lotus. The Eleven can be a bit of a challenge."

"I warned them about that." Quinn's tone was dry.

Kincaid added, "While we're gone, Babcock and Rossington will stay here to protect you and Derek in case of a double-cross."

"And what about you?" Allyn asked. "Who will be protecting the two of you?"

"Don't worry about us. We have SWAT, who is already planning the strategic details. They'll be getting into position as soon as it's dark. Sergeant Taglia and I'll both be armed as well.

"I will need your help with costuming, though. We've got a wig, but the clothes are up to you. In character, but nothing too flashy. No bright colors — I don't want to stand out like a neon sign. A vest or jacket of some kind if you have one, so I can hide my gun. We don't want Irons to realize I'm carrying. Don't give me something to wear that you have your heart set on getting back in one piece." Kincaid glanced at the skin-tight jeans the singer was wearing. "And I'd appreciate it if the jeans were loose enough I can move around. Not like the ones you've got on."

Quinn laughed, "You have no idea how much movement he can get out of those jeans!"

The evening dragged, but eleven o'clock was finally behind them. Quinn lay in his recliner, head tipped back, observing events unfold around him through the filter of his lashes.

Rossington and Babcock sat on barstools, talking quietly to Taglia. He couldn't hear what they were saying, and he didn't really care. The conversation he was interested in was on the other side of the room. Kincaid and Allyn stood by the Christmas tree, as fine a pair of doppelgangers as Hesse could have imagined. With the blonde wig and Allyn's clothes, Kincaid's resemblance to Allyn was uncanny.

"There're no words for something like this," Allyn said. He unfastened his belt and pulled it off. He held it for a moment, weighing the buckle in his hand, before passing it over to Kincaid. "Here, put this on. Rick knows I go nowhere without it. It'll add the final fillip of reality."

"Thanks, Allyn." Kincaid's expression was solemn as he removed his own belt and replaced it with Allyn's. Quinn thought it almost seemed a courtly ritual, knight to knight, exchanging tokens before battle.

How appropriate, on this longest night of the year. Winter Solstice. The old year dies tonight, bringing with it the birth of the infant Sun. He closed his eyes for a moment of not-quite prayer. *Please, let that be the only thing that dies tonight.*

"Time to go, Paul." Kincaid's voice brought him back to the present. He opened his eyes in time to see the cop secure his holstered gun to the belt behind his back, underneath Allyn's black leather jacket.

"I'm ready," Taglia replied, nodded at Babcock and Rossington, and strode for the door.

Quinn rose and followed them to the porch. He was aware of Allyn's warm presence on one side, Rossington's cool watchfulness on the other. "Good hunting, gentlemen," he called as they opened their car doors. Kincaid nodded soberly in response; Taglia gave them a wave and a smile. He watched the cars out the gate then returned to the den, pausing to glance thoughtfully toward his room.

"Is it that time already?" The irritation in Allyn's voice stopped him in his tracks.

"No. I'm still thinking about that tune. I got it mostly worked out in the studio, but I'd like to transcribe it while it's still fresh."

"Oh. Yes. Of course." Allyn sounded abashed. "Forgive me? I'm more than a little anxious."

"Would you rather I stay out here with you? Or you're always welcome to join me if you feel the need for company. Watching me write notes on a piece of paper should at least be amusing. I have to work so hard to get it right. Not like Gilley. He transcribes like it's his native tongue."

"I may do that. But I think I'll take some time for myself as well."

Quinn sat on the edge of his bed with the four-legged bench from the vanity drawn up before him, a composer's notebook spread out across the top. He balanced an acoustic guitar on his knee and held a pencil clamped between his teeth as he frowned in concentration. He played a phrase, repeated it, then took the pencil out of his mouth and jotted down the notes.

As he started a new phrase, there was a soft knock at the door. He reached for the cigarette smoldering in the ashtray. "Come in."

Allyn entered. Quinn noticed the blue cloak slung around his shoulders. "You're going out?"

Allyn fastened the clasp at his throat. "I thought I'd go for a stroll in the back yard. Collect my wits, like. It feels so... *unnatural* in here, just waiting. I'm suffocating."

Quinn nodded, took a long drag on his cigarette and crushed it out in an already-overflowing ashtray. "Would you like company?"

"On a contemplative stroll?" Allyn smiled and shook his head. "No need to disturb you for that. Besides, I'll have my faithful companion, Detective Babcock, in any case."

"There you are, then." As Allyn turned to the door, Quinn set the guitar aside. "Half a moment." He rose and ambled over to the dresser. He pulled open the top drawer and rummaged through its contents.

"You've got a lot of undergarments for a man who seldom wears any," Allyn observed.

"Mostly socks. None of them match... ah, here it is." He brought out a bundle wrapped in soft gray cloth. Laying it on the dresser, he unwrapped it. Light seemed to disappear into the blue steel gun barrel as he slapped a full clip into the well-maintained old Luger and offered it to Allyn. "I know you'd rather it was three feet of cold steel, but this is what I have. I agree with our bodyguards that Rick may not deal fairly with us."

Allyn made no move to take the gun.

Quinn sighed. "You've always been a flower-child at heart. Do be careful."

"I will," Allyn said and shut the door as he left.

Quinn stood for a moment staring at the closed door. At last, he unloaded and rewrapped the gun, tucking it back in the drawer.

He looked back toward the music. He knew he wouldn't be able to concentrate. Restless and uneasy, he left the music behind, drifted down the hall to the bar in the den, and poured himself a drink.

The room was quiet. He snapped the radio on, just for the pretext of company. Warren Zevon was singing about werewolves in London. When he turned around, he discovered Rossington on the couch, holding a magazine and watching him.

"Here." Quinn raised his glass. "Would you like some?"

"No, thanks. I'm on duty."

The phone rang. Quinn set down the glass, staring at the phone.

"Better answer it." The cop was already moving toward the tape machine.

"Allyn's supposed to be the only one who answers."

"No time," Rossington snapped. "Take it."

Quinn worked to keep his breathing even as he picked up the receiver. "Hello?"

"Hey, Derek." A familiar, hated voice, rasped along his nerve-endings. "I figured you'd still be there. Too scared to face me, eh?"

"I'm not afraid of you, or anything like you, Rick."

"Sure you are, but not for yourself," Irons interrupted with a chuckle. "I'll win this time, Quinn. You know how I know? Because there's been a change of plans. I'm not at the Greek. I'm at the Hollywood Bowl. That's where I'll be waiting. Better get Peacock on the road to me. Or his kid..."

"No. You can't! They've... I mean he's already gone...."

Irons roared with laughter. "I got you! I knew it! I knew you'd call the cops. I knew you would! Allyn's still there, isn't he? Cool. Man, this is so cool." His tone changed, suddenly icy. "You tell him to shake his ass. Now, Quinn!"

"Wait — Rick." Quinn spoke quickly, sensing Irons was about to disconnect. "Tell me why you're doing this."

"I'm gonna do what you should have done. What you don't have the balls for. He'll give his love to the one who breaks him. You know that. You've always known it."

"Love?" He could barely speak past the aching in his chest. "What kind of love breaks the object of its affection? A broken thing is less than the thing itself, Rick."

Bird of Paradise
G.J. Paterson

"All slaves love their masters."

"It's only a twisted illusion that lets the master believe it." Quinn was aware of Rossington's impassive regard. There was no knowing what the cop thought. Quinn was past caring. "This is nothing Allyn desires or understands. Let Carys go. Settle for his money and his gratitude. You've proven your power. He'll never love you. He can't be forced. He will die first."

"You've got him brainwashed into thinking you're God. I'll change him. You'll see. Maybe after I've tamed him down real good, I'll send him back to you. If you'll still have him."

"I accept Allyn on his own terms." As he spoke the words, Quinn realized they came from the center, the still-point of his being. "I always have. I always will."

"Sure you do. Well, you've had him long enough. Now it's my turn. Tell him I'll see him at the Bowl."

The connection went dead. Quinn hung up the receiver, shaking so hard it took two tries to do it. He braced a hand against the bar to keep from falling. After a deep breath, he frowned at the cop. "I kept him talking as long as I could. Were your people able to trace the call?"

"I'm gonna get word to the troops first," Rossington snapped, "then I'll worry about the trace." His face was grim as he reached for the phone.

"I'll go get Allyn." Quinn headed for the sliding door at once, not giving the detective a chance to object.

Outside, Quinn paused a moment to let his eyes adjust to the night and to try to guess where Allyn might be in the darkness. Instinct led him toward the little Japanese koi pond, its left side still festooned with yellow police tape.

Allyn sat beside the pool. The fish were barely-moving shadows in the limpid water. Babcock stood a few yards away. The scene should have been tranquil, but when Allyn raised his head at Quinn's approach, there was nothing gentle in his starlit face. "What is it?"

"Rick just called."

Allyn surged to his feet. "What did he say?"

"It's the Hollywood Bowl."

"What?"

"He's changed the drop site to the Hollywood Bowl. Not the Greek. He guessed somehow the police were on the way with the money — but you weren't. I don't think he cares about the money. He just wants you to come to the Bowl."

Allyn was already in motion, heading to the house. His cloak swept back like vast wings, shadows against shadows. Quinn hurried after him.

The light indoors was painfully bright after the darkness outside. Allyn's face was tense and drawn as he stopped just inside the doorway, waiting for Quinn. "We've got to get word to Paul and Jeff."

"He's trying to do that right now." Quinn jerked his head toward Rossington, who was still at the bar, arguing with someone on the phone. He glanced at his wristwatch. "They've been gone just a bit past fifteen minutes."

"Paul's car has a radio," Allyn pointed out.

Rossington slammed the receiver into its cradle in disgust. "It doesn't matter that he's got a radio — we can't use it. They still have radio silence on this thing. Our information can't go out over the air."

"We'll have to catch them, then." Allyn fished a set of keys out of the front pocket of his faded jeans.

"Can you do it?" Quinn asked.

"Of course." Allyn's smile was a dangerous flash of teeth. "They don't have twenty minutes on me. I'll catch them and tell them. Then I'll come back."

Quinn expected him to head for the front door, but instead Allyn ran down the hall. A door opened and closed, then Allyn was back with a tattered, one-eyed stuffed lion in his hand. Quinn smiled as he strode for the front door, realizing Allyn had raided Carys' off-limits bedroom to get Muffin.

Babcock yelped, "Not alone!"

Bird of Paradise

G.J. Paterson

253

"Certainly not." Allyn paused in the doorway, and his deadly grin was back. "Hurry."

Quinn and Rossington followed them to the front door. Allyn yanked the canvas off the Lotus Eleven. The sleek little car, painted British racing green, crouched like a well-trained mount. Quinn smiled at the expression on the cop's face when he realized what they would be riding in.

Beside him, Rossington muttered, "Wish I'd spoken first."

"Not if you've eaten recently."

There was a rumbling snarl from the Lotus as the engine caught. The lights came on, the eyes of a great beast waking up. *The eyelids of morning.* Quinn was sure this wasn't what Allyn had meant when he'd written the lyrics to *"Dragon Fire,"* but it seemed appropriate. The car trembled like a living thing as the motor settled into a steady growl.

Then tires sprayed gravel, sharp as machine-gun fire, against the Chevrolet that Babcock and Rossington had arrived in. The Lotus turned onto the road in the space between one breath and the next. Quinn sighed. There was nothing left of Allyn out here in the darkness save the fading howl of his engine and the settling dust that left a sharp bite in the nostrils.

He left Rossington to fend for himself in the den and returned to his bedroom, paused to light a cigarette, then lifted Sweet Fire from its stand, slipping the shoulder strap over his head. He caught sight of the acoustic leaning against the bed and the untidy sprawl of his unfinished work on the makeshift table.

There's still time for it, he told himself as he flipped the power switch on his amp. He turned to face the speaker, a savage movement, and began the agonizing, power-chorded opening of *"Dragon Fire."* In his mind, he could see the harsh face of the driver. Allyn would catch them, if anyone could.

Quinn went on playing, hearing a strong, phantom voice singing the words to his wailing, doom-laden accompaniment,

"There will be weeping in the valley,
When the child of the gods goes to war."

Bird of Paradise
G.J. Paterson
254

WINTER SOLSTICE
FRIDAY,

DECEMBER 22, 1978

Thirty-Five 35

Allyn lay back in the seat, watching the gauges come up and breathing deeply to steady his nerves. He could feel the tension in the cop beside him. He was more aware of the urgency, the hideous press of time, than he had ever been in his life. He knew he must put it all away. He mustn't think of his daughter, or Babcock, or the ticking clock, or the car itself — nothing at all. He had to narrow his focus down to the moment.

Professional drivers, his true heroes, had complimented his ability to do this. They had paid him their highest tribute, acceptance. Several had told him he should give up music. Racing, they said, was what he was born to do.

Let it be true, he prayed, invoking his own patron saints. *This once, let me drive like Nuvolari, and Fangio, and the man I changed my name to honor, Stirling Moss. Let me become the car and the road the way Quinn becomes the music.*

Bird of Paradise
G.J. Paterson

The gauges leveled off. He untied a leather thong from the steering wheel where he kept it and scraped his hair back from his face, binding it in a rough ponytail. The power plant settled into its steady, galloping rumble. A glance to his left assured him Babcock was strapped in. He put on his goggles and handed the cop the extra set.

He knew he wouldn't be running flat out for more than a few seconds at a stretch. *It's the seconds that count,* he told himself and eased off the clutch. Gravel sprayed from the tires and the little green Lotus shot down the drive. He turned left. There was asphalt under the car, and he wound her up through the gears, careless of the neighbors.

Houses flashed past him, most of them dark as it approached midnight. *Rock stars and movie stars and little old ladies with cats have lived up here for thirty years.* His engine howled down the canyon walls. *There'll be more lights on now.*

He forgot the houses and their occupants as he dodged around a station wagon, narrowly missing a German sedan coming the other way. Both cars honked their terror at his tailpipes as Babcock stiffened in protest.

Allyn laughed a little, settling into the drive. Only concentration mattered, traveling the speeds he was going down these twisting roads, moving fast enough that other cars seemed to be stationary objects, like trees to the downhill racer.

Turning off Oak Pass Drive onto Hutton, he wished he had brought his stopwatch. Taglia and Kincaid were just over ten minutes ahead. He meant to catch them at the Coldwater Canyon junction.

The Lotus ripped past a VW Minibus and a Dodge pickup, running up hard on a Porsche 916. The Porsche saw him coming and punched the accelerator. Allyn stayed on him through several sharp curves. A straight stretch beckoned, but there were too many cars in the uphill lane.

The Porsche didn't turn with them at Benedict Canyon, and the road was clear. Allyn was able to open her up and run as hard as she would go for several seconds at a time. He drifted through a tight series of curves, pushing each one to the edge. His lane hugged the rock cliffs, going down. Beyond the other lane, the road dropped away to the depths below. Miscalculation by a hairsbreadth would either catapult him into space or slam the delicate car into the mountain at something over a hundred miles an hour.

His headlights picked up a slower moving vehicle ahead and he backed off the accelerator, heeling-and-toeing, then double-clutching ruthlessly around the Cadillac. Beside him, his passenger shouted something. The sound was lost in the wind. Allyn tapped his ear and shrugged.

The cars he chased flickered through his mind. The Firebird might as well have been standing still. It was an American designer's idea of a grand touring car and did all right on open American roads. It was too big, though, set too high, and the power-to-weight ratio was all wrong for these hills. It could never do much over seventy safely through the canyon roads. Quinn's Jag, a true grand touring car, suffered from the same problems, sacrificing speed and cornering for comfort.

There was precious little of that in the Lotus. Allyn shifted in his seat, trying to ease his cramped frame.

For a second, he longed for Taglia's presence. He had come to trust him, and trust was never easy. It went deeper than the moments of intimacy they had shared. Taglia had a sense of surety about him.

Like Quinn's strength. He shied away from the idea and brought his attention back to the road as he reached Mulholland.

In the light of passing street lamps, Babcock stared at him. His eyes were huge behind the goggles. His jaw was clenched, and his lips were drawn down in a tight line. Allyn spared him an unsympathetic glance as they moved onto Mulholland.

Halfway through the turn, the steering slipped, and he knew he had other concerns. He cursed under his breath as he fought the Lotus' increasing tendency to pull right. He hoped the tires would hold up against the speed and misalignment.

The night air was fresh, full of the scent of eucalyptus and a piquant fragrance he couldn't identify. Beyond the drop to the left, he could see the lights of Los Angeles and surrounds spreading out like a nightscape from Faerie. *It, too, is beautiful, and perilous.*

He was coming up fast on something low-slung. He passed a red Ferrari Berlinetta Boxer and nearly went head-on into a van on a blind hill. The Lotus whipped back into its own lane with seconds to spare. Behind him, the Ferrari screamed defiance as its driver put it into pursuit.

The two of them swooped uphill and down again into a fast-descending right hand curve, moving in perfect synch. They swung downhill through a series of bends, the road unwinding behind them. Allyn gained a few yards. The road straightened and the Ferrari closed, then lost ground again as they went through another group of turns. Allyn struggled with the steering, the Lotus' inclination to pull right becoming more and more marked. The Ferrari regained the distance as they swept uphill, crested, and dropped down around another long, sloping curve.

Allyn's ears popped with the pressure change. The Ferrari was dueling with Allyn's Lotus. Allyn's opponent was unseen. Still, the other car gave him something tangible to fight against. The two cars ran as though they were alone on the road, passing lesser vehicles as if they were ghosts, insubstantial and unreal. They swept into a rapid descent through an undulating string of bends, and Allyn began to pull away.

They were approaching Coldwater Canyon when Allyn passed the Jaguar. He was pressing Taglia's distinctive black Firebird when he realized he had found his checkered flag.

The road took a sharp bend. The Ferrari had caught the Jag and was closing the gap between them. Allyn over-steered the Lotus, slipping past Taglia around the turn in a perfect four-wheel drift, knowing the move was brilliant, precise, and dangerous. Still, it gained him seconds over the Ferrari.

The opposite lane remained empty. Allyn pulled in front of the Firebird and began to ease off. The Ferrari flashed past, the driver making rude hand gestures out of the window.

"Probably thinks I've broken something," Allyn muttered as he slowed, dropping below the speed limit, in front of Taglia. "Considering how this cow steers, he could be right."

He put on the turn indicator and was gratified to see Taglia do the same. Behind them both, the Jag was preparing to turn in too. Part of him was listening to the engine, pleased to hear the steady rumble as he brought the car to a halt, levered himself up out of the seat and stepped over the side, not bothering with the door.

He glimpsed Taglia fling open the Firebird's door as sirens wailed in the distance, drawing closer. Two black-and-whites snarled past. The lead car went on in pursuit of the Ferrari, but the second braked hard, fish-tailing on screaming tires. It stopped at an angle across the road then swung around, coming to a halt nose-to-nose with the Lotus. Both spots flared on. Allyn flinched away from the light and pushed his goggles up.

"Allyn." Taglia's voice was sharp with urgency. "Put your hands up and don't move until I talk to them." Taglia raised both his hands, badge case in one of them. The golden shield glinted in the light. Beside him, Babcock was pulling out his badge and holding it up as well.

"All right, freeze!" an authoritative voice commanded over the PA, then the squad car doors opened. Allyn held still. He hadn't managed to get his hands in the air, but they were away from his body. He could hear the sound of his own rapid breathing, certain that beyond the lights were police officers with guns drawn.

"Hold it," Taglia shouted back. "We're police. Sergeant Taglia, Missing Persons. The guy in the Jag is my partner, Lieutenant Kincaid. The guy with the long hair is our witness. The guy with him is one of ours, too."

"Paul? Jeff?" Without the amplification, Allyn realized the speaker was a woman. "You guys okay? What's going on here?"

"Emma, is that you?" Kincaid stepped out of the Jaguar, tall and almost unrecognizable in his spotlit disguise. He too held out his badge. "We're working a case. We need to talk the witness right now."

"Oh, yeah?" The driver's spotlight shut off. The relative darkness was almost as blinding as the light had been. Leather creaked and the two patrol officers came out in the open, guns holstered now but hands resting casually on their weapons. "We clocked your 'witness' doing a hundred and twenty-three down Mulholland."

"We'll write him a ticket." Kincaid turned to Allyn. "What's happened?"

"Rick called again. He's not at the Greek — he's at the Hollywood Bowl. He wants me to meet him there."

"When?"

"Same time. Jeff, he knows the police are involved." Allyn was cold and shaky in the aftermath of the adrenaline rush. He had to force himself to speak with a steady tone. Cars passed along the road, slowing because of the tableau on the shoulder. There wasn't much room.

The singer turned away from the road, facing the hillside beyond his car. Something grew there with yellow flowers, leaves shimmering silver in the spotlight's glare. He drew a deep breath. *Nothing is going according to plan.*

Plans change. It still has to be Jeff. Allyn had given his power over to the cop. He looked back at the man standing there in a wig and his clothes. *It was my choice to let him do this thing. He'll find a way somehow.*

"What about backup?" Allyn's passenger spoke for the first time.

"Babcock?" Kincaid peered past Allyn at the cop in the car. "Glad to see you made it."

"You and me both. What about backup?"

"Did Rossington call in the change?"

"He was trying to get through when we left."

"Emma, can you get on the radio, see if you can get through to Captain Ortiz? Find out if he's received a message from Rossington. Nothing more specific than that." Kincaid sounded calm and confident. Allyn's shoulders sagged with relief.

The patrolwoman nodded once and slid behind the wheel of her car. Her partner drifted over to join the congregation around the Lotus.

"The Bowl, huh? Good." Taglia's grin was ferocious. "It's easier to get there from here, anyway. We don't have to deal with the One-Oh-One."

Allyn paced, nerves still jumping from the flight down the hills. "What now?"

"We go to the Bowl," Taglia replied.

"We?"

"Jeff and me. You take a few minutes to chill, then you and Babcock go back home."

"This is gonna be dangerous, Sarge," Babcock interrupted. "Are you sure you don't want me to go with you?"

"No. Stick with your assignment."

Allyn turned and walked away. He hated the helplessness binding him. He was out of his depth and knew it, but he still believed there must be something more he could do.

The flashing red and blue lights reminded him of a concert. Nothing seemed real except the gravel pressing into the thin soles of his lace-up moccasin boots as he paced beside the road.

There's a song in this somewhere. I wonder if I will ever sing it? I wonder if I will ever sing again? It depends. It all depends.

Babcock was still inside the Lotus, deep in conversation with Emma's partner. The uniformed officer had his back to Allyn, shielding Babcock. Neither noticed the singer's approach. "...Are you telling me those two have their asses on the line for a bunch of faggoty long-hairs?" the patrolman demanded.

"Oh, man. You should've seen the pictures," Babcock said. "I wouldn't be in Kincaid's shoes for anything. It's going down all wrong."

Allyn deliberately scuffed his moccasins hard against the gravel. The patrolman spun on his heel, hand on his pistol butt. Babcock stared at Allyn, his expression a comical mixture of disgust and surprise.

The singer stopped, holding his hands away from himself, palms out. "It's okay, you know. It's only me..." *The faggoty long-hair.* Allyn kept his voice neutral with a careful balance of humor and anger. Neither man could know for certain if he'd overheard their comments, and Allyn decided to leave them their uncertainty.

"Paul," Emma called out. "Dispatch can't get through. Do you want us to go with you?"

"No, it'll be better if you and your partner go to the Greek. Let them know the location has been changed to the Hollywood Bowl. Code Three."

Emma's partner returned to the squad car at a run. Backing up in a tight turn, they burned rubber as they peeled out onto the asphalt highway. Sirens howled and lights flashed as they headed for Griffith Park.

Kincaid and Taglia headed toward their cars. Allyn caught up with Taglia at the Firebird. "Paul?"

"You did good tonight, Allyn." Taglia smiled in the darkness. "Go home and try not to worry. Rossington will get through, or Emma will. It'll be okay."

Allyn reluctantly headed back to his own car. After a moment, Taglia called to him, "Hey, Allyn." The singer paused to look over his shoulder, meeting Taglia's grin. "*'Here's looking at you, kid.'*"

"*'Here's looking at you, kid.'*" The words ran through Kincaid's mind over and over as he slid into the Jaguar. *The two of you have your own secrets. Your own code. How the hell did that happen?*

Kincaid struggled to keep his breathing steady as he watched Taglia approach, a lithe shadow in the general darkness. *I don't know how to talk about this, anyway. I'm scared, Paul. Scared to death of myself. Of you. You change everything. I don't know if I'm ready for this kind of change.*

He discovered his jaw was clenched as he reached for the window handle. He forced himself to relax. *Get a grip, Kincaid. You're a professional. This is the time to pull yourself together. As if nothing ever happened.*

"Hey, I've been thinking." Taglia laid one forearm on the Jag's roof and leaned down to the look in the window. Kincaid was painfully aware of how close their faces were. *Keep thinking about Carys,* he told himself firmly. *About trading this briefcase full of money for the kid.*

Taglia continued as if he hadn't noticed his partner's distraction. "Your car should be the only one to go into the Bowl parking lot. I'll park farther down, beside the fountain with the ugly harp player."

Kincaid couldn't resist a smile, even though a part of him insisted this was not the time to be charmed by his partner's sense of humor. "It's the Muse of Music, Paul. It's Art Deco."

Taglia shrugged, casually tossing it off. "I'll have to take your word for it. About the art part, anyway. So, back to my plan, you go on inside, past the box office and concession stands, as near to the escalators as you can get. Take your time. I'm gonna have to run like hell, uphill and through the damn woods, to get into some kind of position."

"Okay. Then what?"

"I take out the bad guy. You rescue the girl. We fill out some paperwork, then go out and get a beer. You're buying."

Kincaid nodded briskly. "Sounds like a plan to me. Let's go."

He followed the Firebird onto the long stretch of Mulholland Drive, turning right onto Cahuenga, then pulled into the outer parking lot, the Muse of Music looming over them.

Taglia got out of his car and crossed to the Jag. Kincaid shifted into park, rolling down the window. "Nothing going on here tonight?"

"Not this time of the year. Too cold and too late." Taglia glanced around at the otherwise empty lot then brought his gaze back to Kincaid. "Do me a favor, Jeff. Don't take any chances."

"Don't worry, I'll be careful."

Taglia flashed a grin. "Time to get this done, then. See you on the other side." He took off running toward the back of the Bowl.

"You be careful too," Kincaid murmured as the sounds of footsteps faded. Wishing he'd said the words sooner, he shifted the Jag into gear and headed for the front parking lot.

Thirty-Six   36

Allyn climbed into the cockpit and cranked the key. The engine caught on the second try. He settled down and buckled his seatbelt, pulled down his goggles. He took one last glance at the Firebird, still parked on the shoulder of the road, then backed the Lotus and swung it around in a tight turn as soon as the traffic permitted. He punched the accelerator with enough force to snap Babcock's head back hard, but carefully topped out under the posted speed limits.

Shouting over the engine noise, he told the man, "You'll want your goggles."

The cop shot him a venomous glance and put them on. Allyn ignored him, concentrating on floating the car back up the hill. *Careful. Careful drivers live longest.*

"So tell me," he shouted over the engine and the road noise, "what do you think will happen at the Bowl? Do you think SWAT will get there in time?"

"I don't know."

"I'm just asking your opinion."

Out of the corner of his eye, he caught Babcock's shrug. "Okay, then. SWAT's not the fucking cavalry. Franklin Avenue's a bitch any time of day, and it'll be hard for them to switch locations... even if Rossington got through to them on his first try — which we know he didn't, 'cause if he had, we wouldn't be here."

"What about those patrol officers? Emma will get through, even if Rossington can't — won't she?"

"Still takes time. Damn! Sarge should've let me come along as backup."

"What do you think will happen if SWAT doesn't make it?"

Babcock shook his head silently, turned his head away to look out toward the side of the road.

Allyn pressed his lips together grimly, as his stomach twisted with anxiety. He forced himself to remember Paul's confidence. *I trust them. Not this guy. Why am I listening to this man? He has no idea. It's them I trust.*

The road beckoned him, and the fresh breeze was full of night-scents. He drove on in silence.

When Babcock tugged at his shirtsleeve a few miles down the road, it broke his concentration. The Lotus' rightward pull nearly yanked the wheel out of his grip. He held on until he got it back in control then shouted, "What?"

"Gotta piss!" Babcock shouted back.

"What? Here?" There were houses on both sides of the road now.

"Well, somewhere."

Allyn sighed and pulled to the shoulder of the road, rolling to a stop. He put a hand on Babcock's arm as the cop started to climb out of the car. "Wait. You never told me."

"Told you what?"

"What you think will happen at the Bowl without backup."

"Huh," Babcock laughed shortly. "Taglia and Kincaid are good, but they're going against a crazy guy. You know that. I think the

Bird of Paradise
G.J. Paterson
268

chances are better than even that a good cop will take a bullet tonight because they don't have backup." Babcock spat the words contemptuously, then levered his body up and over the side of the car. He walked a few feet back down the road, turned away from the highway, and fumbled with his trousers.

His gut burned, and he wanted to vomit again. *'A good cop is going to take a bullet tonight.' For me. And they're going in alone. If Jeff gets shot, what will happen to Carys?*

He drew a slow, deep breath. *If I were there, it wouldn't have to come to shooting. Rick won't start shooting if I'm there, because he wants me alive.*

Allyn glanced in the mirror. Babcock was still pissing, his head cocked back in relief. *I have to be there. Without me, Rick could kill everyone. Without me, Rick has nothing to lose.*

Babcock was finished, zipping his slacks and rearranging his clothes.

Decide now.

In seconds it would be too late. *It isn't always the safe driver who makes it through. Look at Jimmy Clark. Nobody safer than him, and yet it was Moss who retired alive at the end of the day. I can't sit back and take the safe line.*

Allyn depressed the clutch and shifted into gear. He saw Babcock one last time in the mirror, spinning toward him, shouting wordlessly, at the snarl of the Lotus's wind-up.

Allyn slipped the clutch, brought the car around in a flat, hard turn and slid back down the mountain, careful to keep to the speed limit.

Traffic began to pick up as he neared the valley floor. Allyn was in no mood to wait for anyone else on the road and passed where he could. Finally, a long, empty stretch of road opened up — the signal he had been waiting for. He let the speed creep up a little as he followed the line of the turn into the final hairpin. One hard squeeze of the brakes brought it down off the edge in a couple of seconds. He dropped into second gear and pitched it into the left-hand turn, powering his way around with the tail cocked. The Lotus wailed as he shifted into third for a fast series of s-curves. He put it back into second for a long bend to the right, braking deep into the corner as the car groped for traction. He hoped the already-abused tires would hold out a little longer.

The instant before the road opened up again, he fought his instinct to punch the accelerator. He reached for third without the fast build up of torque which would put it over the top in a hurry. He turned right onto Cahuenga and backed off the power even further as he briefly wished he hadn't dumped Babcock. *The man may be an arse but at least he has a gun.* He wished he'd accepted Quinn's offer of the Luger, then shook his head and made the turn onto Hollywood Bowl Drive.

Allyn rolled up to the Firebird, parked alone and empty by the fountain at the entrance to the Bowl grounds. He parked beside Taglia's car, yanked off the goggles and threw them onto the seat beside him.

He realized he had been wishing Captain Ortiz would be there to tell him everything was under control. He had hoped to find everything already resolved, with flashing lights, Jeff and Paul with a prisoner in handcuffs, and the nightly news team with their cameras and microphones and professionally-concerned smiles to explain what had happened in a fifteen second burst.

And Carys. Most of all, he had longed to find Carys.

Instead, there was darkness and a floodlit glow on the marble statue. There was no sound except the occasional car on Cahuenga and the steady hum of traffic on Highway 101. In the midst of the restless cauldron of the L.A. basin, he had never felt so alone before.

Allyn untied the leather thong holding back his ponytail and shook out his hair. Levering himself out of the cockpit, he reached back in for his keys and the stuffed lion. A glance at the dashboard showed him the Lotus was nearly out of fuel. He surveyed the tires as he circled the car, noting the blistering on the right rear. He smiled grimly to himself: he was committed to this course of action now. *No way out.*

His moccasins made no sound as he rounded the statue and trotted up the long hill to the Bowl. It was the hardest quarter mile of his life. His frame, cramped from driving in the sports car, was now called to stretch itself in the uphill climb, but the difficulty was his worry not the terrain.

He had been to the Bowl for performances. Carys knew the place, too. She loved the symphony. His heart ached for her, and that pain, more than any other thing, carried him up the hill to the parking lot. Loving her was the only constant in his chaotic life. Fear for her had persuaded him to do what he was doing. He knew the truth about himself. He would never have come for Taglia or Kincaid alone. *Carys is everything. I said I would buy her back with my life, and now I will.* He clung to the shabby stuffed lion as a token of hope.

The parking lot was empty save for Quinn's Jaguar and a dark, late-model American sedan, parked in the fire lane, pointing down the hill.

Allyn passed the sedan, paused, then went back. He circled the car, studying it thoughtfully. The driver's door was locked but ajar. "Oh, Rick, how careless of you," he whispered and bumped the door hard with his hip. The door clicked shut, latch popping open. The singer slipped inside to release the hood then was out again, relocking and easing the door closed.

A quick yank freed the distributor cap. He closed the hood quietly then set off again on his original path, disposing of the distributor cap in a handy trash bin on the way up the hill. He wiped his hands on the seat of his jeans and smiled. He had learned many skills on the streets of London back in that cold winter.

His satisfaction faded as he ran the rest of the way to the steps leading into the Bowl. The calves of his legs ached from the angle of the hill. He knew in his heart it was fear, not lack of conditioning, which shortened his breath to gasps. Allyn was heading into Irons' chosen territory, and the deserted air of the place oppressed him. He had been a part of a crowd when he had been there last. He never thought of how isolated the Bowl could be when the music stopped.

Allyn stopped and stared up the short, sharp ascent to the amphitheater. The canvas barrier at the first entrance was pulled back invitingly. Instinct agreed with tactics, and he went on past it. He crossed to the second entrance, where the canvas was still in place.

He mounted the steps, keeping close to the dark shadow of the escalator, then slipped through the heavy canvas sheet. He paused at the next canvas, listening.

His stomach roiled with a compound of fury and fear.

Darkness was speaking with Rick Irons' voice.

Thirty-Seven

37

*T*he last chords rang into silence. Quinn laid his right palm flat across the strings and stood gazing down at the old guitar for a long moment.

He switched off the power to the amp then slipped the shoulder strap over his head, dropped the pick he held onto the dresser top, and wiped the vintage instrument with a polishing cloth before putting it back on its stand. Whatever release he had hoped for in the music eluded him.

He glanced at the acoustic guitar by the bed and the untidy clutter of papers on the bench. He needed to work on the new song while it was still fresh in his mind. It was a promise to the future. He knew it, but it didn't comfort him.

If only Allyn will get back. If only Kincaid and Taglia will bring Carys back to us. If only... He wasn't sure what else to wish for, so he let the thought hang. He considered taking a little bump to ease the worry, but Allyn was facing all of it without buffers. It would be wrong not to do the same.

Quinn rose, stretched, then headed for the door. Maybe Rossington had heard something. Maybe he had gotten through, and the forces of order were converging on the new location, even now.

The phone rang as he stepped into the den. Rossington grabbed the headphones and turned his attention to the recorder as Quinn crossed to answer it.

"It's Babcock," a voiced snapped before he had a chance to speak. "Let me speak to my partner."

Quinn silently handed the receiver to Rossington.

"Hal?" Rossington met Quinn's glance, brown eyes wide with surprise, then he shed the headphones and reached for the receiver. "What's up? Where's Sterling?" There was a pause. Rossington clapped his free hand to the back of his neck.

"...roared off down the damn road!" Babcock' voice was so loud Quinn could hear it without the speakers.

Rossington jerked the phone away from his ear. "Damn, Hal, you're gonna blow out my eardrums! What happened?"

"I don't know!" His voice didn't lose much volume. "We stopped so that I could, uh, we stopped for a minute, and he took off back down Mulholland toward town. I figure he's headed for the Bowl."

Rossington shook his head. "You were supposed to stay with him, Hal, not take a leak in somebody's flower bed! Where are you now?" After scribbling notes on a napkin, he snapped, "Sit tight. I'll send somebody after you." He slammed the receiver into the cradle, muttering, "Idiot!"

Quinn smiled grimly. "You must go after him, you know."

"Babcock? Hell, I'm tempted to let him stew in his own juice. By the way, I didn't get a chance to tell you. Just before the phone rang, I got through to the station. SWAT is on the way to the Bowl."

"That is good news, but I actually meant Allyn. You have to go after Allyn. Can you get to the Bowl before Ortiz's people do?"

Rossington considered. "Maybe, if I run Code 3 all the way. Depends a lot on the traffic."

Quinn lit a cigarette. "You could pick up Babcock and go on to the Bowl. You might have to be their backup, in case SWAT gets delayed."

"Can't do it. I'm not supposed to leave you here alone." Rossington began to pace, then paused. "You'd stay here?"

"Where on earth would I go? How would I get there? Everything with wheels is on the road to the Bowl right now — saving your car, of course. I sincerely doubt Rick is going to come here after me. And if he does, I have a pistol. I'm a reasonable shot. I will be fine. Just go."

Rossington frowned doubtfully before nodding. "All right. Come lock the door behind me."

Quinn followed the cop into the foyer. He shut the door and locked it, listening until he heard the sound of the Chevy fade down the road.

Silence swelled, filling the house as he returned to the den. He glanced at the radio but had no patience for anyone else's recordings and least of all for his own. Fear gnawed at him. He had no idea where either of them was. He had no idea if either one of them would come back. The pressure of that thought shook him to his core.

He had no idea what he would do if they didn't.

There's a way through. There's always the heroin.

He shook his head. *Not yet. There's always later. Not yet.*

He wandered back to his bedroom, sat down on the edge of the bed, gathered the acoustic guitar in his arms and rested his lips on its smooth side. The wood was cool against his mouth. Dread stalked him, and he had only the fragile box of wood and steel to shield him.

It took less time than Taglia expected to crest the hill that formed the back wall of the Bowl's natural amphitheater. He crouched low in the brush at the top of the hill and took a moment to catch his breath. The amphitheater stretched out below him, the four main aisles curving through the seats as they sloped down to the stage. To Taglia, the paths looked as though someone had drawn the image of a hot-air balloon on the ground with the stage as the gondola.

The white, domed stage was dimly lit by overhead spotlights, revealing the tall pillars that outlined the back of the stage and spread out to either side like wings. Taglia slipped his walkie-talkie off his belt and raised it to his lips. "I have lights on the stage," he whispered into the mesh screen covering the microphone.

"The downside entrance is open," Kincaid's voice whispered back. "If you're ready, I'm coming in."

"Ten-four," he replied and returned the walkie-talkie to its holster. He quietly worked his way the last few yards out of the shrubbery to the back row of audience seating.

A tall figure with a briefcase in his hand walked cautiously through the left-side entrance nearest the stage. He paused and looked around warily. Even though Taglia knew the man was Kincaid, he admired his performance. Allyn, he suspected, would have entered just the same.

"Come on in, Allyn," an unamplified voice called from the wings, carrying to the back seats as the stage lights came up to bright. "I've been waiting for you long enough."

Taglia slipped over the waist-high wall and crouched behind the last row of seats, raising his head just high enough to see the stage. After a few seconds, a man and a child emerged from stage-left. The man was dressed in a bulky black sweatshirt and jeans. The girl was dressed in a white nightgown. Her face was a pale blur, and her tousled hair caught the stage lights. Her wrists were secured behind her back, and the man held her by her right arm. There was no doubt in his mind that this was Carys Sterling.

She walked quietly with Irons until she saw Kincaid. *"Daddy! No!"* she cried, trying to jerk her arm away from her captor.

Irons forced Carys to move forward, stopping when they reached center stage. He pulled her close in front of himself, wrapping his left hand around her slender throat to hold her still. His other hand held a revolver, pointed at Kincaid.

Kincaid started forward again, following the aisle between the Pool Circle and the Garden Boxes, where the rich and the lucky had their seats. He halted a third of the way around the stage and turned to face it, holding up his free hand to shield his eyes from the stage lights, obscuring his face. Taglia moved with him, staying low and using the bench seating as a shield. Their plan was that by coming in from Irons' left, while Kincaid stayed to his right, they'd be able to keep his attention on "Allyn" so that he would miss Taglia's stealthy approach.

"Daddy," Carys whimpered. The acoustics carried the fear in her voice.

Irons grinned. "Hey, Peacock. Glad you made it. Not much traffic, I guess. Did you bring the money?"

"Yeah." Kincaid held up the case. The single syllable could pass for a Welsh accent.

"Okay! I knew you'd come through. I knew you couldn't resist being a fucking hero! Assholes — you and Quinn both. I deserve this money! You know why? Because the two of you put me through hell. When I was on tour with Leviathon, I spent all my time keeping the audience from finding out what a lousy guitarist Quinn really is. And how did he thank me? He destroyed my career. He tried to destroy me!"

Good. Taglia smiled as he drew his gun. *He's going to be a talker.* He started toward the stage, moving slowly but steadily. In the dark, he had to feel with his feet for the steps as he reached them. A fall at this point would be disastrous.

"So," Irons went on cheerfully, "now it's your turn to spend your life in living hell. You think you know what that means? You think you've seen the worst hell has to offer in the last couple of days? You're wrong. This is the beginning. You're going to learn — both of you. You know how? Little Miss Carys here. I'm not quite through with her yet.

"You're pretty soft on her, aren't you? I remember how you always talked about her. You always wanted to go home to her, even while you were teasing me and tormenting me and leading me on. Well, here she is, Peacock. You know, I could kill her right here in front of you and there'd be nothing you could do to stop me." Irons shifted his gaze to the gun in his hand. Still smiling cheerfully, he raised the gun and pressed the muzzle against the side of Carys's head.

"Don't!" Kincaid's spoke sharply, taking a single step forward.

Irons' eyes jerked back to Kincaid. His voice turned into a snarl. "Stay where you are!"

Kincaid stopped. Taglia, midway down the aisle, froze in place as well, hoping Irons' wouldn't take the opportunity to look around the arena.

Long seconds passed, then Irons' express softened into a smile. "There. That's good. See, Peacock? You *are* learning to listen to me." He glanced down at Carys, still smiling, then looked back at Kincaid. "So, where was I? Oh, yeah. I could trade her for you. I could keep you for myself, the way Quinn has. In case you haven't noticed, tonight's my night. I can do anything I want."

Taglia started moving forward again.

"Do you know what my favorite part of my plan is? It's Quinn. Moody thinks he'll hunt me down, but Moody's an idiot. I won't even have to lay a finger on Quinn. Once he realizes he'll never get you back, he'll save me the trouble. He'll drink some booze, pop some pills, shove the old needle in his arm and pull the plug himself. And then you are mine forever."

Taglia was a third of the way down the aisle. He gritted his teeth, wishing he could move faster. He felt for another step and kept going.

Irons paused, eyes still on Kincaid as he lowered the gun to his side. When he spoke again, his voice was soft, persuasive. "It doesn't have to come to that, Peacock. No one has to die. All I want is for you to come with me. Of your own free will. You know you want to. You've wanted to give yourself to me since we first met. Come on up here now. Bring the money, and we'll all three walk out of here together."

"No. Leave Carys here."

"I can't do that, Peacock. I've grown to like her company. We just want you to join us."

Taglia had reached the halfway point when Kincaid finally lowered his arm from in front of his face. He held up his shield, which glinted gold in the lights from the stage. "I can't do that either, Rick" Kincaid's tone was calm, authoritative. "You need to let Carys go. I'm a police officer, and this place is surrounded. You aren't going to make it this way, Rick."

Taglia had reached the last benched aisle, behind the high-priced box seats. He was still at least fifty feet away, and it wasn't close enough. He never took his gaze off the figures on the stage as he crept forward.

"Lousy fucking coward!" Irons' cry of rage was tinged with fear. He swung the gun back at Kincaid. "Where is he? You get that blond bastard out here, or I'll send his brat home in pieces."

"She's just a little girl, Rick. She hasn't done anything to you." Kincaid held out the briefcase again. "There's a quarter of a million in cash in here. Just like you asked. Let's work a deal. The money for the girl."

Irons licked his lips. Silence followed.

Taglia froze in the quiet, then Kincaid stepped forward to the wall surrounding the Pool Circle. He set the briefcase on the wide top edge and opened it. "Come on, Rick. Let's trade."

"No." Irons was still angry, but something was gone from his voice — some edge of conviction. "I don't want the money. I don't *need* the fucking money. It's Moody who wants it. Him and Harry. I — I want Allyn." His voice roughened and he bellowed, "You get your ass to a phone. You call him, and you tell him I want to see him. *Now*. We do it my way, or she's dead."

"Moody's dead, Rick. Harry's in jail. You're alone in this, Rick, but we can make a deal. Let me help you out of this mess."

"You don't understand!" Irons' shout cut him off, and Taglia used the man's attention on Kincaid to slip forward to the Pool Circle wall, and crouching low, follow it to the right toward the stage-access stairs.

"They *used* me, man. They used me, and when they were done they said 'fuck off' and didn't care what happened to me. My whole career went down the toilet because of them. Allyn was always such a fucking rock-god. You couldn't touch him. Everybody thinks he's something special, and nobody believes it more than him."

Kincaid stepped forward again, and Irons straightened. He held the child like a shield, his gun still aimed dead-center at Kincaid's chest. "Him and Quinn," he went on hoarsely. "Taking whatever they want and too good for anybody but each other. Allyn came on to me all the time, but it was one big private bullshit joke. I saw them when they didn't know anyone else was around. I know all about them. I don't want the money. I want them. I'll get them, too. You wait and see. Even if I take the money and go right now, I won't stop. I'll never stop. You get Allyn out here. Now!"

He stepped forward, dragging Carys with him. She stumbled and fell, twisting out of his grip. Sobbing, she landed in a sitting position, hands still tied behind her back. She scrambled toward the back of the stage as fast as she could move.

Taglia realized something was wrong when Irons let her go.

A shadowed figure walked down the outside aisle to the edge of the Pool Circle. When he drew next to Kincaid, light from the stage flamed unmistakably in Allyn's hair.

"Get out of here." Kincaid's low voice was taut with anger.

Goddamn it, Allyn... Taglia's concentration shattered. Allyn's presence changed everything. Any possibility of Irons' surrender was gone. He stood, gun aimed at the kidnapper. "Police!" he shouted. "Freeze!"

Kincaid reacted to his partner's shout, picking up the briefcase and hurling it at Irons. He spun on Allyn, catching him around the chest and bearing both of them to the ground.

Irons' gun roared, the bullet going wild above the two prone men. Taglia fired and missed. Irons hesitated, then fired again, this time at him.

Taglia felt a punch in the chest like a mule's kick and breathing was suddenly difficult. There was a bright blossom of pain, and he felt himself falling. The ground at the foot of the stairs rushed up to meet him.

Bird of Paradise
G.J. Paterson
280

Still covering Allyn's body with his own, Kincaid heard Taglia fall. He rose to his knees, shooting as soon as he was sure the little girl was clear. The bullet caught Irons in the right arm above the elbow. The man screamed and doubled over as the gun flipped out of his hand, arcing upward and crashing down again at the back of the stage.

"Stay down!" Kincaid hissed at Allyn through clenched teeth, then scrambled to his feet and ran for the stairs.

Taglia lay curled on his side at the foot of the steps. His eyes were wide but unfocussed, his breath coming in bubbling gasps.

Kincaid knew he had to get to Irons before more damage was done. "Hang on, Paul," he said. "I'll be right back."

"Go," Taglia whispered. "Get... Carys... Hurry."

Thirty-Eight 38

Irons stumbled toward Carys, his right arm hanging at his side at an awkward angle, blood dripping from his fingertips. He caught her arm with his left hand. Carys fought for all she was worth, wrenching and twisting her upper body, kicking with her bare heels. Her struggles distracted Irons, keeping him from reaching his gun.

Allyn jumped to his feet and vaulted the railing separating the audience from the flat surface of the empty Pool Circle. He ran across the wide, open Pool Circle, put his hands on the stage, boosted himself up and leapt to his feet.

He was across the stage in a few long strides. He swung his right fist over Carys's head and caught Irons full in the jaw. He glimpsed Kincaid beside him, catching Carys and pulling her to safety.

"You bloody fucking bastard!" He grabbed Irons' shirtfront to keep him from falling. Irons clutched his arm with his left hand.

Allyn jerked free, drawing back for another punch. In the distance someone shouted his name. It wasn't Carys's voice, so he ignored it.

His second blow smashed into Irons' nose and blood spurted. Irons screamed, stumbling backwards.

"Oh, did that hurt?" Allyn swept a leg, kicking Irons' feet out from under him. He released his grip, and the stocky man dropped hard. Irons landed on his broken arm and sobbed, gripping his shoulder.

"Too fucking bad!" He caught the man's shirtfront and hauled him to his feet again. "If you ever — " a short jab to the stomach, " — so much as think — " a hard knee to the balls bent Irons double, retching, " — of Carys's name again — " something irritating grabbed his cocked arm, trying to pull him backward, " — I *will* kill you!"

The irritating something didn't let go, and he whirled to face his new attacker.

He came face-to-face with a black clad SWAT officer.

The sight of the cop's face brought back sanity. Breathing hard, Allyn lowered his arm. He released Irons' shirt and let him fall to the floor. Irons curled up in a ball, moaning.

"You okay?" the cop asked as another officer grabbed Irons' arm to cuff him. "You aren't going to keep trying to kill the guy if I let go?"

"Yeah. I'm good. Where's Carys?"

She was standing a few feet away, Kincaid's arm wrapped loosely around her shoulders. When Allyn saw her, he dropped to his knees. She raced into his arms, and he wrapped his arms around her and buried his face in her hair. Kincaid ran back to the stairs and down to his partner.

Sirens blared in the distance as Kincaid searched feverishly for the source of the blood on Taglia's shirt. He murmured, "Easy, Paul. Carys is safe, and everything's all right. I'm here. I've got you."

Taglia stirred and moaned at his touch, then he choked. Blood, pink and bubbling with the air from the wound, trickled out of the hole in his chest. Kincaid immediately tried to staunch it with his hand. Blood covered his fingers, and he could feel the flow of air back and forth from the wound. "Medic!" he yelled. "Officer down!"

It felt like hours before the paramedics arrived, swarming into position with their gurney and bags of equipment. A medic replaced his barehanded pressure on the wound with a thick wad of gauze. Kincaid stayed where he was, taking one of Taglia's hands in his as he whispered, "Stay with me, Paul. Just stay with me."

A second paramedic arrived and took him by the shoulders, forcibly moving him aside. "Give us room to work, officer," he said, then Kincaid found himself standing outside of the circle of professionals as they swiftly prepared Taglia to transport.

"Jeff?" Allyn said. He stood behind Kincaid, Carys in his arms.

"What do you want?"

"Is he badly hurt?"

"He saved your life."

"I know. I... Oh, gods." The singer's voice sounded strained.

The swirl of people separated them from Kincaid, and he lost sight of the singer and his daughter. Kincaid looked back toward his partner but Taglia was hidden behind a wall paramedics. He bit his lip and turned away, watching bedlam seethe around him. Detectives and patrolmen were pouring through the entrances as SWAT swept through the amphitheater. More paramedics hustled a stretcher and large totes of equipment onto the stage for Irons.

The activity in the amphitheater felt as distant as watching a poorly-written movie. His only reality was Taglia's blood on his hands.

Then Ortiz was there, handing him a cloth for his hands and trying to move him away from where the paramedics were working. "Get out of these men's way, Lieutenant. I need your help talking to the little girl." The captain's voice was brusque but steady.

Kincaid tried to focus. "But Paul..."

"Let the medics do their job, Kincaid. You can't help them."

"I want to stay with him.

"They need room to work. Come over here, with me."

Kincaid followed his captain to Sterling and Carys. He couldn't help noticing the paramedics onstage working on Irons, who was sitting up on the gurney. He sucked in a breath. *I shot a man tonight. Just this one case and we've both shot someone. I.A. is going to have a field day.*

Ortiz had found father and daughter. Allyn's eyes met his with anxious gaze. Carys, still wrapped in his arms, held her stuffed lion and pressed herself close to her father. Fear and incomprehension darkened her cornflower blue eyes.

Allyn looked away first. He brushed a light kiss against Carys's hair as they approached then whispered something in her ear. She nodded. Allyn freed her from the folds of his cloak and put her down. He didn't let go of her hand. "Carys, I'd like for you to meet two friends of ours. Captain Ortiz and Lieutenant Kincaid. Gentlemen, this is my daughter Carys."

Carys gazed at him with round, solemn eyes. She was taller than he'd imagined. Even with her hair in disarray and a dirty nightdress, she was a pretty child.

Fuck I.A. Saving her was worth it.

Ortiz crouched in front of her to meet her at eye-level. Kincaid did the same. "I can't tell you how glad we are to meet you, Carys," Ortiz said. "Your dad has told us a lot about you. We've been very worried about you. Are you okay? Did he hurt you?"

"No, sir. But he scared me."

"I bet he did. How did he scare you?"

"He talked about Daddy all the time. He hit me once. And grabbed me by the neck." She lifted her free hand to her throat.

Ortiz nodded. "We'd like you to go to the doctor. He can look you over and make sure you're all right. Would it be okay with you?"

"I guess. Can Dad come, too?"

"We want for you to ride in an ambulance. We'll have a lady officer going with you, and I don't think Dad will fit — but he can meet you at the hospital."

"Oh." She bit her bottom lip, then met Kincaid's gaze. "I knew you weren't Dad right away, but I kept calling you 'Daddy,' so Rick wouldn't know. Was that okay?

"You did exactly the right thing." Kincaid smiled at her.

"What about the other policeman?" she asked. "The one Rick shot?"

"He'll be fine," Kincaid replied. There was no way he was going to frighten this child further with any other possibility. Still, he glanced toward the paramedics as he spoke. Taglia was on the stretcher now, and they were rolling it toward the entrance.

Carys is fine, and they're both alive. Because of us, partner. Hold on, dammit! Hold on!

"I'm sure you want me to explain myself," Allyn said to Ortiz as the ambulances departed with their passengers. "I promised Carys I'd meet her at the hospital. Can I give you my statement there?"

Ortiz nodded. "I'll drive you down, if you'd be willing to wait awhile."

"Thank you. I have a car." He drew his cloak close and set off across the parking lot alone.

Ortiz watched him a moment, then turned to Kincaid. "What was Sterling doing here?"

"Fucking things up."

The Captain nodded. "Why don't you go on to the hospital? I've got to check on things here, then I'll be down."

"Thanks. I'll see you there." Kincaid pulled his keys out of his pocket and stared at them. He had a key to Taglia's car. Taglia had one to his. "I think I'll take Paul's car. Can you get the Jag back to the house?"

"No problem."

It seemed a long way to the Muse of Music. The wind rustled in a pile of leaves and discarded paper as he crossed the empty expanse of concrete, stretching away into the darkness. The shoulder of the hill beyond it loomed, cutting off the city lights. Kincaid walked down the sidewalk toward the white fountain where Taglia had parked the Trans Am. He rounded the statue and was almost to the car before he noticed the figure waiting.

Allyn stood beside the Trans Am. His dark cloak moved in the breeze. The light from the statue bleached the color from his hair and cast his face in shadows.

"What are you doing here?" Kincaid stopped a few paces from his car.

"Waiting for you."

"What do you want?"

"To hitch a ride." Allyn's voice was quiet, vulnerable. Kincaid hated the sound of it. "I forgot — My car's not safe to drive. I was hoping I might go down to the hospital with you, if you didn't mind."

"What if I do mind?"

Allyn sighed. "I understand, but there's something else. An officer told me the barricade down at the turn into Bowl Drive is swarming with reporters. I'd like to avoid them if I can."

Kincaid snorted, unlocked his door and got in. He shut it and glanced over at the seat where, if the world was as it should be, he would be bracing himself for another of Taglia's wild rides. If the world was as it should be. *It isn't though. The world is just the world, and Paul is riding down to the hospital with a bullet in his chest. Jesus what am I going to do if he dies?*

He leaned over and unlocked the passenger door, then pulled off the wig and threw it into the back seat while Allyn got in the car.

When the passenger door shut, Kincaid started the car. Allyn ducked below the windows as they passed through the barricades and flashbulbs. He sat up again as the car turned onto Cahuenga. Finally, Kincaid glanced across at his unwanted guest and asked, "Do you ever think about anybody but yourself?"

"I beg your pardon?" Allyn asked stiffly.

"I said, do you ever think of anybody but yourself? Or are you as sure of your worth as you seem?"

"I'm not certain I understand what you mean."

"Oh, no? Well, let me help you. For starters, you almost got Paul killed back there. He still might die. Because you had to be in on the action."

"No, Jeff. Irons insisted I be there." Allyn sounded desperate for understanding. Kincaid ignored the appeal. "It was a bad deal, everybody said so. Detective Babcock said you might get shot if there wasn't any backup. I just got... scared."

"I almost had him talked down when you butted in."

"I wasn't going to go in as long as everything sounded like it was under control. Would I take that kind of chance with Carys?"

"That's not the point," Kincaid said. "The point is I don't think you came down here to save Carys as much as you did to be in on the action and be a goddamned hero."

"I stood outside listening for a long time. Then I heard what he said about wanting me there." He sighed and glanced out the side window. "I never meant for anyone to get hurt because of me. What else could I do?"

"You could've used your head! If anybody's a hero tonight, it's Paul."

"Jeff, I..." There was a moment of silence. At last Allyn said, "I suppose you feel I deserve this?"

"If I told you what I thought you deserved, I might be tempted to do something about it myself."

Allyn didn't respond. All in all, Kincaid had to admit, silence was Allyn's wisest choice.

The hospital emergency parking lot was well lit and crowded with police cars. More were coming in behind them. Kincaid wheeled into a space marked "Police Only" and cut the engine. He got out and headed for the glass double doors without bothering to notice if his passenger followed or not.

Allyn laid a hand on his arm as they reached the door. Kincaid spun to face him, knowing from the way the singer stepped back that fury blazed in his eyes. Allyn let his hand fall away. "Jeff, you make it sound as if I wanted Paul to get hurt. I never meant..."

"The hell with that," Kincaid snapped. "And the hell with you, too."

Thirty-Nine   39

Quinn dropped his bedroom curtain back into place and glanced at his watch for what had to be the twentieth time in as many minutes. He shrugged and looked back to the bed where his work waited. Worry had replaced interest, and he couldn't focus on the new song.

"No use trying to do anything in this state," he muttered and headed out the door, making his way down the hall and flipping on the den lights.

He crossed to the bar, hesitated, then switched on the FM radio, hoping there might be news. Just the sound of another voice would be some comfort. Instead, the last few bars of "Don't You Leave," from Leviathon's first album, rang into the quiet. He listened to the end of the song with bemusement. It was always a little disconcerting to hear his own music on the air.

The announcer's voice at the conclusion of the song interrupted his reverie. "Repeating a story we broke here about four minutes ago, early reports are coming in — Allyn Sterling of Leviathon has reportedly been shot and killed. Reports from the Hollywood Bowl indicate Sterling was cut down when he attempted to intervene between police and the kidnapper of his eight-year-old daughter. At the present time, police haven't released a statement, but we'll keep you up-to-date with the latest information as we receive it. We'll continue with our tribute to Leviathon's world-famous lead singer after these messages..."

A commercial began. Quinn stood for a moment gazing down at a pair of hands clutching the edge of the bar with white knuckles before he realized they were his own. Taking a deep breath, he forced his grip to relax. Without haste he turned off the radio.

He found the yellow file box and searched under "P" for photographer. He found the number and dialed.

"This is Chris," a voice on the phone said.

"Is it true?" he asked.

"Who is this? Derek?" Chris Derry asked, worry tingeing his voice. "Oh, man. I am so sorry."

"You believe it then?"

"I've heard it from two separate sources. Something serious went down at the Bowl, judging from all the police chatter. I was heading out the door to find out more information when you called."

"I see," Quinn said. "Thank you." He hung up the phone without waiting to hear more.

It seems odd you should be gone. He had always assumed he would know somehow if anything happened to the unpredictable golden sun at the center of his orbit. Somehow he would know.

He opened a fresh bottle of whiskey and carried it back to the bedroom. He sat on the edge of the bed, set the bottle on the floor, picked up the acoustic guitar, and went back to work.

He passed the next forty-five minutes methodically working through the music. When he put down the pencil at last, he sighed and stood, took another swig from the bottle and carried his acoustic guitar to its stand beside the others. Standing there, gazing down at Sweet Fire, his throat tightened. His eyes narrowed, and the muscles in his jaws clenched as he fought down the wave of blackness threatening to swamp him.

He ran his fingertips across the face of the headstock, feeling the tiny difference in texture when they crossed the word "Fender." He squatted down before the guitar and touched the polished surface. Eyes alone were not enough to commit its being to memory. His moving fingers found all the familiar dents and chips in the finish. He paused for a moment, tracing the burled knot that resembled a dragon's head. It was still beautiful, though battered and worn. It had seen many miles and many years.

He touched the strings. They sounded back to him softly. Good strings, at their prime. At the perfect stage before they go flat and dead.

Dead.

The word echoed in Quinn's mind as though filtered through a harmonizer. The next breath was hard to draw. The words engraved on the gleaming silver pick-guard swam before his eyes. *Sweet Fire.*

He had completed this ritual many times. This time he took special care to be aware of every movement as if he were preparing the Tea Ceremony for an honored guest. He lit a candle, set it on the nightstand beside him and began the process of dissolving the heroin.

He pushed up the sleeve of his shirt, strapped a length of rubber tubing around his arm above the elbow and pumped his fist a few times. The large vein in the crook of his arm popped up. He hadn't used it in a long time, but he no longer cared if the mark showed. He didn't wince against the negligible prick of the needle, watching as its steel sank into his flesh. After a moment he pushed the plunger home.

He loosened the tourniquet and withdrew the needle in a smooth one-handed movement with the grace of long practice. He let them fall to the floor and lay back on the bed as the rush swept over him.

It sped like loosening fire all along his veins and spread outward from his loins until his whole body seemed to melt with chemical ecstasy. Even in the heat of the fiery embrace, his heart reminded him this surrogate was in no way an acceptable substitute for what was lost.

He surrendered himself to the aftermath without hesitation or resistance. Languidly he moved his head on the pillows. His gaze found the flame of the candle and he stared into the golden brightness, he remembered a day long ago, standing and watching the sick man on his tattered couch and wondering what impact his enemy's Trojan Horse would have.

A ghost of his old smile touched his lips. *Ah, Sammy. Now we know. Now we know.*

Time dragged toward stop. He was conscious of a floating sensation, drifting on an endless warm pink sea. Soon, he knew with detached certainty, he would follow his thoughts down to the fathomless depths of that ocean.

A phone rang nearby. He ignored it. He was free of such considerations and responsibilities now.

The bell rang on.

Forty 40

"Hello, hello, hello," cried a man from the emergency room entrance. "What's all this, then?"

Allyn recognized the drummer's voice and raised his head from his hands. Avery Potts smiled and waved at him. Gilbert McConathy was a pace or two behind him, holding Lydia Calhoun's hand. Jackie Carlisle came next, with Milton Ables, Martin Cohen and Blaine Harris bringing up the rear.

Allyn found himself smiling back with relief. He stood up as they pushed their way through the sea of cops packing the waiting room.

Somehow, Lydia reached him first. "Oh, Mr. Sterling!" Tears ran down her face as she clutched her hands together at her breast, almost as if praying. "I've never been so happy as when you called to say you got Carys back! Where is she?"

Allyn took her shoulders. "She's fine, Lydia. The doctor has checked her out and she's just fine. She's in talking to a psychologist right now, but I think we'll be able to take her home once she's finished."

Her smile vanished, and Lydia was instantly back in nanny mode. "We'll not be taking her back to that awful house, Mr. Sterling. I'll take her to the hotel and she can stay in my room with me until you make other arrangements!"

With a grave nod of agreement, Allyn said, "Absolutely right."

"I shall speak to Mr. Ables about it immediately, sir."

Avery pushed into the space Lydia vacated as she marched away, followed by Gil, Cohen and Harris. The musicians seemed happy, but Harris's face was pasty white. Cohen was haggard. "Good to see you again," the drummer interjected angrily. "Especially since the radio said you were dead."

"Avery..." Gil sighed.

"Dead? Me?"

"Yeah, we heard it as soon as we got into the limo to come over here. They said Irons shot you. Well, they didn't say Irons. They called him 'the kidnapper.'"

"No one was killed. But Paul — Sergeant Taglia, was shot. Irons was too. I'm waiting for Carys, but I'm also waiting to see how badly Paul's hurt. They've taken him into emergency surgery."

"That explains the room full of coppers, then, don't it?" Avery grinned at last and shook Allyn's hand. "I knew you'd get our girl back."

"So where's Derek?" Gil asked.

"He's still at the house with his bodyguard. I'm supposed to be there too, but... well, it's a long story, and I'll give it to you some other time. I tried to call him a few minutes ago to let him know all's well but I didn't get an answer. He may be in the studio. He has a new song he's working on. He's was transcribing it for you, Gillie."

Avery interjected, "We tried to call him too, from the phone in the car. We didn't get an answer either. You said he has a bodyguard there? Strange the bodyguard wouldn't answer the phone."

A chill brushed across the back of Allyn's neck as he remembered Derek explaining the studio phone to Taglia. *I know there are times you like your solitude, Dee, but you'd never shut yourself away from the world, especially not now. Why didn't you answer the phone? Why didn't Rossington answer it?*

His chest suddenly felt tight. He gestured toward the waiting area where Ortiz sat. "Listen, lads, I'm going to go call again. Why don't you sit over there and I'll be back in a few minutes." He turned and strode away quickly, heading for the nearest pay phone.

The phone rang for nearly two minutes before Allyn hung up. His breath caught in his throat, and he ran a hand over his face in an effort to stay calm. *"No one knows what will happen."* The memory of Quinn's voice was immediately followed by the memory of Iron's laugh. *"You know the best part of this? It's Quinn. I won't even have to go after him... he'll save me the trouble..."*

Bile burned the back of Allyn's throat as he looked around the crowded hallway for Kincaid. *Damn him forever! Rick's going to prison, but he can still reach out and take you away from me. Oh gods, Dee, what have you done?*

He couldn't find Kincaid anywhere inside the emergency area, so he went back to where Ortiz was waiting. The Leviathon entourage sat nearby, talking, and didn't notice when he leaned down to Ortiz and asked him, "Where's Lieutenant Kincaid?"

"I think he went outside," Ortiz responded, coming alert. He kept his voice quiet as he went on, "Is something wrong?"

"I hope not." He headed for the exit as swiftly as his long legs could carry him. Ortiz followed. They found Kincaid in the parking lot coming back from Paul's car.

Allyn ran to him. "Derek's not answering the phone, and the radio is broadcasting that I'm dead."

Kincaid replied, "Rossington's not at the house. He and Babcock are both here." His fierce stare spoke volumes. The captain's expression went taut and angry in agreement. "Quinn's at the house by himself. Would he hurt himself?"

The words turned Allyn's blood cold. "Will you take me there?"

"Paul's still in surgery."

"I know, and Carys's still with her doctor. I have to leave without telling her."

"I'll watch over them both," Ortiz interrupted.

Kincaid glared at Allyn for several seconds. The singer could see the contempt in that level, blue-eyed gaze. "Shit," Kincaid said at last. "Are you ever anything but trouble? We'll take the Trans Am."

They drove with red lights and sirens all the way. Kincaid was amazed Allyn didn't urge him to greater speed. He tried to concentrate on driving, but he kept remembering the feel of Paul's blood on his hand as he pressed his palm into his partner's chest. The rasping of Paul's breath had wrenched something in his soul. *What will happen if he dies? What will happen if he lives?*

He clenched his fists on the steering wheel and knew he was facing his own personal crossroads.

The singer slouched in the passenger's seat, nibbling on the knuckle of his right index finger and gazing out the window while the night whipped past. "I wonder...."

Kincaid was almost relieved by the momentary distraction as they turned onto Benedict Canyon Road. "What?"

"Oh. Sorry," Allyn glanced at him. "I didn't know I was talking out loud. I just wondered if Quinn heard the same radio broadcast as Avery."

"Why?"

"Because then we should have some indication how long ago he OD'ed. If that's what he's done."

"I get the feeling you're pretty sure he's done something," Kincaid said. He told himself he shouldn't care, but he did. He liked Quinn and hoped Allyn's fears were wrong. Besides, in spite of his earlier anger, his sympathy was aroused.

"My grandmother had the Sight, you know," said Allyn at last. "I... I get these feelings sometimes. Usually I'm wrong. I hope I am now."

"Do you really think he'd OD?"

"He's got a gun," Allyn replied bitterly. "He'd use it on someone else if he had reason, mind you. But he wouldn't shoot himself. A famous rocker dying of a drug overdose doesn't look so much like a suicide that way, if you take my meaning. 'Live fast, die young, leave a good-looking corpse.' Just another flaming crash out of the fast lane."

Kincaid glanced at the singer. Allyn's face was tense. Pity stirred. "We'll make it."

Allyn gave a small smile. "You're a good man, Lieutenant. I can understand why he loves you."

"What?" Kincaid glanced at him again, startled. *"Quinn?"*

"No, you arse," Allyn said with a hint of laughter. "Paul."

"What the hell do you know about who Paul does or doesn't love?" Kincaid snapped, his anger back in spades.

"He told me."

"Why the fuck would he tell you? He never said anything to me."

"Perhaps you wouldn't let him."

There was no time to respond to that. They were finally at the house. Kincaid killed the siren as he turned the Trans Am into the driveway. Gravel crunched under the tires as they pulled up to the empty carport.

Allyn had his door open before the car rolled to a complete stop. He ran up the shallow steps and unlocked the front door, flinging it open. Kincaid followed him in

They paused inside the den door, and Allyn shouted, "Derek!" There was no sound in the house anywhere. Allyn glanced toward the kitchen and the studio beyond then turned abruptly and strode down the hall to Quinn's room. At the door, he paused with his hand on the knob and took a deep breath. He entered without knocking.

Forty-One

41

"Oh, my gods," Allyn whispered. He gripped the doorjamb with his left hand for support. Kincaid peered around his shoulder into the room.

Quinn lay sprawled on the wide bed. His right hand rested on his breast. His left arm stretched along his side, palm up, the long fingers unflexed as if in a gesture of appeal. His face was white and bathed in sweat.

Holding his breath, Allyn leaned over him and touched his left hand. It was cold and clammy.

"How bad is it?" Kincaid picked up the phone to dial 911.

"I don't know yet." He searched for a pulse and found it — thready and rapid, but present.

Quinn's breathing came in a slow, shallow effort that seemed ineffectual, as if each breath was more exhausting than the one before it. Allyn could hear a faint rattle on the inhalation, sure proof of the failing struggle.

He unclasped his cloak and spread the heavy wool mantle over the unconscious man. He cradled Quinn's head while he pulled the pillow out from beneath it. He let the guitarist's head down and tipped his chin up to allow for easier breathing. With gentle fingers, Allyn brushed unruly strands of dark hair from Quinn's forehead. His eyes stung, and he bit his lower lip as he turned away. "Will you watch him for a moment? He may have trouble breathing. I'll be right back."

Allyn hurried out of the room and down the hall to his own room. The Narcan box was still in the drawer.

Quinn was already in the restricted area of the ER when Kincaid walked into reception. Allyn, who had ridden in the ambulance, stood by the registration desk. He saw the haunted look in the singer's eyes as he approached. The silence between them was awkward.

After several seconds, Allyn drew a deep breath. "Miltie will take care of all the admission paperwork, but they had me sign as Quinn's 'responsible party.' That's rich, innit? I'm responsible."

Kincaid shook his head. "It's not your fault, Allyn."

"You think not? I only wish that were true." Allyn cleared his throat, "Is this a good hospital, then?"

"Yeah, it is. Derek is in good hands."

"Good." Allyn's gaze drifted toward the doors leading to the treatment area. "Thank you for your help."

Kincaid nodded but couldn't bring himself to acknowledge the comment. "Let's go sit down with the others."

The waiting room was slightly less crowded than it had been earlier, but there were still a couple dozen police present. Ortiz was back in his chair near the band. The band was passing time by reading magazines or talking quietly. The only person missing was Lydia Calhoun.

Kincaid and Allyn pulled up chairs on either side of Ortiz.

"How's Quinn?" Ortiz asked. Despite his quiet tone, everyone associated with the band turned to Allyn for the answer.

Allyn cleared his throat. "He's in for treatment right now. I don't know anything else."

"What's Quinn gotten himself into this time?" Avery asked.

Allyn said, "We don't know for sure. He was barely breathing when we found him."

"Ah, well we all know what he is." Avery nodded. "Bound to catch up with him sometime."

"I'd hoped we were done with that after Paris," Gil said while looking over his latest hand in the gin rummy game he was playing with Jackie.

"Paris was *not* his fault." Allyn looked back at Ortiz. "Where's Carys?"

Ortiz smiled. "The nurse brought her back just a few minutes ago and said she could go home. Mrs. Calhoun wanted to take her to the hotel right away, but Carys insisted she wouldn't go until you got back. They've gone to the ladies' room to get her cleaned up."

Kincaid had waited as long as he could stand. "What about Paul, Captain? Any word on how he's doing?"

"A nurse came out a little while ago. The bullet nicked a lung, and he had a pneumothorax — his lung was leaking air, is how she described it. It wasn't as bad as it could have been, though, and she said the surgery is going well."

"Thank the gods" Allyn whispered.

"Daddy!" a little girl's voice cried, and Allyn shot to his feet, spinning toward the sound. Lydia and Carys were approaching, holding hands. The child's long blonde hair had been brushed and some order restored to her nightgown. Her face glowed when she smiled. She pulled her hand away from Nanny's and broke into a run, racing to him. "You're back!"

Allyn opened his arms, and she sprang into them. He enfolded her in his embrace, the cloak closing around her. He pressed his lips to the top of her head. When he spoke his voice was soft and muffled. "Are you all right, my little love?"

"Yes, Daddy. I'm fine. I love you."

He lifted his head to gaze at her, drinking in the sight. Kincaid was struck by the remarkable likeness between father and daughter. "I love you too, my heart."

"Nanny told me Uncle Derek is sick. Is he okay now?"

"That's why I had to go get him, sweetheart. We had to bring him to the hospital."

Bright blue eyes filled with tears. "It's because of his medicine, right? It didn't work like it's supposed to."

"The doctors don't know yet, but they're taking good care of him."

Lydia interrupted briskly. "Your father is right, young lady. They'll take very good care of Uncle Derek. So now it's time for you to come with me. You've been up all night, and you can hardly keep your eyes open. Time to be abed."

"I don't want to go," Carys protested. "I want to stay with Dad and Uncle Derek. Please, Nanny, don't make me go now."

"Now, sweetheart, Nanny's got the right of it. Go along to the hotel. I'll be there before you know it."

"Will you come and tell me about Uncle Derek?"

"I promise. First thing."

She suppressed a yawn. "All right, then. Since you promise."

"Good girl," Nanny approved. "Come along then, my dearest." The grandmotherly woman and the child took a sweep through the room to hug Avery, Gil and Miltie. When they got to Jackie, he offered Carys the stuffed lion. "I still have Muffin here, Miss Carys. He told me he's tired and ready to go to bed, too. May I have the honor of taking you, Nanny and Muffin to the hotel?"

Carys giggled. "Oh, Jackie, you can be so silly. Of course you can."

Allyn smiled and followed them to the car. He returned to the ER once the headlights had faded out of the parking lot and into the night.

Nearly two hours had passed and Kincaid, Allyn and Ortiz were still awake, thanks to numerous cups of machine-made coffee. Kincaid's stomach burned, but he couldn't tell if it was from anxiety too much caffeine.

The sky was finally beginning to lighten when a man in surgical greens approached. "Is one of you Captain Ortiz?"

"I am." Ortiz rose. "Do you have any word on Sergeant Taglia?

"Would you like to come to an office to talk privately?"

Ortiz gestured toward Kincaid, who scrambled stiffly to his feet. "This is Sergeant Taglia's partner, Lieutenant Kincaid. Paul hasn't got any relatives out here. Please, just tell us his condition."

The doctor smiled. "So far, the surgery appears to be successful. We got the bullet out, and the lung is doing well. Paul is in stable condition. The way it looks right now, he'll be with us for a few days, but he's come through surgery in good shape. He's in recovery. It won't be long before he'll be transferred to a room in ICU."

Kincaid grinned. "That's great news! When can I see him?"

"Well, he'll be taken to ICU in the next thirty minutes or so. He's not really in any condition for visitors yet, though. It might be better to come back this afternoon, when he'll be completely conscious."

"Just a couple of minutes?" Kincaid said. "I don't care if I can talk to him, I just want to see him. He's my partner, and he got shot on a case we were working...."

Saunders shrugged then nodded briskly. "I understand. Paul isn't the first police officer I've treated. You can see him once he's settled, but please make it short. Two minutes, max."

It took about 45 minutes before he could go in. Finally the ICU nurse came out and told him to go ahead.

He pushed open the glass door and went in. Taglia lay on a bed surrounded with beeping machines. His eyes were closed in sunken hollows. A half-full bag of clear fluid dripped into his left arm. An oxygen mask covered the lower half of his face.

Kincaid stood close to the bed, his thighs pressed against the mattress. He pulled up a chair, sat down, and took Taglia's right hand in his. He rested his forehead against the cold chrome bars on the bed. After a few moments, Taglia's fingers stirred. Kincaid jolted to his feet and the chair scooted back. His partner's eyes were on his face.

Taglia pulled his hand away from Kincaid's, reaching for the mask, trying to dislodge it. *Trying to talk. It figures.* Kincaid's heart took a painful lurch. *Damned Italian, anyway.*

"Don't do that. Just lie there and relax. You're gonna be fine. The doctor said so. Carys is safe and so is Allyn. You're a hero, man."

Taglia frowned, then his eyes drifted shut, only to fly open a few seconds later. He started to reach for the mask again.

"Stop it, Paul," he said. "You aren't supposed to talk. But I can. Let me, instead, because you have to know this. I have to tell you. I do remember, Paul. About last Saturday night. I remember everything. I just... it was just too much for me. I couldn't admit how you made me feel. How right it was in spite of anything else. It's only that I almost lost you. You almost died. That can't happen... I can't let that happen without telling you. Because I love you, and I think you love me."

Kincaid sighed as a bone-deep weariness settled over him. "If you want a new partner I won't fight it. It's up to you. I'll understand. But I love you and I am not going to stop, no matter what you decide." He turned to reach for the chair, too depressed to keep standing.

Taglia's right hand caught his wrist and he looked back to meet his partner's eyes. Taglia tried again to brush the mask aside. Finally Kincaid moved it for him. Taglia's hand reached up toward him. Kincaid leaned down close to listen and felt his partner's hand close in his hair, drawing him down.

"Nobody else," Taglia whispered. "Only you."

Their lips met with the lightest of touches, the softest brush of physical contact, an exquisite sharing of breath. Kincaid held the kiss a few moments before he straightened.

Taglia lay back in the bed, eyes drifting closed, all that he had been through finally claiming him.

Bird of Paradise
G.J. Paterson

Kincaid repositioned the oxygen mask, sat back down and reclaimed his partner's hand. He knew it was time and past time for him to go. In another minute or two and a nurse would come and politely throw him out. He'd wait anyway. "Sleep, Paul," he whispered. "We have all the time in the world. Now we do."

Forty-Two   42

ow odd. I never thought hell would smell like a hospital. Quinn's throat hurt, and his body seemed twice its normal weight. The effort of opening his eyes required an amazing amount of concentration. He had to blink several times before he could bring the room into focus.

Oh dear. It would be a bit much for the afterlife to look like a hospital, too, I suppose.

Speech seemed the logical next step. It would attract attention, then he would be able to tell whether or not he was dead by judging whether he attracted a demon or a nurse. Although, he reminded himself, drawing on past experience, the distinction was by no means certain.

"Hello?" His voice was a ragged croak. A face swam into view in response. A young face. Female. Not especially pretty, but not obviously demonic.

He lowered his eyelids and gazed at her through his lashes. It broke the light into many colors to avoid the blue of her eyes. "Where..." She leaned closer, and he guessed his voice was weaker than he'd realized. "Where am I?"

"Central County Hospital," she said.

Not dead then. He closed his eyes and wished her away. There was a receding rustle and he knew she was gone. He focused his awareness on the mere rushing in and out of air through nose and throat and lungs.

He had given his soul over to death. The coming back to life was like a slow spring rising. It must have been like this for Orpheus as he came back alone from the mouth of Hades, the shade of Eurydice dispersing behind him like smoke on the wind.

I didn't go down to the Halls of the Dead to wrest life back for the fallen. I didn't presume that far. How should I hope to succeed where a greater man failed? Desolation, cold as a winter wind, swept through him.

His body grew freer of the bonds wrapping it and fed him greater and greater awareness of quickening life. He lay and listened in respectful silence as the sturdy donkey of the flesh began to bray in protest and triumph.

His mind though, once again set stirring, refused to stay still.

I should have died. I knew what I was doing. Someone interfered. I wonder who it could have been? Could Gillie or one of the others have found me? Or did one of the inspectors guess?

Allyn would have known, but Allyn is dead.

He tried to banish thought and just lay there breathing — in and out, in and out. The cold air rasped in his throat. He opened his eyes when firm fingertips took his wrist. The nurse had come back. He gazed up at her. "Who are you?" His voice sounded like a rasping whisper, even to his ears.

"Miss Jensen." She stared at her watch.

"Someone... brought me here."

Bird of Paradise
G.J. Paterson

"You came in by ambulance." She sounded a little bored. The drama had faded, perhaps, through overexposure.

"Do you know... who found me?" The effort to speak was enormous, coming back from such a vast silence.

"No."

"Have you any way of finding out?"

She sighed and moved out of his sight. While she was gone, he flexed his fingers and found his right hand seemed to be lashed down somehow. He became aware of an IV bottle hanging on a rack over his head.

She came back with a manila folder in her hands. "There's a name here, but I can't read it."

"Could I see it, please?" He tried to reach for the paper with his left hand, but the effort was too much. Instead she held the paper to let him see.

At first he couldn't focus on the thin yellow paper. Then, as though an obscuring veil had been lifted, he saw the signature in every detail. Bold, black, illegible, unmistakable. The date was listed too. It was the winter solstice.

He laughed shakily and closed his eyes, immediately reopening them. *There's no more reason to shut out the light.* He gazed up at Miss Jensen with the infectious, carefree smile of his youth.

"You feel like getting up?" She smiled back.

"Yes," he said, "I think I do."

The waiting room was quiet as Quinn came in on the nurse's arm. A familiar sound slid into his heart. Allyn was playing something bluesy on his harmonica, soft as a whisper, full of pain and loss.

Gil sat next to him, his right arm flung across Allyn's shoulders. The gesture spoke of comfort and support. Kincaid sat nearby. Avery was across from them, with his chair tipped back on two legs, reading a newspaper. Jackie sat next to him, reading over his shoulder. Ables was engaged in a low-voiced conversation with Cohen and Harris.

Quinn knew they were there more for Allyn than for him, and he greeted that fact with equanimity. Where Allyn was, there would always be others. It was part of Allyn's nature — the thing that drew people to him for songs and light and laughter, for whatever he would give them. Quinn understood that and had made his peace with it long ago. But there was a steady fire burning in the heart of the man that only he could grasp.

It's all down to the music that binds us both. I've no better way to say it.

The full light of dawn filled the windows of the ER, silhouetting Allyn as he sat slumped, cupping the harmonica to his mouth with both hands. Exhaustion was in every line of his body. The sound of Quinn's halting footsteps attracted Gil's attention. The bassist let his hand drop forward and touch Allyn's shoulder.

The singer lifted his head and gazed at Quinn. There was nothing in his face but bleak endurance. He needed a shave and was pale and worn. He looked dreadful. Quinn was certain he had never seen anyone more beautiful in his life.

"*Sol Invictus*, Invincible Sun," he whispered. The heat of Allyn's stare scorched him, drying up anything else he could say.

"Skimmed through another one, I see." Allyn's voice was inflectionless.

Quinn nodded, leaning harder on the nurse's arm that supported him. He was wearier than he cared to acknowledge, even to himself. After a lengthening silence he said, "Is Carys all right?"

"Carys is fine. Lydia took her to the hotel."

"Ah, good. She's safe." Speech began to come more easily. "She wasn't hurt?"

"No. Nor was I." Allyn said bluntly. "Paul was."

"Oh, dear." Quinn knew Kincaid's eyes were on him. He knew how inadequate his words sounded and knew he should be embarrassed. But Allyn was alive, and his daughter was safe. Nothing else mattered as much. "Not badly, I hope."

"He's not dead, nor likely to die." So much Taff in Allyn's voice was a promise of violence. The singer rose to his feet, the convulsive

Bird of Paradise
G.J. Paterson

movement without grace. He crossed the room to Quinn, who transferred his weight to Allyn's forearm with unfeigned weakness.

They walked away from the waiting area, moving slowly. A covert glance at Allyn's profile told Quinn nothing, but he could feel the suppressed tension in Allyn's muscles beneath his fingers.

"What possessed you?" Allyn's whisper was an explosive hiss.

"It seemed reasonable at the time."

"It was stupid, and it was selfish. You aren't to do anything like this again. Do you understand?"

Quinn pondered this ultimatum as their stroll continued, moving into an open stretch of hallway where the occasional passerby moved swiftly toward unknown destinations. "Oh?" he asked at last. "Why not?"

Allyn stiffened. Quinn imagined he could feel the hot blue gaze rake his face. He didn't turn to meet Allyn's eyes.

The singer cleared his throat and spoke with deceptive calm. "I can't talk to you out here." He looked at a door to their right. Quinn followed his glance and saw that it led to the stairwell. Allyn pushed it open.

The door shut heavily behind them. Quinn released his grip on the singer's arm and leaned back against the door for support. Allyn spun to face him, placing one hand flat against the door, on either side of his head. His breath was hot on Quinn's face when he spoke. "Vocalists are easy enough to come by, after all. Your talent is irreplaceable. Stupid for it to be snuffed out for no reason."

"No reason?" Quinn echoed, stung by the rebuke. He knew full well where his next words would strike. "The music must come from somewhere, you know. One makes music for a reason. I thought all my reasons were taken away."

He didn't flinch from the fury he saw gathering in Allyn's face. "I can't live like this anymore," he said, with more courage than hope. "Love me or kill me, but let's have an end."

Swift and merciless as a striking hawk, Allyn brought his mouth down hard against Quinn's. He leaned against him, using his greater weight to hold him against the door.

Bird of Paradise
G.J. Paterson

Quinn opened his mouth to the bruising onslaught, surrendering himself to the sensation of Allyn's mouth against his for the first time. Tears ran down his face, and he didn't care. Allyn's hands were on him now. The touch was hard, almost hurtful. With Allyn's body pressed close against him, he could feel the singer's desire quickening against his thigh.

He lifted his arms and wrapped them around Allyn's waist, pulling him close.

A door opened somewhere above them, and footsteps echoed on the stairs, drawing closer. Panting, Allyn pulled away and moved across the landing to peer through the window blinds. Taking a deep breath, Quinn joined him. He leaned against the window frame, still unsteady on his feet. They were silent as a woman in nurse's whites went by. She was from India exotically dark, with glistening black hair falling down her back in a thick braid. She gave them a veiled glance through thick lashes as she slipped on past them down the stairs.

Quinn laughed as her footfalls faded in the distance.

Allyn frowned. "What's so bleeding funny?"

"Oh." Quinn went on laughing. He couldn't help it. "We are."

Allyn stared at him.

"Look at us," Quinn explained when he could. "No, I mean it. You've been out playing cops and robbers, bargaining for your daughter's life. I've almost died and feel I still might. We've got a tour looming over us, and we could both do with a shower. Yet here we are, in a clinch, ducking apart like two schoolboys dodging the headmaster. We're ridiculous."

"Are we?" Allyn's chin lifted.

"Allyn." Quinn sobered abruptly. "I know why you reacted as you did when you saw the police photos. I know what happened in London, before we met. I've known for years, almost from the first."

Allyn's voice came out as a whisper. "No. It isn't possible. About St. James' Park, yes."

"Not that. About what came before. It doesn't matter to me. It never has."

"H-How can you know?"

"There was a blackmail attempt after our first album did so well. Just the one. It won't happen again." Quinn smiled grimly. "Enrico Paglio took care of it. Syn-Syn helped for reasons of her own."

"Splendid." Allyn's lips thinned. "Mafioso and drug dealers. And what did it cost you, I wonder?"

"Not as much as it cost you. All debts were paid in full long ago. There was a fire at the warehouse. The films were destroyed. You're free of it. Clear and free."

"Did you watch them?" Allyn's voice trembled.

"Of course not." He reached out a hand to touch Allyn's cheek. The red mark where he had struck him was long faded. "It's over. Don't ask me anything more."

Allyn leaned into the touch and sighed then moved away to look out the window. After some time, he turned back, eyes bright with unshed tears. "Let's go home, Dee," he whispered. There was the faintest shiver on the last word that thrilled Quinn to hear. "Please?"

"Hungry for the sight of your Welsh hills, eh, lad?"

"Oh, yes," Allyn said. "I think I need a holiday from my holiday."

Quinn chuckled and searched his shirt pocket for his cigarettes. He came up empty. "Out of smokes."

"We'd best get back to the others, anyway. They'll be out searching for us, thinking I've taken you out to murder you."

Quinn pushed himself off the wall. Allyn held out his arm and guided the guitarist through the door. They resumed their slow walk, heading back the way they had come. The silence between them had become easier, companionable.

Finally Quinn said, "It's been a long time since I saw a hillside blanketed with snow."

Allyn glanced at him with surprise and pleasure written in the angle of his head. "Would you care to come out for a bit?"

Quinn shrugged as if it were the most casual idea imaginable. "Oh, I dunno. I could do with a bit of country air, I daresay. I've got these few tunes which could do with some work. It'd give you a chance to put vocals down to them, if you like, without you having to tear back and forth."

"True." Allyn nodded with the same studied nonchalance.

"Well then," Quinn said. "We'd best have Miltie book a flight tomorrow, early as he can."

Forty-Three

43

Kincaid took one look at the formidable wall of speakers on either side of the stage and decided the earplugs Taglia had given him were a good idea, after all.

During the preceding months, in anticipation of Leviathon's upcoming tour, Taglia had coached him rigorously on the band's musical history. Then, on the day tickets went on sale, they were caught on a stakeout. The tickets sold out long before their shift was over, and Paul had been deeply disappointed. He'd have done almost anything to cheer Paul up, and even considered buying scalped tickets but the prices were way beyond what their combined paychecks could handle.

So it had been an enormous surprise when Jackie showed up in the squad room the day before the concert with tickets for *"the best seats in the house."* There was no way he would have declined the gift — especially after seeing the pure, unadulterated delight on Paul's face.

Now he found himself packed into the Forum next to his partner and more than 16,000 other souls on a warm August night. The concert was scheduled to start at 8:00. They'd arrived at 6:30 and still had to struggle for a place to park.

He had to admit, their seats were good, three rows back, dead center in front of the stage. The crowd behind them wore mostly t-shirts and jeans, but all around them were celebrities and gorgeous women in rock and roll glitz. Almost everyone in their section was wearing a pass of some kind on lanyards around their necks. His and Taglia's said *"All Access."* Someone had already offered him a surprisingly large amount of money for his. Kincaid saw Blaine Harris in a group of others who looked very much like him, more disco than rock and roll, and concluded the nearby seats were also taken up by record industry people. Reporters and photographers in sports jackets and slacks with cameras slung next to their passes stood toe-to-toe with impassive security guards down by the stage. The crowd noise was ear splitting. The smell and haze of smoke — legal and illegal — hung in a pall over the seats.

Just about the time he got used to the sound level, the crowd began chanting, *"Leviathon! Leviathon!"* and pounding the floor deafeningly. A glance at his watch told him it was a few minutes before eight. Twenty minutes later, the chanting continued, climaxing into a roar of adulation as colored stage lights began to swirl. The lights continued playing across the stage for several minutes, then went dark. Sounds of preparation were picked up by the live microphones, then the lights came back up and with a crash of Avery's drums the first song began. Allyn and Quinn came down to the front of the stage. Gil hung back by the drums. Taglia shouted something incomprehensible into his ear then turned back to the stage and began clapping, yelling and stomping with the rest of the crowd.

Kincaid was proud of himself for recognizing *"Don't You Leave"* and *"Mirror, Mirror"* as Leviathon performed their classics during the first half of the concert. Allyn whipped across the stage, a golden whirlwind, dancing and singing without pause. Taglia's high-priced stereo speakers — no matter how loud they were cranked — couldn't begin to compare with the massive power pouring out of the towering speaker stacks on either side of the stage and slung by special rigging above it. Kincaid wasn't certain why they needed speakers hanging from the ceiling, unless it was to make sure that the upper seats left as deaf as the rest of the crowd.

His introduction to Allyn as a performer in the small studio at the house on Oak Pass Drive, hadn't prepared him for the energy of the concert. Allyn was dressed in leather pants tighter than anything Kincaid had seen him wear at the house, but they didn't slow him down. He wore a pale blue poet's shirt, heavily embroidered down the front and around the cuffs. As the evening progressed and Allyn's skin gleamed with sweat, he ripped the shirt open, buttons flying into the crowd, exposing his finely-muscled chest.

He flashed across the stage, his bright hair streaming behind him like a banner as he sang. The vocal line of the song was often rendered down to a soaring, amazing wail. Allyn's voice swooped around the guitar lines as it had in the studio; but here it was transformed by the magic of immense power. He whirled and strutted and played to the audience, creating a web that wove them all together. The audience sang and clapped with him, some of the ones nearest the stage surging toward him like a rising tide. They were pushed back repeatedly by the security force.

At the back of the stage, Avery was almost completely shielded by his enormous drum kit. His face — rarely visible — was usually hidden by his flying, sweat-soaked hair. He had a trick of unexpectedly twirling one drumstick 15 feet into the air and catching it on the beat. Kincaid was so startled the first time he saw it, he broke out into a spontaneous cheer at the smooth recovery. The power of his blows convinced Kincaid that there was no way the drum kit would last the night.

Gilbert stood to one side, watching the other musicians as he played his bass. He was dressed in dark blue silk with embroidery down the legs and sleeves, and his hair was, for the most part, neatly brushed. He played steadily, laying down a bass line solid enough to walk on, as he watched everything going on around him. His expression indicated he found his bandmates — particularly Quinn and Allyn — as entertaining as the audience did.

But it was Quinn that Kincaid found himself watching most. His style was nothing like he expected. He had supposed that Quinn would stand up there, cool and aloof with a sneer curling up one corner of his mouth, sinister and world-weary. He wasn't prepared for the smiling, perpetual motion machine clad in white satin, that stalked and glided and duck-walked, covering the stage non-stop from one side to the other all evening.

The crowd loved the energy the guitarist and the singer wove between them. They stalked each other and teased one another, trying to crack each other up. They rocked out, shoulder to shoulder, their intermingled hair flying. There was something compelling in the Dionysiac flamboyance of their display. Ultimately, Kincaid realized, the music seemed less the production of four men than something akin to a primordial clash of nature.

More than an hour into the show, Allyn took his only break, leaving the stage during Quinn's set piece, *"Don't You Leave."* Quinn disappeared from the stage as well once he was done, leaving Avery to a 15 minute drum solo.

"Nobody can say Leviathon doesn't give their fans their money's worth!" Kincaid shouted in Taglia's ear, meaning it.

Paul nodded enthusiastic agreement and turned his attention back to the stage, patting his hand on his thigh in time to Avery's rhythm. Kincaid smiled, reflecting that Quinn and Allyn certainly deserved a breather. Their performance was much harder work than he'd expected. *I wonder how much longer they'll be performing tonight?*

The audience's cheering ratcheted up again when the music began again. Quinn and Gil reentered the stage, picking up the melody where it had been left off. Allyn danced back to the microphone stand, ripping the mike free as his voice tore back into the lyrics. They finished the song with one last verse and several choruses, finally slamming the song to a halt.

The crowd screamed for more.

Kincaid had lost track of time by the time he heard the opening strains of *"Bird of Paradise."* The audience let out a communal shriek of pleasure, then Kincaid was surrounded by people standing on the seats of their chairs.

He looked at his chair and decided there was no way he was climbing up there, no matter how badly he wanted to watch the performance. The air was thick with marijuana smoke, and the kid standing on the chair beside him offered him a joint. He shook his head. He was feeling light-headed enough without actually taking a toke, and flashing his badge in this place would cause a riot.

Taglia grinned at him and bent down to tug on his arm. Kincaid shook his head, but Paul waived for him to get up. Reluctantly, he shrugged and climbed up onto his chair seat. He found himself almost on an eye level with the band and receiving the full force of the speakers. He felt precariously vulnerable and clung to Taglia's arm until he caught his balance.

All around them, people joined hands and swayed to the slow, gentle opening lyrics. The tempo began to pick up, and by the end of the second verse, the drums and bass came in. Audience members punched their fists into the air and sang along with the music. Kincaid could see their mouths moving as they sang, although their voices were lost against the band's sound system. He smiled at them, then laughed at himself when he realized both he and Paul were singing along with them, too.

This is actually kinda fun, he thought.

Allyn sang, leaning on Quinn's shoulder then breaking loose to dance at the edge of the stage, his arms flung out to the audience. His face was suffused with more than simple sensuality. He loved those people out there in front of him. Kincaid was sure of that, as sure as he was that the audience loved him back.

Looking at the barbaric golden face, suddenly Kincaid felt an interior shift — and he was caught up in the tidal wave of emotion flowing back and forth between the four men on stage and the thousands in front. It wasn't just a band playing for some people who'd decided to have an evening out. They had all become one thing. They shared some strange unity of experience. Kincaid felt himself open up to the flow of energy, and he was suddenly a part of it.

When *"Bird of Paradise"* ended, he hollered and stomped for more along with the rest.

There was a pause between songs while Quinn traded Jackie his Strat for a custom double necked guitar. As Jackie darted back stage, Paul shouted in Kincaid's ear, "This is something new! He's never played a double-neck in concert before! I wonder what this is going to be?"

Allyn clipped his mike onto the stand. He pushed his hair back from his face with both hands, and put his palms on his hips. He was breathing hard, and his skin was slick with sweat. "Since our last tour and this one, we've managed to get an album done. Now, usually we just come up with some tunes and go in and record them. And then Quinn usually wants to add something at the last minute, so we find some way to fit it in. That's what usually happens. But this time, he waited until the masters were all done, and we had to rearrange the entire album."

The audience laughed. Allyn laughed with them and glanced at Quinn, who gave him a thumbs up.

"Anyway," Allyn continued, "tonight we have a new song, and we'd like to dedicate it to some very good friends of ours. We owe them a lot — more than we can ever repay, actually — and I hope that our gift of music is some measure of compensation. So then, for our two White Knights, here is a little thing we call 'Guardians of the Light.'"

With the volume and the electricity and the lyrics, it took Kincaid several bars to recognize the song as the one Quinn had written on that Monday afternoon so long ago. The lyrics told a tense and complex ballad, but it was the chorus that stayed with him:

Daggers line the path they tread
Into the night alone.
Guardians of the silver path
Seldom reaching home.
For now, side by side they ride
For love, the good man's pride.
Demons storm the breach they hold
Against the hearts of stone.

One by one at first, then in tens and hundreds and thousands, points of light appeared through the vast arena until the hand-held lighters were a galaxy of stars. Then the roar began. It went on and on. Grinning, Kincaid clapped even harder and whooped along with the rest of them. Taglia leaned over and shouted "That song's for us, you know!"

"I know," he shouted back. For a few seconds their hands touched and grasped, then they let go, for fear someone else might see. But nothing could keep them from smiling.

The band members were smiling, too. At last Allyn called Avery out from behind the drums and Gil over from his corner. They all joined hands and the whole band took a bow. Even with repeated bows, it was several minutes before Allyn could make himself heard over the cheering.

"Thank you!" he shouted. "Thank you. That wasn't the end of the show, you know. We have more. We can go on, if you like?"

The question was met with even greater approval from the music-intoxicated crowd. The cheers continued for another minute, then the music started up again.

The rest of the show passed in a blur for Kincaid. It left only disjointed impressions, like snapshots taken at random. One thing he remembered clearly was the audience, the young women in particular. They were like hordes of Maenads whose screaming was a high, endless keening as they rushed the stage, throwing flowers, scarves, blouses and more intimate articles of apparel across the footlights.

Some of them stood as though rooted to one spot, staring lost-eyed at the stage while tears ran heedlessly down their faces. Over them all hung Allyn's face, both present and remote, like the face of Apollo on a Greek vase; the face of an elven prince or a Viking warrior, the face of ecstasy and madness.

They reached the final encore, their third. Through blazing guitar riffs and the bass roaring along under them, the thundering drums sounded like a storm at sea. Quinn's guitar screamed and wailed like the voice of creation, and Allyn became, in the pouring ice-fog and flickering lights, the flashes of flame and billowing smoke, an avatar of the cosmic dancer who brings pandemonium and ringing silence.

fin

G. J. Paterson lives in Tulsa, Oklahoma, sharing 3 dogs and 5 cats with her partner of 33 years (and spouse since 2008). She writes book reviews for The Gayly, a regional LGBT newspaper, and is working on a new novel. G.J. is active in the LGBT civil rights struggle and is a proud member and volunteers regularly at the Dennis R. Neill Equality Center.

www.ingramcontent.com/pod-product-compliance
Lightning Source LLC
Chambersburg PA
CBHW051636050726
47502CB00011B/555